W9-BGF-326

HARD STOP

(signature)

CHRIS KNOPF

HARD STOP

 VINTAGE CANADA

VINTAGE CANADA EDITION, 2010

Copyright © 2009 Chris Knopf
Published by arrangement with The Permanent Press

All rights reserved under International and Pan-American Copyright
Conventions. No part of this book may be reproduced in any form or by
any electronic or mechanical means, including information storage and
retrieval systems, without permission in writing from the publisher, except
by a reviewer, who may quote brief passages in a review.

Published in Canada by Vintage Canada, a division of Random House
of Canada Limited, Toronto, in 2010. Originally published in
hardcover in Canada by Random House Canada, a division of
Random House of Canada Limited, Toronto, in 2009. Distributed
by Random House of Canada Limited, Toronto.

Vintage Canada with colophon is a registered trademark.

www.randomhouse.ca

Library and Archives Canada Cataloguing in Publication

Knopf, Chris
    Hard stop / Chris Knopf.

ISBN 978-0-307-35753-3

    I. Title.

PS3611.N66H37 2010   813'.6   C2009-905332-2

Printed and bound in the United States of America

10 9 8 7 6 5 4 3 2 1

To Mary Jack Wald,
without whom, quite literally,
none of this would have happened

ONE

I DIDN'T LIKE ANYTHING about that big, dumb, ugly SUV. I didn't like the way it looked. All black, with a toothy gold grille. I didn't like the windows, tinted nearly opaque. I mostly didn't like where it was parked—a half block from my house.

I'd seen it driving around Southampton Village, a standout among other moronic excess. I'd also seen it on Main Street in Sag Harbor and on the Montauk Highway. In fact, I'd seen it so often I was getting sick of seeing it.

It was now parked up on the lawn of a house rented by a guy who would never do that. He was fastidious. He was also still in the City, at Mount Sinai, being treated for something bad enough to mean missing out on a whole season bought and paid for in the Hamptons.

It was about nine o'clock at night and I was just getting back from dinner with my friend Paul Hodges at his little fish joint in Sag Harbor. I pulled my old Grand Prix in behind the tail of the SUV and into the sick guy's driveway. Eddie, the mutt who lives with me, jumped into the driver's seat expecting to follow me out the door. I told him to sit, stay and be quiet, words he understood, but considered only advisory.

I walked the rest of the way to my cottage, getting close enough to see the light above the side door, which was supposed to be on, and a light inside the house, which wasn't. I walked around the rear of the house to the other side, past another exterior door, and then up to the screened-in porch that faced the Little Peconic Bay. I could see the light left on in one of the bedrooms, something I wouldn't do. My father never allowed such profligate use of electricity. I didn't argue about his rules when he owned the cottage, and though he'd been dead a long time, I wasn't going to start now.

I saw another light, this one moving. A flashlight darting around the walls of the kitchen. You could get to the kitchen from that side of the house by going through a small pantry. It was a good route for me because it was close by and I could pick up my three-quarter-sized Harmon Killebrew baseball bat along the way. I kept it next to the door so I could hit tennis balls for Eddie to shag off the grass or chase over the breakwater down to the pebble beach by the bay.

I probably should have taken a moment to develop a better strategy, but my adrenal glands had already opened the floodgates, relieving my judgment of command and control and turning them over to my lousy temper. This is how you end up doing things like confronting nighttime intruders with a kid's baseball bat and a simple question:

"What the hell's going on?"

I was in the pantry by now. I saw the flashlight in the kitchen flick off. I jumped toward the light switch on the far wall, but before I could get there a big black mass plowed into me.

We fell back into the pantry. Before we hit the floor I twisted so the guy wouldn't land directly on top of me.

This didn't completely solve the problem, but kept the worst of the blows he threw from doing serious harm. I wriggled out from under him and got back on my feet. I needed space to get my fists into play and protect my head, my greatest vulnerability.

In my hurry to stand, I lost my bat and almost lost my balance, stumbling backwards into the kitchen. This was fortuitous, as it allowed more room to maneuver.

The guy came at me again, his head down like a fullback trying to blow a hole through a defensive line. I sidestepped and sank a sharp uppercut into the vague black shape, connecting well enough to snap the guy into a full standing position. He staggered back against the wall. Before he could recover his momentum, I socked him a couple times in the general direction of his head. He was bigger than me, but not as quick, and not much of a fighter. At least with his fists. When the gun came out I wasn't so sure.

There was enough light seeping in from the living room to see the big black automatic. Since it takes less than a second to pull a trigger I wasted little time grabbing the barrel and pushing it toward the ceiling. When it went off the sound was literally deafening, though I could hear myself yelling a string of startled obscenities as I held the hot barrel with my right hand and shoved a series of enthusiastic jabs into the guy's face with my left.

When his grip on the gun weakened, I pulled it out of his hand. I managed to get the thing into the rear waistband of my jeans without letting up on the left jabs, which seemed to be having an effect. With the gun secured I got my right involved, using my left forearm as a shield against his faltering resistance.

I'm too old to be much of a power hitter, but I was motivated that night. The guy was now slumping forward, covering his head with his hands, so my last important punch came from above, dropping him hard to the floor.

I sank one knee between his shoulder blades and stuck the automatic against the back of his neck. I held my index finger along the barrel and away from the trigger so I wouldn't accidentally kill the guy before I had a chance to find out who he was and what he was doing in my house.

"Fuck you," he said.

I racked the slide on top of the automatic, ejecting the round that was already in there and putting another one in its place, just to be sure.

"Come again?" I asked.

"You're not going to shoot me," he mumbled into the floor.

"You're right." I stuck the gun back in my waistband, gripped him by the hair and pulled his head up off the floor. Then I reached around, grabbed his windpipe and squeezed. "I'm going to strangle you."

He started to thrash around from shock and pain, so I squeezed a little harder.

"Unless you want to chat," I said.

He gurgled something that sounded like a yes, so I let go of his throat and stood up. I turned on the kitchen light and retrieved the bat from the pantry. The man in black was now up on his hands and knees, though none too steadily. A gentle push with my foot sent him to the floor again, rolling him over and giving me a better look at his face. As good a one as I could get, through all the blood.

He looked somewhere in his late thirties, though jowly, which can add years. White face, black hair, small upturned nose probably made more so by recent events. He was wearing a black turtleneck shirt, black pants and black shoes. His eyes were sunken and set too close together, and he coughed as he tried to catch his breath.

"Take your wallet out of your pants and put it on the floor," I told him.

It took him a while, but he did it. I kicked it out of his reach and picked it up.

"Honest Boy Ackerman," I read off his New York State driver's license. "Honest?"

"That's my mother's fault. Nobody calls me that."

There wasn't much else in his wallet. A few credit cards and some cash. No baby pictures or membership cards for Breaking and Entering Professionals of America.

"So what do they call you?"

"H.B."

"Okay, Honest, you're going to tell me what you're doing here, and why, or I'm going to beat you with this baseball bat until you're almost dead, or just wish you were. Whichever comes first."

He looked hesitant, so I moved things along with a little tap on the noggin.

"Ow, Christ!"

"That was nothing. I'm only getting started."

"You're not."

"I am," I said, then tapped him again, a little harder.

"Shit, okay. I was just looking around."

"Of course. Why didn't you just say that?"

I tapped him again. He put his hands over his face.

"Okay, okay. I was looking for dirt. Stuff we could use on you."

"Huh?"

"I don't know. Dope, illegal guns, a wad of cash. Photos of you sleeping with a llama."

"I've never even dated one," I said.

"You don't do shit, pal. Not even a computer."

"Sorry to disappoint you. You still haven't told me why."

"I don't know why. I'm just supposed to get the stuff. Why is somebody else's job."

"Is shooting me part of your job?"

"I wasn't trying to shoot you. It went off accidentally. You should know better than to grab a gun like that."

"So who hired you to look for dirt?"

"I tell you that, I'll never work again."

"You tell me that or you'll be drooling on yourself and shitting in a bag for the rest of your life."

I knelt down, got another grip on his larynx and cracked him on the forehead again, in case he'd forgotten what it felt like. He nodded ferociously and I let go.

"You're a harsh son of a bitch," he croaked.

"Out with it."

"I work in security for Con Globe. I'm on special assignment to George Donovan, Chairman of the Board. I don't know what it's about. I just do what he tells me and that's that."

I sat down on my butt as if Ackerman had landed a decent punch of his own. Con Globe. The snappy corporate nickname for Consolidated Global Energies. My former employer. My only employer for twenty years of my professional life. Run by George Donovan, the guy who helped make sure twenty years was all I'd ever get.

—

Joe Sullivan could have sent Will Ervin, the patrolman who took over the North Sea beat after Sullivan was promoted to Southampton's investigative unit. But this was way too interesting to pass up, and anyway, Sullivan was a friend of mine.

Ackerman ran out of things to say while we waited in the kitchen, except about the end of his professional life.

I soured his mood even more by promising an avalanche of felony charges.

"What do you get for hitting me with a baseball bat?" he asked.

"Exercise."

When Sullivan made detective he hated giving up his uniform, so he designed a new one. Olive drab T-shirt and camo pants stuffed into a pair of steel-tipped boots. He wore an official ID around his bull neck and a non-regulation S&W 627 in a shoulder harness. At almost six feet tall with blonde hair in a buzz cut and about fifty extra pounds hanging on a weightlifter's build, he rarely had to take the Smith out of the holster.

I could tell the outfit made the right impression from Ackerman's moan when Sullivan came through the door.

"Yo, Sam," said the cop, "what do we got here?"

I tossed him Ackerman's wallet.

"Who says you can't find an honest man?" I said, as Sullivan looked at the ID.

I made him hold his questions while I freed Eddie from the Grand Prix. He was happy to see me, and happier to get to the nearest tree.

"Sorry, man. I got held up."

He raced ahead to the house to say hello to Sullivan, having seen the cop's Bronco drive by. When I got there he'd already been introduced to the idiot lying on the floor.

"Want some coffee?" I asked Sullivan. "How 'bout you, H.B.?"

While I worked on the coffee Sullivan pulled Ackerman to his feet and sat him in a kitchen chair. Then he brought a washcloth from the bathroom to wipe off the blood and assess the damage.

"I better get him to the hospital," said Sullivan. "That lip should be sewn up."

"Can you keep him from talking to anybody while you do that?" I asked.

"First tell me what happened."

I went through the whole story, everything I knew, including the name of Ackerman's employer, my old boss.

"Jesus," said the cop. "Why would he do something like that?"

"I have no idea. I haven't spoken to the guy in years. Or had anything to do with his company. It makes absolutely no sense."

Sullivan went and stood over Ackerman, who shrank involuntarily into his seat.

"I guess we'll find out when we book this lard-ass ninja."

"Could we talk about that? In private?"

I got the look I expected from Sullivan. After cuffing Ackerman to a radiator, he followed me outside.

"I'm not going to like this," he said.

"Don't I have the option of pressing charges?"

"Sort of. A B&E is pretty serious crap. At night, with a gun, assaulting the homeowner. Bad shit."

"I've got to know what's going on. Donovan's a very heavy guy. The worst Ackerman's statement will do is prompt a firm denial and cause a little embarrassment. If you bring him in now we'll lose whatever leverage we got."

"What are you talking about?"

"I want you to take him to the hospital and get him patched up. Don't let him talk to anybody or get near a phone. Then figure out a way to burn up some time. Lose him somewhere. Give me eight hours. Then I'll call you and tell you what I want to do."

"What *you* want to do? Doesn't work that way."

Sullivan was a straight-ahead type of cop. He not only followed the rules, he liked following the rules. He wasn't self-righteous about it, it was just the way he was. For him, proper procedure was sacred doctrine.

But then again, there was such a thick ledger of debt between us that we both knew he'd try to do what I wanted, no matter how much it endangered his career. A career we also knew was partly my doing.

"This is not a typical situation," I said. "This guy's only here because I'm here. I'm the target. Nobody else."

"That's a fine point."

"Just give me the time to do some things. Figure out how to deal with this."

"I may not agree with what you figure out."

"I understand. It's your call. I just need a little wiggle room."

Sullivan had his hands on his hips, skepticism etched on his face.

"Wiggle room for what?" he asked, then abruptly put up his hands. "Forget it. I don't want to know."

"You don't."

He'd given in. Though I could see the warning in his eyes—*do not fuck this up.*

Sullivan retrieved Ackerman from the kitchen and marched him over to the battered Bronco. Along the way he recited Miranda. He didn't mention that Ackerman was about to disappear into a hole before all those hallowed rights could be exercised. But Sullivan said the legal bit like he meant it, which he mostly did.

———

I'd finished my coffee by then so I felt okay about switching to an aluminum tumbler filled with Absolut on the rocks, to bring over to Amanda Anselma's house next door. I needed her to look after Eddie while I was gone and I wanted to brief her on the situation. Get it all out right from the get-go. See what it felt like to have complete trust in another human being, something we'd been working on lately. Something neither of us were very good at.

She met me at the door in one of my favorite flimsy white things. Her thick auburn hair was pulled back from her face, which this time of year was tanned a deep mahogany, creating an even sharper contrast with her brilliant green eyes.

"I was just about to jump into the shower," she said. "Care to join?"

I surprised her by asking for a rain check. Instead I started sharing details of the evening's events, and as much as I dared of my plan for where it might go from there. While I talked she gripped my arm and searched around my body, staring into my eyes for signs of dire injury.

My first go at candid and complete disclosure went about as well as I thought it would.

"This makes me very unhappy," she said. "You need to go to the hospital."

"I'm okay. Nothing bad happened."

Age was less an issue with an old boxer than the accumulated damage, of which I had more than my share. This meant I'd have to live the rest of my life walking along the edge of a precipice, one step away from the mental abyss. And that assumed no more shots to the head. I'd promised as much to Amanda, an easy promise to make provided the situation was entirely up to me, which I pointed out to her.

"You didn't have to go in that house," she said. "You could have just called the police. You have your own cell phone now, just like a regular person."

I have a general rule when it comes to arguments with people I love. I don't have them. At the first sign of genuine conflict, I do the brave thing and concede defeat, or if I'm really feeling courageous, I turn and run the other way.

I decided on a combination of the two.

"You're right. I'm still a work in progress. Can I borrow your Audi?"

She looked incredulous. I liked that a lot better than pissed off.

"It's only two weeks old. I've hardly driven it."

"That's why it needs some highway miles. I know this for a fact. My father was a mechanic."

"Your father bought that ridiculous Pontiac. What did he know about zippy little station wagons?"

"You've got the pickup. You look great in it."

"You still haven't told me what you're going to do," she said.

"Get dressed, throw some crap in the car and be on the road in ten minutes. Eddie ate at Hodges's. Let him stay with you tonight. I want to know he's safe. And Will Ervin will be hanging around keeping an eye on things."

I snatched the keys off a ring by the side of the door and wrapped my arm around her waist. She put both hands on my chest and pushed back, looking at me with a mix of annoyance and resignation.

"Some day you might learn to trust me," she said. "You might learn I can handle the truth."

My beat-up brain still knew enough not to tackle gigantic relationship issues when you were trying to make a fast get-away. So all I did was give her a sloppy, theatrical kiss on the lips and got the hell out of there.

———

As promised, I was out on Sunrise Highway heading west ten minutes later, feeling the silken surge of the torqued-out little car as I ran through all six gears. I'd have enjoyed it more if I hadn't felt a little bad about the conversation with Amanda. Which would have been distraction enough without the hurricane of confusion and conjecture brought on by the unexpected resurrection of my dead past.

"What the hell is going on?" I asked for the third time that night, with no improvement in the result. So I concentrated on the only thing I knew for certain.

George Donovan had some explaining to do.

TWO

I USED TO DRIVE through Greenwich on the way from my house in Stamford to the office in White Plains. Every time I passed the Greenwich commuter lot off the Merritt Parkway I'd think of George Donovan's house, just up the hill and secured within what they call a gated community. There wasn't an actual gate, just a little hut that was usually empty, though sometimes there was a guy inside you got past by giving your name and the names of the people you were going to visit. The commuter lot always made me think of George's house because there was a path up the hill from the lot that bypassed the hut at the gate, proving its utility had more to do with status than security.

I'd been to George's house at least a half dozen times when I worked for the company. These were occasions of soaring elation for my ex-wife, Abby. She saw them as unambiguous signs of my rising fortunes within the firm. She'd walk into the foyer of the majestic limestone mansion, take a deep breath and gaze about as if to say, "In a few years this shall all be mine."

What she got instead was spectacular loss, though at least she lost me in the process.

It was about midnight when I pulled into the lot. Even this late, there were plenty of silver and grey imports parked there to camouflage Amanda's Audi. Awaiting their owners' return from Jersey City or Kuala Lumpur.

First I put on my clever disguise—a blue blazer over an Ivy League tie and blue oxford cloth shirt, and pressed khakis. Then I stuffed a leather knapsack full of tools and electrical equipment and headed up the path.

I had a lot of worries at this point, even with the adrenaline rush of three hours ago still itching at my nerves. My biggest worry was Mrs. Donovan. It was the middle of the week, barely past Labor Day, so she was probably still at their house in Montauk, wrapping up the season. I truly hoped so, since she'd have the dogs with her, eliminating one more irksome variable.

As I followed the gentle curves of the main road, I tried to look like a titan of industry out for an evening stroll, willing the backpack full of burglar's tools into invisibility.

George had about a quarter mile of driveway. Spotlights buried in the ground illuminated the tangled branches of sycamore trees overhead. I took a parallel course over the lawn, staying well inside the dark edges.

When I reached the house I went around back and located a basement window. I took off the backpack and sat cross-legged, listening. All I heard were bugs in the woods and the monotonous swoosh of traffic washing up from the Merritt Parkway.

I pulled on a pair of surgical gloves. Then I took the glass cutter, and, using the window frame as a straightedge, started drawing the tool across the glass. Certain repetitive motions bore me to death, but I put up with myself long enough to carve deep scores into the glass. Then, after wiping everything clean with a paper towel, I stuck two wads of plumber's dope to the center of the window. I twisted galvanized screws into the dope to give me something to grip, then, using my fist like a hammer, gently tapped until I felt it bust inward. I turned the glass in the hole and drew it out, placing it carefully on the ground.

Then I sat and listened to the bugs and traffic for a few more minutes. No screeching alarms, no sirens.

I used a miniature Maglite to examine the window. As expected, there was an alarm sensor mounted to the frame, a magnetic type that went off by breaking a circuit when the sash was opened. Something I didn't need to do with the glass out of the way.

I slithered through the hole and dropped to the floor, dragging my pack behind me with a string tied to the straps. Using the Maglite, I searched around for the electrical panel, which I found near the furnace. Predictably, the controls for the security system were in a locked box mounted next to the panel.

It took a few minutes to jimmy the lock. I could have done it faster, but I was afraid of the noise. I'd always been good at working locks, a skill put to good use as a teenage car thief. Or car borrower, as I liked to think of it, since I always gave the cars back.

Inside was a chaos of multicolored wires, but I knew what it all meant. I'd installed a system in my house in Stamford and this didn't look that much different.

Before I touched anything in the box I used a heavy pair of wire cutters to sever the phone trunk that emerged from a conduit sticking through the concrete floor. I waited again for the hot scream of alarm, but nothing happened. I sorted out the lines that fed the sirens inside and outside the house and snipped those. Still nothing. For good measure I disconnected the 120-volt line and backup batteries for the system.

The house was now deaf, dumb and blind.

I climbed the basement stairs and came out into the kitchen. It was lit by the glow of the LEDs on the kitchen appliances—coffeemakers, ovens and microwaves. I scanned the ceiling corners for motion detectors and found two. No blinking red lights. I moved on in search of stairs to the second floor.

It must have been somebody like Nathaniel Hawthorne or Zane Grey who wrote that Indians understood that absolute silence was impossible, so instead moved in random patterns, blending in and mimicking ambient sound. They probably didn't have to deal with creaking floorboards or the hum and whir of central air-conditioning.

It took a long, nerve-wracking time, but I finally found George Donovan's bedroom, which I was deeply grateful to see was free of Mrs. Donovan. Better yet, it had Mr. Donovan, lying flat on his back on top of the bedspread, snoring like an unlubricated chain saw.

I took the last few steps and stood by his bed. I flicked on the little Maglite and stuck it in my mouth. Then I vaulted onto the bed, landing with my knees astride Consolidated Global Energies' Chairman of the Board. His eyes popped open.

"Hi, George," I said, after taking the Maglite out of my mouth.

Terror and confusion raced across his face.

"What's this?"

"The cops call it a home invasion. Pretty unsettling, isn't it?"

"I don't understand," he said, buying time while he corralled his faculties.

One of my worries going in was shocking Donovan into a heart attack. He had to be in his late sixties, in good shape, but nevertheless. Looking at him harden under the light of the flashlight took care of that worry.

"Who are you?" he asked.

"You don't remember?"

I moved the flashlight to the side so he could see my face.

"I thought I was unforgettable."

"Good God. You have to be out of your mind."

"Maybe."

"What the hell do you think you're doing?"

"You know."

"Of course I don't."

He looked down at where I was sitting on him, struggling with the sensation of being pinned by one of his former divisional vice presidents. It was only a little less weird for me, and I'd had a few hours to get used to the idea.

"You're not going to lie about a guy named Honest, are you?" I asked.

"I don't know what you're talking about."

"Honest Boy Ackerman. You sent him to study me. In his words, to find some dirt. What he found was a busted lip and a free night in a secure place. This surprises me, George. I thought you were more circumspect than that."

He thought his face wasn't betraying him, but he was wrong. Few people can keep strong emotion out of their eyes.

"He's Marve Judson's hire," he finally said.

"This is where you have to ask yourself," I said to him, sticking the flashlight closer to his face, "can you convince Marve Judson to tell a jury that he ordered Ackerman to break into my house and assault me, with criminal intent, at night, with a gun? That it was his idea, even when Ackerman says it was all yours? And even if Judson could persuade the court, why would he want to? You think he's prepared to destroy his career and do years of hard time for you just because you're the Chairman of the Board? Have you gotten that delusional?"

He just looked at me, running the calculations. We both knew which way the math would work out.

"I got you, George," I said. "You're sunk."

"That must give you some pleasure, Sam. You probably think I ruined your life."

"You didn't ruin my life. I did that all on my own. You're not that good."

"You were always mentally unstable," he said.

"I'm unstable? Did I hire a guy to attack you in your own house?"

"That's not what I was doing," he said, quietly. He tried to shift under my weight. "And if you don't mind, I prefer discussing things with people who aren't sitting on top of me."

I moved the Maglite closer to his face. He squeezed his eyes shut and turned his head.

"You got anything to drink in this house?" I asked.

He opened his eyes.

"Everything."

"Okay. But before I get up, here's the deal. I have Ackerman on ice. I can make a call and the whole thing goes away. Or not. The missile will stay in the silo, or it'll go off. You can fire back if you want, but which of us has the most to lose?"

I looked around the sumptuous bedroom. He took the point.

"Just get off me and we'll have that drink."

I got off and scooped his cell phone off the side table. While Donovan rose unsteadily and pulled on a robe, I took the phone into the bathroom and flushed it down the toilet.

I escorted him to the library on the first floor, where he kept his booze and a few thousand books, few of which he'd ever read. His wife once proudly told me they'd been selected by an interior decorator based on the color and composition of their spines.

I didn't relax until we were in opposing Chesterfield easy chairs next to the yawning fireplace. The scotch he poured was probably older than both of us.

"So Ackerman isn't in police custody," said Donovan after a sip of his drink.

"Like I said, that depends on you."

"One would think after forty years in business I would know how to size up a risk."

"You used to be pretty good at it."

"Very good. But not perfect."

"Apparently."

"Experience teaches you to hedge your bets," he said. "But a hedge isn't a guarantee."

"I'll take your word for it. Your hedges have worked out better than mine."

George Donovan could have been the smartest man alive. I didn't know him well enough to say. I knew the way he ran the company made a lot of money for him and the shareholders. It wreaked havoc on the employees, though there might have been good business reasons for that, too. History would have to sort it out.

I really didn't know if he was a good man or not. I'd never seen him be overtly heartless or cruel. Only selfish and greedy. He delegated heartless and cruel.

"You were hoping to get some leverage as a hedge against a risk," I said. "Is that what you're saying?"

Donovan nodded appreciatively.

"That's exactly what I'm saying, Sam. Still sharp as a dart."

I remembered how he talked about me in front of the board. I ran the company's Technical Services and Support Division, which included R&D and product development.

By fact and implication the company's technological brain trust. Since I ran the unit, he felt compelled to joke that *I* was the smartest man alive. Then he decided one day to shed my whole division with about as much concern as you'd flick a bit of lint off your suit coat. This settled the question as to who was the most powerful guy in the company, if not the smartest.

"We signed an agreement, remember?" I said. "I've always held up my end of the deal, and so has Con Globe. What the hell do you need leverage for now?"

"There are two forms of leverage, Sam," he said, with a touch of condescension, "carrots and sticks. I like to have both before entering negotiations. With you, as it turns out, I have a whole garden full of carrots. What I lack is a stick."

He held his drink upright with his elbow braced on the arm of the chair and swirled the ice around the glass, studying me while he continued studying his options.

"Thanks for the lesson, George. People would pay a lot of money for wisdom like that."

"They do."

"I'll start paying when you tell me something I don't already know."

"You'll be able to afford that when I make you a rich man," he said with a soft smile. "Well, not rich exactly, though wealthy enough to allay any financial concerns, which by my reckoning should be considerable."

Okay, I thought. That I didn't know. It must have showed on my face.

"Don't tell me Jason didn't mention the intellectual property dispute we're wrapped up in. The one we'll apparently have to settle, which of course is tantamount to admitting we've lost."

He had. Jason Fligh was the only friend I still had on Con Globe's board. We'd kept in sporadic touch since I left the company. He'd told me that Con Globe and the people who bought my division had been sued by a group of employees— mostly design engineers and bench researchers—who challenged the clause in the company's standard employment agreement dealing with patent rights on products developed on the job. We'd always assumed you signed all that away when you joined the firm, but an entrepreneurial spouse of one of my engineers—a legal expert on intellectual property—had apparently found a gaping loophole. The net result would likely be a nice hunk of dough distributed to some of the people I used to work with.

Jason called me when he heard about the lawsuit, but I had to disappoint him. The severance agreement I'd signed would trump anything in a potential settlement. I asked him not to tell me what that meant financially. I didn't want numbers like that rattling inside a brain already overloaded with regret and self-recrimination.

I told as much to George Donovan.

"I know that, Sam. But what you *don't* know is that I have my finger on a button that will delete that portion of your agreement. Without nullifying the rest of the deal. You'd get your fair share of the booty. If, like me, you'd spent the better half of a year poring through the company's patent filings, you'd know how much that could be."

This is the sort of thing I've always detested. That skip of the heart you feel when some manipulator sneaks around your natural defenses and triggers a flood of hope and expectation. The killer emotions. The greatest peril to the healthful cynicism that sustains life. The last guy in the world I wanted this from was George Donovan.

I took a deep breath.

"God preserve me, George," I said. "But I don't want your fucking money. I do carpentry now for a guy named Frank

Entwhistle. So far I haven't seen strings attached to what he pays me. That's my wealth in the world. I don't have shit but I don't owe anybody anything."

"Including your daughter?" he asked.

That was the other thing I really detested. Being threatened with guilt. Especially since I had nothing to feel guilty about, except almost everything I'd ever done in my life. Especially when it came to my daughter.

"Looks like you could use another scotch," I said. "Don't get up. I'll pour."

I needed something to cover my reaction, though it probably wouldn't work. I'd never underestimated George Donovan before, and it was good to remind myself not to start now.

I topped us off and sat back down.

"I'm getting this vague feeling you want something from me," I said to him. "I don't know. Call it a sixth sense."

He let a pause collect in the air before answering.

"I do. I have a personal situation. One I can't entrust to people inside, or outside, the company, however competent. To even speak the words necessary to explain the situation is a grave risk."

"Hence all the carrots and sticks."

"I know you're indifferent to the fortunes of the firm, but I've stayed abreast of you. Jason Fligh, in fact, has kept me filled in, as a way of expressing his displeasure at the way he thinks you were mistreated. In analyzing my options, it dawned on me you'd be the perfect person to call on for assistance. Amusing notion, don't you think?"

"No kidding."

"I still believe it's true, despite Mr. Ackerman's dismal failure. Assuming your fabled talent for self-destruction hasn't completely overwhelmed your common sense."

Big assumption. I really didn't give a crap about his money.

But I did give a crap about my daughter. She was a full-grown adult supporting herself in the City. She'd never asked her parents for money, but if she did, it would have to come from her mother. I know it's old-fashioned, but that bothered me.

"Okay," I said, "let's hear it."

"There'll be conditions."

"You're right. These are the conditions. You tell me what's really going on and I'll spring Ackerman. Though we keep the gun and the bullet it fired, which is safely lodged in my ceiling. You tell me what you want from me, and if I can do it, you release my royalties without qualification. If I can't, everything goes back to the way it was and you leave me alone forever."

He smiled. "Here I am giving you lessons on negotiation."

"Yeah, I wrote the book on it. It's called *Take It or Leave It.*"

He looked like he was still deliberating, but the climate in the room told me he was ready to get down to business.

"Very well," he said, as if this was all my idea. "It's rather simple, actually."

"So am I. What is it?"

"I've lost my girlfriend and I need you to find her."

"You're serious."

He looked at me like a boa constrictor who'd just noticed somebody'd dropped a mouse in his aquarium.

"Deadly serious."

THREE

I HAD A LOT OF DIFFERENT TITLES when I worked for the company, but my job was basically to figure things out. First as a field engineer with the operating units, diagnosing process and equipment failure. I loved that job. Not for the big hairy catastrophes; those were relatively easy. But for the subtle ones, the failed efforts to optimize, or improve efficiency, or repurpose operations. The tricky stuff that usually had everybody stumped.

I loved walking onto a site, looking up at the gigantic cracking towers and smelling the fragrance of partially remediated sulfur and complex hydrocarbons. The look of confusion and near panic in the eyes of the plant operators and engineers—some filled with hostility toward the asshole from White Plains, whom they assumed was just another ambitious prick fresh out of the corporate grooming salon. What they got was a lot more complicated, but sometimes a lot more dangerous in the long run.

Whether this was adequate preparation for the project George Donovan had in mind was yet to be proven.

"Just give me the whole story," I told him. "Don't make me fill in the holes."

He sighed.

"It all sounds so dreary and predictable. We hired a consultant to help with strategic planning. They assigned a woman who'd worked with us years before, when she was barely out of business school. A brilliant, attractive woman. We spent a lot of time together and you won't believe me when I say I've never done anything like it before, in all my years, despite the ongoing opportunities. I don't flatter myself to think it's my beauty and charm. I know it's just money and power. Nevertheless, this particular woman was different. More exotic, more intelligent, more powerfully compelling in her own right. And there I was approaching that now-or-never age. It all conspired to produce the inevitable."

I looked around for a pad and pen to write things down. With all the craziness and adrenaline poisoning, I wasn't about to trust my memory.

"What's her name?" I asked.

"Iku Kinjo. You may remember her. She remembered you."

I did. Like he said, brilliant and compelling. I could see her sweeping into my office on slender legs and an abundance of confidence. Trying to knock me off balance with the first question of the interview. Smiling at me, like we'd been assigned seats across from each other at the company barbecue, but intent on getting the answers she was looking for.

Instead of answering her question I lit a cigarette, contrary to office policy, and winked at her. She held up her forearm and looked at me over the top of her watch.

"My next interview is at two p.m.," she said, "which means

this meeting has a hard stop at one fifty-five. That gives us exactly forty-eight minutes."

Consultant-speak like that usually makes me sit up and square my shoulders. But I couldn't help liking her. She got her forty-eight minutes' worth, and as it turned out, eventually held up my division as a model on which the rest of the corporation might consider basing itself, which did a lot for her standing with me.

I said as much to Donovan.

"She respected the way you ran your division," he said. "You and your man Endicott, the financial fellow. Have you two stayed in touch?"

I remembered our divisional CFO, though his name hadn't passed through my mind since I left the company. Ozzie Endicott. It didn't surprise me that Donovan remembered. It was one of his political gifts.

"Haven't seen him or talked to him. You recall the severance agreement. No fraternizing with Con Globe employees. Not that I wanted to."

"Ah. Of course. Iku liked Endicott. But she didn't like you very much."

"Like you said, smart girl. What do you mean you lost her? In what way?"

"She'd been spending weekends in the Hamptons. That's where she was the last time I heard from her, by email, nearly a month ago. I haven't heard from her since."

Despite myself I suddenly felt something akin to sympathy for Donovan. Not for losing a lover, but for the pain he clearly felt in having to discuss it with me. Or anyone else. Now I understood why he wanted to extort my help. It would be easier to control the embarrassment from a position of strength.

"I'm going to ask you a lot of personal things," I said. "Don't expect me to be good at it."

"If it was tact I needed, believe me, you wouldn't be my first choice."

"How were things going with the relationship when she disappeared?"

"I thought they were going fine, but something was a little off. Nothing overt. Nothing apparent. She was distracted. Maybe a little distant. I might have imagined it. Conjured the memory after the fact."

"How secret is this thing?"

He thought that was amusing.

"You're now the third person in the universe who knows. Unless there's a God or Iku has a confidante she's hidden from me. I pray she doesn't. Exposure would be ruinous."

He read my expression.

"You know Arlis," he said. "My wife."

I pictured a small woman with iron-grey hair and a face that looked unnaturally young for her years. She was formal, but in a gracious, kindly way, and always looked me in the eye and smiled when I tried to make idle chitchat.

"Sure. I guess you don't want to lose her either."

"The loss would be total. You're probably unaware her family holds a significant share of Con Globe's voting stock. Enough to compel the board to review the chairmanship."

Now I understood why he wanted a stick to go with the carrots. Better yet, a hammer.

"I might've known that back then," I said. "Not the kind of thing I'd pay much attention to." I was probably the only VP in the place who could've said that, but that was one of my career specialties. Political myopia.

"Arlis Cuthright is her maiden name. Back in '38 her grand-father sold off his coal mines and cargo ships and needed to reinvest the proceeds. Hydrocarbon processing seemed a good bet on the future. The dot-com of its time. The family never thought much of me. Just another shanty Irish in their eyes. So the connection did little to help me on the way up. But it would surely grease the slide in the other direction."

I looked around the room and breathed in the aroma of leather and oiled furniture. I once thought people who lived like Donovan had discovered a secret tunnel that led from aching nervous want to a paradise of eternal security. Until I got to actually know people like George Donovan.

"I know I'm taking a monstrous risk involving you," he said. "But it's no worse than having this thing just hanging there. I couldn't possibly trust a private investigator. I'm even afraid to do a computer search. Afraid of leaving a trail. I know you're a capable man. The best troubleshooter the company ever had. And even if you hate me, I believe you'll honor a deal."

Now that I had a chance to focus on him, he didn't look so good, even in the dim light of the study. Older, wan. He prided himself on physical fitness, showing off his straight posture and knuckle-grinding handshake. But no exercise routine could counter this stew pot of uncertainty, loss, embarrassment and dread.

"What about family and friends?" I asked.

He looked around at the ersatz erudition that surrounded him.

"I don't think she has any friends. Just a boyfriend. Ostensibly. A man named Robert Dobson. She calls him Bobby, of course. I have no idea what he knows, or where he lives, or what he does. Just the name."

"Do you have a picture of her?"

He nodded with a half smile.

"Not in a frame on my desk. But she's part of a group photo in Eisler, Johnson's annual report. You can see it on their website. It's not very big, but you can make out her features.

I visit the site as often as I dare. Rather wretched of me, but there you are."

"Parents?"

"She was the product of an army officer's liaison with a woman on Okinawa. Adopted by an American couple as an infant. Raised in Brooklyn. Parents now dead, reportedly. Again, that's all I know. No other details."

"I don't remember much about Eisler, Johnson," I said.

"Management consultants or legal extortionists, depending on what you think of their reports."

"No word from them?" I asked.

"Her most recent assignment with us concluded several months ago. She and I continued. With all the lust and romantic fervor of addled adolescents. And then suddenly, no word. After a few days, I asked my assistant to get in touch with Eisler, Johnson on a simple pretext. The people she spoke to said Iku had left the firm, but to have her contact them if we heard from her. That's when I started to worry in earnest."

I tried to fix Iku Kinjo in my mind. I thought she'd be in her late thirties by now. A little older than Allison, my daughter, another princess of New York City, working hard in the graphic arts, the right brain division of the professional community. Talented and willing to wreck herself over vast, meaningless projects, though not the best at yielding to authority. Cursed with genetically determined behavior.

"Okay," I said.

"Okay?"

"I'll do it. The deal I laid out. If you don't remember the terms, I'll send you a copy of the transcript."

I pulled a small digital recorder out of my backpack and held it up. It was an exotic, highly sensitive device Allison had given me to record messages to send her over the computer. Not having a computer, I was glad to have a chance to finally put the thing to use.

"How thoughtful," said Donovan.

"Only one other condition."

He raised an eyebrow, waiting.

"All I have to do is find her."

"Of course," he said.

"No matter what I find."

I moved the little recorder closer to his face. He paused, catching the implication.

"I understand."

I downed the last ten-dollar gulp of scotch and got up to leave.

"You have a hole in one of your basement windows," I said. "Better get somebody to reglaze it before the critters start crawling inside."

Donovan stared back at me from his lustrous leather chair.

"With all the dust stirred up when you left the company, I wasn't able to express to you what I truly felt," he said.

I held up my hand to ward him off. This wasn't part of the deal.

"You don't have to. It doesn't matter anymore."

"Yes it does. I'm sorry about what happened. I know it was partly my fault. I didn't realize all the implications at the time. If I had, I might have chosen a different course."

I could feel two balls of something forming somewhere around my midsection. One fury, the other regret, leavened with a strange, brainless kind of concern for George Donovan. Loathsome emotions all.

There were things I could have said to him at that moment, but none of them sounded right in my head, so I kept my mouth shut and just left, with Donovan watching me go—pale, thin and alone in his silent house, his stone and mortar fortress home.

—

I half expected to be pulled over by the Connecticut State Police on the way down the Merritt Parkway, George Donovan having had a sudden change of heart. But I made it all the way to the border without incident.

From there I went into the City and booked myself into a hotel I used to stay at when I had an early meeting at Con Globe headquarters on Seventh Avenue. It was a stubby little place sandwiched between high-rises, a real City hotel with Italian doormen, Nigerian desk clerks and twelve-inch base-boards groaning under two inches of off-white paint. The radiators rattled and the carpets smelled of cigars and the elevator still had a guy working the sloppy brass controller, sitting on a milk crate, his belly stuffed inside a pair of grey polyester pants, his nails chipped and yellow, his breath a dank, sweet tribute to cheap liquor.

I slept until the sun came up, then I called Joe Sullivan on his cell phone. He was at the twenty-four-hour diner in Hampton Bays having breakfast with Ackerman.

"What did you do with him all night?" I asked.

"I took him over to Hodges's boat and cuffed him to a hand-hold inside the quarter berth. I took the salon. The wind was up and the boat rocked like a cradle. We slept like babies."

"I need you to let him go."

"I was afraid you'd say that."

I told him about my discussion with George Donovan, including everything about his involvement with the missing Iku Kinjo, and his attempt at extorting my help in finding her, but leaving out the preceding B&E. No sense further straining his already strained sense of propriety. Instead, I worked on persuading him that Ackerman posed little threat to the community.

"He's not a criminal, just criminally stupid," I said. "Anyway, you like it when I owe you a favor."

That tipped the scales. Sullivan kept me on the line while he told Ackerman he could go, as long as he left behind his gun and a promise to stay clear of Eastern Suffolk County for the next twenty years. I didn't hear Ackerman's reply, but I guess he'd agree to anything to get out from under Sullivan's baleful glare.

After I hung up I called Amanda and told her everything that had happened. Every detail I could remember. She almost seemed convinced that I was being fully candid and forthcoming. Which I was, almost. I diverted her by asking about the morning walk she took with Eddie and what she was making for breakfast. She didn't fall for it.

"Can I ask you to take care of yourself, even if I don't believe you truly will?" she asked.

"I will. In fact, I'm going back to bed for a few hours. Try to catch up on my sleep."

Which I did, with surprising success. Then I showered, shaved and put on jeans and a black T-shirt under the blue blazer. And black shitkickers. City garb. Then I called Allison, waking her up.

"Time to get up, honey. It's the crack of eleven-thirty," I said.

She said something like "mumph-umph" and coughed into the phone.

"Hold that thought," I said. "I'll be there in a half hour with coffee and bagels."

"You can't get here that fast," she squeaked out.

"I can if I'm only thirty blocks away."

Allison had a studio up on the West Side where she lived and designed on her own computer after recognizing she couldn't manage a regular full-time job. She didn't want it and full-time employers didn't want her. Luckily, graphic arts was the kind of thing you could do as a freelancer and still do pretty well.

I visited her place whenever I could. I always fed her lunch, which would take about the time needed to catch up and stay clear of the big emotional bear traps that would open in front of us if we lingered too long in one place.

But that was fine. Compared to where we used to be, this was paradise.

I was always glad to see her. I'd be glad to see anyone for whom I feel blind, unconditional love and devotion. Even when she met me on the sidewalk outside her apartment, red-eyed, with her dirty blonde hair looking like her mother's did when I first saw her walking across Kenmore Square, clutching her books to her chest as if expecting someone to leap out of a manhole and snatch them out of her arms.

"I can't let you see the place right now," she said, grabbing my arm and moving me down the sidewalk. "I've been cranking on this big crappy job all week and there's crappy stuff all over everywhere. And no, there's no boy in there."

"If there was I could get him to clean up the place."

She pulled me along quietly before asking the usual questions.

"Are you alright?"

"I'm great," I said. She looked suspicious. "Honestly. Everything's great."

"Everything's always great. You sure there's nothing you need to tell me?"

"Such trust."

She trusted me enough to stop asking, though she didn't look entirely convinced. I couldn't blame her.

She brightened considerably after her first cup of coffee. I listened attentively while she told me about her big job. I held eye contact and asked questions to help propel the narrative and demonstrate how well I was listening. These were things I'd learned from my friend Rosaline Arnold, a psychologist. Things that hadn't come naturally to me when Allison was growing up, when she really needed them. But Rosaline had convinced me that late was better than never, and based on how things were going with Allison, she was right.

When I thought it was safe to take the floor, I told her that Amanda and I were getting along reasonably well. Better than ever. I told her before she had a chance to ask, voluntarily sharing intimate emotional information. Something else I'd been taught by Rosaline. Both the content and delivery were pleasing to Allison. She adored Amanda, and the feelings were returned. This was a total, joyful mystery to me. Maybe some day Rosaline could explain it all.

When we were back on the sidewalk she actually hugged me for the first time since I'd left her mother.

"If you mess this up with Amanda I'll knock you on the head," she said into my shirtfront before letting me go, and without another look headed back to her messy apartment and big crappy job.

—

Eisler, Johnson occupied the top fifth of a glassy skyscraper on Madison Avenue. I breezed past the airtight security in the building's lobby and took the elevator, which opened directly into a starkly appointed reception area—all sharp-edged metal furniture, pale grey walls and Pop Art.

The receptionist was a reedy little guy with a shaved head and a complexion that matched the decor. Eisler, Johnson must have hired a first-rate interior designer. I walked up to him and asked for Iku Kinjo. What I got back was a blank stare. I asked for her again.

"She's not here," he said.

"When will she be back?"

"I don't know."

"Then please call someone who does."

"Do you have an appointment?" he asked, still looking colorless and blank.

"Yes. And I expect someone here to honor it."

"Can I have a name?"

"Burton Lewis. Lewis and Shanley."

Dropping Burton's name always had a predictable effect. He was a big deal in the City, running a gigantic law firm and sitting at the top of everyone's society shortlist. Though I didn't drop it too often. I hated exploiting our friendship, especially since he was always so eager to help out. But at least I knew I wouldn't get arrested for impersonating a very important person.

The receptionist was wearing a thin black headset, so all he had to do was hit a button on the console in front of him to connect with the offices behind a set of massive grey doors.

He spoke in hushed tones I had trouble making out. My hearing had never quite recovered from the effects of a big explosion I'd lived through a few years before. Lived to reach deep into my fifties, an age when even people who hadn't almost been blown up or repeatedly socked in the head had a little hearing loss. I leaned over the top of the desk to get a better angle with my good ear, causing the guy to look up at me with a touch of alarm, the first honest expression I'd seen him make.

He stuck his index finger into the console and said someone would be out to see me. I leaned farther over the desk, forcing him to lean back in his chair, increasing his alarm.

"Good," I said, then went and sat in a square chair that felt like a solid block of upholstered wood.

A few minutes later a tall, slim man with a head shaped like a lightbulb came through the big grey doors. He was wearing a dark green rayon shirt and black trousers that flowed when he walked. He was about my age, with close-cropped white hair that exaggerated the lightbulb effect. When he got closer I could see his eyes were a brilliant fluorescent lavender. Contacts.

When he saw me he turned and went back to the reception desk.

"Where's Mr. Lewis?" he asked.

"Probably at the Gracefield Club having a beer and a tuna sandwich," I said to his back. He turned. The pasty guy behind the desk shot me a look.

"You asked for a name. You didn't ask for mine," I said, getting up and walking back to the desk. I offered my hand to Lavender Eyes. "Floyd Patterson."

He took my hand, studying my face.

"That name rings a bell," he said.

"That was somebody else's job. You got a name?"

"Jerome Gelb. What is it you want?"

"I want to know if you've heard from Iku Kinjo."

He raised both eyebrows and pulled back his head, as if trying to get me in better focus.

"Your interest?"

A perfectly reasonable question. I just hadn't worked out an answer. I wondered what my friend Jackie Swaitkowski would do in a situation like this. She was great on improvisation.

"I have to serve her papers," I said.

"Oh?"

"Eisler, Johnson's named, too, but I'm supposed to give them directly to her to make it official."

"Really."

"Those are the rules."

"Who's the plaintiff?"

"Where's Miss Kinjo?"

I smiled at him. He smiled back and reached out his hand. "Maybe if I could just take a look."

"So you haven't seen her or heard from her."

He dropped his hand.

"No. Not for about four weeks. Officially, she's no longer employed here. So if there's some sort of action against the firm, tell whoever sent you to change the name of the recipient."

"She have any friends here? Anyone who might know where she went?"

Gelb shook his head, then frowned, caught giving me an ounce more information than I deserved.

"I'm not in a position to discuss this any further," he said. "Do you want the name of our attorneys?"

"Sure."

While he wrote out their names on the back of his business card I asked him, "Was she a friend of yours?"

He handed me the card.

"I was her boss. There are no friends at Eisler, Johnson."

"But you must be a little worried about her. I'd be, if one of ours went missing."

"Maybe I'll try a little worry when I finish digging out of the hole she left me in with our clients."

"When I find her I'll let her know that," I said, as I stuffed his card in my shirt pocket, turned and headed back to the elevator. He was still standing there as I watched the elevator doors close on Eisler, Johnson's cheerful reception area, a lanky, coutured centurion, off-balance but alert. Poised for battle.

FOUR

WHEN I GOT BACK TO Southampton I drove right past the turn off Route 27 that led up to Oak Point—the peninsula in North Sea I shared with Amanda—and headed east. It was about four in the afternoon, so I thought I'd just catch Jackie Swaitkowski at her office above the shops that lined Montauk Highway in Watermill. I probably could have stopped at the cottage and switched back to my Grand Prix, but I was reluctant to let go of the zippy little station wagon.

Jackie was nominally my lawyer. I'd never paid her anything and she hadn't done much for me but keep me out of jail at a few critical junctures, for which I was sincerely grateful. Actually, I owed Jackie a lot more than simple gratitude. So I didn't think it would hurt to toss a few more items on the bill.

I jogged up the outside stairs and tried the door to her office. It opened only partway. So I gave it a shove and pushed a bankers box clear of the passageway.

"Hey. I wanted that there," she said from somewhere behind the piles of paper on her desk.

There were a half dozen more bankers boxes on the floor, since there was no room to put them on the desk, or the sofa and chairs, or work tables, or any other horizontal surface in the room, all of them already groaning under a year's accumulation of professional detritus, indispensable possessions, *objects d'art*, flotsam, jetsam and the unimaginable heaps of worthless junk that gathered around Jackie like the drifting snow of an arctic blizzard.

"If you can't get out the door you'll starve in there," I said to her. "Unless you've put up survival rations."

Jackie stood up so I could see it was actually her. She was a medium-sized, curvy thing with a lot of freckles and a head full of kinky strawberry-blonde hair. It was only the second week of September, so she was still in her summer wardrobe—a scoop-necked cotton dress and flip-flops. Her glasses were pushed up into her hair, where she also stored a pair of number two pencils. An unlit cigarette bobbed between her lips when she spoke.

"No, but if you could find my lighter, I'd really appreciate it."

I tossed her mine.

"Keep it. I don't need it anymore."

"Yeah?"

"I'm giving it up. After I have one of yours."

"In other words, you're giving up buying and moving on to mooching full-time."

I scooped the piles off the two easy chairs that faced the loveseat and waved her over. I found an ashtray under a wet beach towel and balanced it on the last six months of *The Economist*.

Jackie flung herself over the arm of the chair and landed

with her knees already tucked up under her butt. We lit our cigarettes.

"Where's the mutt?" she asked.

"With Amanda. I left him with her so I could go into the City."

"Biz or pleasure?" she asked.

"A little of both. Though mostly manipulation, extortion and threats of violence."

She blew a lungful of smoke up at the ceiling.

"I hope that's just the amusing way you express yourself."

I disappointed her by telling her the whole story, beginning with the visit from Ackerman straight through to my conversation with George Donovan. I filled in as many details as I could remember. I was starting to appreciate the concept of free and full disclosure. It was liberating. Rosaline Arnold was right. If you just open yourself up to people you care about, you get so much back in return.

"You've got to be fucking kidding me. You're out of your fucking mind."

I tossed her the micro-recorder.

"Download it for me, will you? I'll probably never need it, but you never know."

"Sure, why not. Anything else I can do for you?"

"Yeah, a bunch of things, actually."

Her shoulders dropped.

"Goddammit, Sam."

"Come on, Jackie. What's so bad about tracking down a missing management consultant? How hard can that be? I'm not asking you to do anything illegal."

"Not yet."

"I need her background information. Her parents' names and where they lived. Her address in the City, which I don't even have for Christ's sake. The boyfriend, Robert Dobson.

All those vital statistics. You just have to climb back over to your computer and look it up."

"Or you could buy a computer."

"Donovan said she was heading for a weekend in the Hamptons right before she disappeared."

"We've heard that one before."

"I need to know where she stayed. Who she stayed with."

"Sure. I'll just do a search—'Iku Kinjo weekend Hamptons.'"

"You can do that?"

She sighed.

I remembered something Donovan had told me.

"Let's look at her," I said.

I coaxed her back to her desk and watched her call up Eisler, Johnson's website, click on the annual report and scroll through the pages until we came to a photo of a half dozen bright-looking young professionals sitting around a conference table pretending to be engaged in earnest and penetrating deliberations. One of the women had an Asian cast to her features, and the caption confirmed it was Iku Kinjo, EJ associate and specialist in the energy and chemical-processing industries.

"Can you isolate her face, blow it up and print it out?" I asked.

"This is a basic office PC. It's not Industrial Light & Magic."

"What can you do?"

"I can put the whole group shot on a disk and give it to you, and you can take it to a guy I know in the Village who can isolate her face, blow it up and print it out."

Ten minutes later she was still trying to figure out how to capture the image. It was all pure alchemy to me, so I wasn't much help beyond offering cheerful words of encouragement. I could smell her starting to smolder.

"How urgent is all this?" she asked, glowering up at me.

"Believe it or not I have people who pay me to do things for them. Quite a few at the moment."

"It's pretty urgent to George Donovan. Enough to risk a loaded gun at his head with my finger on the trigger."

She frowned, but kept at it until she had what I needed transferred to a disk, which popped out of a little door on the front of the computer.

"He must really want her back," she said, handing me the CD in a flat plastic case.

"Oh, yeah."

"You know why? Beyond the obvious?"

"Mostly fear. Maybe love. Those are good enough 'whys' for starters."

"Good enough for you?"

"Sure. I've seen what fear and love can do. You have any other theories?"

I could almost see the imperceptible tug as the hook caught. It was hard to know all the forces that drove Jackie's busy, chaotic brain, but I knew one of them was curiosity. And its co-conspirator—the fear of boredom.

"Do you think Donovan will hold up his end of the deal with you? If you find Iku?" she asked.

"I'm wondering the same thing. I want you to take a look at my severance agreement and the settlement of the intellectual rights suit. Let's see if Donovan's as omnipotent as he thinks."

"Could be a lot of money."

"That's what Donovan thinks."

I spent another half hour making sure Jackie had what she needed to do whatever she did on the Internet. The potency of the Web was just starting to take hold about the time I evolved from divisional vice president to finish carpenter, and I'd seen my friend Rosaline Arnold pull off some astounding online research. I promised I'd learn how to do it myself someday. After I evolved a little more.

I left Amanda's Audi Avant back in her driveway before sunset, which was just starting to heat up over on the western shore of the Little Peconic Bay. Clumps of luxuriant clouds were getting into formation, bathing in the first golden wash that radiated from the horizon. Eddie ran up to me just long enough for me to rub his head, then darted back toward Amanda's. A true loyalist.

I peeled out of my clothes and put on a pair of swim trunks. The September air was only slightly cooler than late August, but the bay was still warm. I walked gingerly over the pebble beach and dove through the miniature waves, feeling the salty grey-green water scrub off a coating of City grit, startling disruptive revelations, and unexpected possibilities.

I'm not a great swimmer. My body's too dense to float, though as a little kid I'd mastered a sort of hybrid dog paddle–Australian crawl that would keep me from drowning as long as my stamina held up.

I swam out as far as I dared and looked back at the tip of Oak Point. My cottage and Amanda's stood side by side a few hundred yards apart, two Foursquare testaments to the power of hope, forbearance and weathered cedar. My father built mine during the Second World War. Amanda's had also been raised by her father, though not with his own hands. He built about thirty other houses along with it, most of which she still owned, along with a big piece of abandoned industrial property at the base of the lagoon that bordered her lot. This alone would have made Amanda a very wealthy woman, even without the bulging portfolio of investments she'd inherited along with the real estate.

Besides the cottage, all I inherited was a debt from the nursing home that looked after my mother during the last years of her life. I was able to pay it off before taking my career, my marriage and my financial wherewithal off a cliff, leaving me with just enough to live on for a while before I had to reacquaint myself with finish hammers, nail sets and miter saws.

I wanted to think the financial discrepancy between us didn't matter, but it always does. I didn't feel I had to match her net worth to be worthy of the relationship, but having nothing versus having enough to underwrite a small country was a pretty big gap. Not a rich girl growing up, it had taken Amanda a little while to get used to fathomless resources, but she was getting there. She'd never be extravagant, but she had a right to have as full a life as her means would allow. It had never been an issue between us, but I wasn't about to let it become one. I'd never let her let me hold her back.

So it wasn't only concern for my daughter that caused me to drop for Donovan's offer. Sitting there in his library—funded by the river of technology royalties that had flowed daily into his company, technology I'd had a major hand in developing—I felt an unfamiliar tug of self-interest. It wasn't until I was out there trying to float around the Little Peconic Bay that I fully understood what it really meant.

I wanted some of my past back. A past I'd shed like a suit of flames. I didn't want my job back, and surely not my ex-wife. I didn't want the icy, faux-modernist house we had in the woods above Stamford, or the garden parties on the velvet lawns of Fairfield and Westchester Counties. I didn't want the crushing responsibility or nerve-searing professional stress. I didn't want to stand in front of the Board of Directors and sell them on the need to preserve one of the few assets they owned that actually contributed to the long-term health of the corporation—an asset they then threw away for eighteen months of stock lift. All I wanted was something I had truly lost all hope of ever having again.

I wanted the money.

———

The next evening Amanda and I hit the nightclubs.

It was more like late afternoon, since I wanted to talk to the bartenders and waitresses before things heated up. Not long ago all the clubs would have been closed by mid-September, but seasonal boundaries in the Hamptons were steadily blurring. There was still a big drop in population after Labor Day, but not like the old days when everyone from the City and beyond—renters and owners alike—would suddenly vanish and the locals would have the South Fork to themselves again. The socioeconomic Left Behind, and happy for it.

On the way to the first club on our list we stopped at the small shop off the main parking lot in Southampton recommended to me by Jackie Swaitkowski. It was called Good to the Last Byte and its purpose was akin to that of the auto repair shops I used to work for as a kid: basic computer maintenance and repair. It was cleaner and smelled better, but looked as if somebody'd set a bomb off inside a bank of mainframes—wire racks crammed with cartons, boxes and devices with faceplates splattered with tiny LEDs, heaps of printed circuits, loose CDs, stacks of packaged software, monitors of every vintage and size, plastic crates disgorging tangles of cables and surge protectors, pizza boxes and a full-size trash barrel filled with empty Mountain Dew cans.

"No wonder Jackie likes this guy," I said to Amanda as we picked our way to a rolling wire rack recruited as a service counter by the owner of the place.

"Randall Dodge," I said.

"That's me, Sam. Nice to see you again," he said, unfolding his full six-foot-eight frame and putting out his hand to shake.

Randall lived on the Shinnecock Reservation and was a racial gumbo of African, European and indigenous peoples. I knew him from Sonny's, the boxing gym I went to north of Westhampton Beach. I met him one day when he found himself at the top of a bench press with a bit more weight then he could safely put down. His request for a little help was remarkably calm and polite, given the circumstances. From then on we spotted for each other, and I had a chance to show him some things, like how to hit the speed bag and how to stay on his toes when moving around the ring. Like me, he almost never sparred, which was lucky for the rest of the kids who worked out at the gym. He was thin and slower than an earth mover, but he could reach halfway across the ring, and if he ever managed to connect with a punch it'd be good night, Irene.

"This is Amanda Anselma."

Randall took her hand and gave a little bow.

"My pleasure to meet you, ma'am."

"This your place?" I asked.

"For certain. Used to be my uncle's, but the technology got a little ahead of him. I was sorry to see him go. He didn't talk much, but you get used to the company."

Randall's head was big even for his beanstalk body. Or maybe it just looked big because of his broad face and high cheekbones, framed by a pair of slender, tightly woven braids. I never saw him form a smile, but his eyes were perpetually alight.

"I thought you were going to Hofstra," I said.

"I dropped out after taking all the computer science courses they had. After four years in the Navy I'm too old to be sitting through lectures on poetry and poli-sci. Got to get down and dirty with the circuits, you know?"

"Yeah, I do. What do you know about digital photography?" I handed him the disk.

"I'm a warrior of the Photoshop," he said, studying the disk as if the silvery surface could reveal its inner mysteries. "What are the issues?"

He slid the disk into an aquamarine Macintosh and brought the picture up on a big flat-screen monitor. I explained how we'd pulled the shot off a website, but needed a clearer image.

"The first thing you have to deal with is the low resolution," he said. "The original photo was probably high-res, but you can't have that on the Web. Slows everything down."

I reached over his shoulder and pointed at Iku.

"That's the girl. I'd love a good-sized printout. Clear enough to make an ID."

"Hard to do, boss," said Randall.

"Not for a Photoshop warrior," said Amanda.

Randall's sparkly eyes looked at me.

"Did you tell her pretty women drive me to impossible feats?" he asked.

"Why do you think I brought her along?"

"Go buy her a cup of coffee. I need a few minutes. The impossible could take a little longer."

We got drinks instead, at the big restaurant on Main Street. Seemed an appropriate way to ramp up to the evening. I had vodka. Amanda sipped red wine and filled the joint with radiant beauty. I never tired of looking at her. It was one of the few failings I allowed myself without reproach. When I wasn't feeling charmed by her smile I was lost in her pale green eyes. Or distracted by an ankle or the shape of her neck. I used to like looking at Abby, my ex-wife, but that was different. More an objective admiration of elegant, comely form. There was nothing objective in my appraisal of Amanda. Quite the contrary. The longer I lingered, the weaker my judgment.

"You're staring," she said.

"I am."

"Shouldn't we see how Mr. Dodge is fairing? While we can still see?"

"I'm clear as a bell."

"Of course you are. It's so irritating."

We paid the bill and walked back to Randall's shop. It wasn't a long walk, but I enjoyed every step. It was times like these, random events, that reminded me I'd given a lot of my life to misplaced ambitions and faulty desire. Not to dwell on regret, but to better appreciate the moment.

I watched Amanda as we walked, at once a presence so close at hand the barest twitch would alert her attention, yet as distant as the moon. This was something I'd learned about Amanda. She was there, and then not. And that was okay, now that I knew her better. I'd been through a lot of trial and error, sorting it out. But as long as she was there, walking next to me, I assumed she was willing to press on, even without a confirmed destination.

"You're staring at me again," she said.

"I am?"

"I don't mind as long as I haven't done something ridiculous."

"I'll tell you when you do."

"And they say you aren't a gentleman."

"They do?"

Randall looked hypnotized by his computer screen when we got back to his shop.

"I've got something, not sure what," he said to us without looking up. I walked into his work area and looked over his shoulder. A vivid portrait of Iku Kinjo filled the screen.

"You got what I wanted," I said.

He looked up at me.

"You sure? The skin tone doesn't look right."

"Her father was African-American. A soldier."

"Shoulda known. I got a big dose of that myself. On my mother's side."

"And you're just as pretty, Randall. Give me a half dozen copies."

In a few minutes we were out of there with a big white envelope stuffed with pictures of Iku. The whole experience made me feel as if the world had surged abruptly into the future without me—caught unawares and preoccupied with the Little Peconic Bay, questioning the point in having any future at all.

"You didn't actually box with that young man, I hope," said Amanda as we walked back to the Grand Prix.

"I never fight with techs. Too good at getting even."

The first two clubs were a bust. Nobody remembered Iku or took any interest in helping advance the cause. It wasn't worth the effort. They wore indolence as a cloak of pride. It made Amanda a little tense, glancing sideways to gauge my reaction. But I remained circumspect and polite. Pacing myself.

By the time we hit the third place, a dance club called the Playhouse, the early autumn nightlife had gained some traction. The house system was at close-to-full roar and a quorum of happily scrubbed and perfumed young aspirants were executing arrhythmic contortions on the dance floor. The men, anyway. The women moved much more fluidly, their eyes on each other, or the ceiling, or otherwise disengaged from their partners so as not to betray their amusement or horror at the situation they'd put themselves in.

I waited until we were hard up against the bar before showing around Iku's picture. Safe haven.

"Sorry, man. Haven't seen her. Friend of yours?" was the usual response.

"Sister."

After a long string of blank faces, Amanda decided to take over. As if the beauty of the investigator determined the results.

"Oh yeah. My favorite look," said the second guy she approached. A bartender.

"But did you see her?"

"Oh, yeah. Love the multiracial thing. In a thousand years we're all gonna look like Halle Berry and Tiger Woods. It'll be Earth Beautiful. Until some recessive ugly gene takes over and we'll have to mix it all up again."

"So you know her."

"Not really. Campari and soda is all I remember. Always came in with two other women and a guy. I see those three all the time. Live together at a share. All strictly Caucasoid."

"When was the last time they were here?" I asked.

"Labor Day weekend, I think."

Amanda stuck her thumb at me.

"Any chance they'll be here tonight?" I asked.

"Anything can happen, chief," said the bartender.

"I guess we're forced to wait here at the bar," I said to Amanda.

"No sacrifice too great."

We ordered gin and tonics and took a position where we could watch people coming through the door. We filled the time talking about the houses Amanda was knocking down and rebuilding on Oak Point and around the corner on Jacob's Neck. I worked for Frank Entwhistle, but occasionally consulted for Amanda. For no charge, unless you counted frequent use of her pickup truck and outdoor shower.

The Playhouse slowly filled to near capacity and the volume finally overwhelmed our ability to converse, neither of us inclined to shout over the noise about Sheetrock crews and building permits. So we settled on watching the pulsing throng on the dance floor and the people standing around and drinking, the couples entangled or ill at ease, the packs of men in baseball hats and baggy pants trying to look non-chalant as they surreptitiously scanned the crowd for targets of opportunity.

The bartender who'd seen Iku sidled up to me at the bar and put his hand on my forearm.

"There's the dude," he said. "Over there next to the pole. White shirt. Heineken."

I watched him for a while. He was apparently there alone, leaning on the pole and looking out on the dance floor, but otherwise disengaged. He had short brown hair and a few days' growth of beard. He was slight, just shy of delicate—Iku would have been close to his height in her bare feet. But he wasn't a bad-looking archetype of the generic young professional class.

"What do we do now?" asked Amanda, shouting in my ear.

"I don't know," I yelled back.

The guy stayed put through a half dozen musical segments—I don't know what else to call them—strung together with the non-stop thump of the underbeat. Then he put his empty bottle on a table and headed for the men's room. I told Amanda to save my seat and followed him.

A short line formed at the door. I stood behind him until we were through and waiting for vacancies at the urinals along the wall. It was a good time to take out the picture of Iku and hold it in front of his face.

"Hey, Bobby."

He whipped around.

"Get away from me," he said in a strained whisper. "What are you doing?"

"Looking for your girlfriend. What are you doing?"

He pushed past me and plunged back into the crowd. I followed him across the club floor to the main entrance. He maneuvered his way through the oncoming flow and shot through the door. When I got outside he was already partway through the parking lot. I ran after him.

"Hey, just want to talk," I called, which had the effect of shooting him into a full run. I saw him point something at a row of cars and the lights inside a Volvo sedan lit up. By the time I got there he was in the car with the engine running, his headlights blinding me as the car pulled out of the parking space and tore down the lane. I turned around and ran for the entrance to the lot, zigzagging through the rows of cars, hoping to cut him off at the pass.

Which I didn't quite do, but as he squealed out onto the street the headlights from the other cars lit the rear of his car and I could make out the license plate. I pulled a pen out of my shirt pocket and wrote the number on the inside of a pack of matches.

A man and a woman I'd nearly plowed over on my way across the lot came up behind me.

"What was all that about?" the woman asked me.

"That guy hit my car when he was backing out. Didn't even bother to look."

"Fucking Volvos," said the man, as if that explained everything.

When I got back to the bar Amanda asked me how it went.

"It went out the door and down the road. In a big hurry," I shouted in her ear.

"Interesting."

"You think?"

"Did he say anything?"

I told her what he'd said, as best I could above the noise.

"Odd," she said.

"I got his plate number. I think."

"So what do we do now? All this shouting is hurting my throat."

I looked around the inside of the club, which was now filled with young bodies and energetic foolishness.

"We dance," I told her, pulling her out on the floor and holding her in a traditional slow dance embrace, contrary to the pace of the music. It was the only kind of dancing I knew how to do, though empirically speaking, it was also the best.

We left after that, which I was happy to do. I was never much for nightclubs, and they made even less sense at this stage of the game. Amanda always looked great to me, but looked best when I could hear her speak, when she was animated by the conversation, whatever the content.

I cashed in my rain check for the outdoor shower before we went to bed. Cleansed by the steaming water, the pinprick stars overhead and the proximity of the sacred Little Peconic Bay, I slept hard. For once the swarm of bitter wives, alienated daughters, conniving plutocrats and light heavyweight contenders stayed out of my normally snarled dreams. Held at bay by the surge of gratitude that commingled with the scent of Amanda's thick brown hair and filled my mind as I let go and yielded to the night.

FIVE

I CAUGHT UP TO SULLIVAN the next day at the boxing gym in Westhampton, as I often did in the late afternoon, both of us preferring to go there after work. He was riding the stationary bike, a towel around his neck and a scowl on his face.

"I'm still unhappy about cutting that stupe loose," he said as I approached.

"I know. I appreciate it."

"Ross never heard anything. I hope he never does."

Ross Semple was the Chief of Southampton Town Police. Sullivan's boss.

"He won't from me," I said.

"You'll be thanking me the rest of your life for that one."

"So then you won't mind doing me another favor."

His expression stayed the same, but he sped up his pace on the bike. "Funny."

"I need to match a license plate with a name and address."

He smiled.

"Sure. Do you want a surveillance crew to go with that?"

"That's okay. I'll handle that part."

He took his feet off the pedals and the bike slowly spun to a stop.

"Explain."

"I found Iku's boyfriend hanging at a club last night. When I tried to talk to him he took off. But I got his plate number."

I stopped him before he could say no.

"There's no official police interest in this, I know," I said. "But so far at least two people consider this woman missing. Her boss and her big-shot lover. These are not minor connections. What if the boyfriend's in the same boat? She was last known to be in Southampton. That's your interest, right?"

"Jesus Christ."

"If I can't do this through you I'll have to go underground. Consort with dangerous scoundrels selling license plate identities out of storefronts in the Bronx."

"I thought you were born in the Bronx."

"Right. The attraction will be irresistible."

He stuck out his hand.

"Gimme the number."

I took it out of the waistband of my workout shorts.

"It was a Volvo. Four-door, black, fairly new. The guy's name is Robert Dobson. Mid-thirties, maybe a little more. Five foot nine, maybe less. Light brown hair, might have a short beard. I'm pretty certain he's out of the City, but might have an address here as well."

He looked at the slip of paper as if he could pull the address out of his memory.

"Why's that?"

"He's here all the time. Even in the off-season. Iku was last known to be here. One and one is two."

"Could still be a renter. Part of a group. Used to be a summer thing, now you see it year-round."

"Good thought," I said.

"You'll have to talk to the realtors. But if it's a private deal, there's no records anywhere. You'd have to go door-to-door."

"Let's try the easy way first."

"What 'let's'? This ain't an 'us' thing. It's a 'you' thing."

"I know. Whatever you can get me on the plate is all I need. Then I'll leave you alone."

"Right."

I spent the next hour doing all the clichéd things you do in a boxing gym—working the bags, jumping rope, lifting weights. I'd never seen the inside of a regular gym where regular people worked out, so I didn't know what that was all about. Having been a fighter as a kid, I'd gotten used to a boxing gym's sweet stink and blunt-force simplicity, its sense of purpose and undercurrent of latent threat. More motivational.

I had to stop sparring on doctor's orders. That was fine with me. I never liked the actual fighting part of the sport. Way too easy to get hurt.

In further acknowledgement of time and the looming menace of infirmity, I'd almost quit smoking, and for the first time put a weekly budget on vodka consumption. I wasn't entirely committed to the idea and the program was still in the experimental phase. But at least it kept at bay my daughter's carping on the subject.

When I was back in my car I made a call on my cell phone, another concession to the inevitable. This was all Jackie's fault. She'd lent me her phone once, and I liked it so much I didn't want to give it back. I blamed her for the new addiction even as I delighted in calling people from the front seat of a '67 Pontiac Grand Prix.

"House Hunters of the Hamptons," said the sing-song female voice on the other end of the line. "You tag 'em, we bag 'em. This is Robin speaking, how can I help you?"

"I think the selling metaphor needs a little work."

"Not if you ask my accountant."

"This is Sam Acquillo."

"Who else. Ready to cash in and move up?"

Robin and her partner Laura were old friends of Amanda's from when she worked at the bank. They'd started their real estate business at the bottom of the market in the early nineties, starved for several years, and now lived in the kind of houses they once dreamed of listing with their agency. Yet success had done nothing to add polish to their operation.

"I'm looking for a guy."

"Can't help you there, Ace. Sales and rentals only. Does Amanda know this?"

"The guy's a renter. Maybe. Though I guess he could be a buyer or an owner," I said, realizing I'd assumed from his age that he couldn't afford to buy in the Hamptons, which was ridiculous given the money often made by the callow youth of Wall Street.

"Why are you looking for him?"

"I'm actually looking for his girlfriend. It's a long story."

"Sounds it. What's his name?"

"Robert Dobson."

"I can check the computer."

"While you're at it, check for Iku Kinjo," I said, spelling out the name.

"That I'd remember, but I'll check."

She put me on hold. I spent the time trying to stay on the road while catching occasional glances of the tiny screen on the phone, checking the connection. I was still getting used to the mystical vagaries of modern telecommunications.

"Nobody here by that name," said Robin when she came back on the phone. "But I can ask around the other agencies."

"You can? That's great."

"Sure. We talk all the time. It's like one big happy back-scratching family. When we aren't back-stabbing. Don't tell the FTC I said that."

When I hit the end button on the cell phone I noticed the message icon on the tiny screen. This was a regrettable consequence of owning the phone. I'd been able to resist an answering machine my whole life, now it just tagged along for the ride whether I liked it or not.

I struggled unhappily through the retrieval process. It was George Donovan.

"Hello, Sam. It's George Donovan here. Just calling to confirm that I've spoken with counsel regarding the intellectual property settlement. I have full discretionary powers to negotiate a resolution of potential claims based on certain provisos being met. It'll need both our signatures. I'll await an update on your progress toward completion of the items we've discussed. Just a heads-up."

I knew circumlocution was the language of commerce, but I never liked listening to it. At least this time there was a good reason for the gibberish. I saved the number he'd called from and tossed the phone on the front passenger seat, letting it cool down before the next irritating interruption.

When I got home I showered off the day of work at Frank's giant rehab over on Halsey Neck and my subsequent workout at the gym. I was so eager to get under the hot water I forgot Eddie's dinner. When I came out of the outdoor shower he bounced around my feet and ran toward the door to show me where it was, then ran back to make sure I understood simple instructions.

"So, I shouldn't take a few hours to get back into the house like I usually do," I said to him.

He ignored me and continued herding, tongue out and lavishly long tail aloft, waving in the air.

Still in my towel, I dumped food in his bowl and a pint of Absolut in my aluminum tumbler. Our rations for the night. Or at least that part of the night. I put on a clean T-shirt and jeans as I always did after a day of dusty carpentry. It meant an almost daily laundry run to the basement, but it was a habit I'd formed early on. A reaction, I think, to my old man's disregard for the effect his greasy clothes had on the already agitated atmosphere of our household. He was a mechanic, and the caustic smell of refined petroleum still reminded me of emptiness and cruelty.

I was about to stroll over to Amanda's when Honest Boy Ackerman's SUV rumbled into my driveway. Eddie bounded up to greet him with his usual "Oh, boy, company!" élan. I bounded up, too. Less convivially.

I put both hands on the driver's side door before Ackerman had a chance to open it.

"What's up?" I asked, when he rolled down his window.

"New assignment."

"I thought Joe Sullivan escorted you out of town."

"That's why I'm here," said Ackerman. "I'm hoping you'll call him off."

"That's not up to me. It was all I could do to get him to let you go."

"I'm just trying to earn a living," he said.

"It's a big world. I'm sure George Donovan could send you somewhere else."

"He did. Right out of my job."

Amanda picked this moment to stroll across the stretch of lawn and over the tumbled-down flower beds that separated our properties. She wore a loose aquamarine dress and white sandals and carried an ice bucket stuffed with a bottle of white wine. I forced my attention back to Ackerman.

"Explain," I said.

"Donovan fired me, but Marve Judson hired me back. As an independent contractor. All on the q.t. He was mightily pissed that Donovan left him out of the loop. You can't do that to Judson. Can't fuck with him like that. He's gone batshit trying to figure out what Donovan's up to."

"Hello," said Amanda, as she tossed a curious glance at Ackerman.

"I'd introduce you but he's not going to be here long enough to make it worth the trouble."

"Hey," said Ackerman.

"Charming, isn't he?" said Amanda.

"Like a root canal."

I wanted to sock him in the mouth again to illustrate my approach to dental health, but instead took a deep, cleansing breath. I knew, despite myself, that Ackerman was a complication not easily done away with. Certainly not the way I'd like to.

"Say, Honest Boy," I said. "You like red wine or white? Or would you rather have a cocktail?"

Ackerman just sat there and looked at me, hunkered into his surly defensiveness. For good reason. I tried again.

"Or a beer? I've got some fancy microbrews in the basement."

"Beer's okay," he said tentatively.

Amanda gently moved my hands off the truck's door and opened it up.

"Come along, sir," she said. "I won't let him hurt you."

"One beating's the limit here on Oak Point," I said, taking him by the arm and starting him off toward the bay. "If you survive, you're invited to join in native rituals. Starting with carrying the ice bucket."

I took it out from under Amanda's arm and passed it to him. She took his other arm and escorted him out to the Adirondack chairs that I keep at the edge of the breakwater above the pebble beach. Eddie followed, sniffing at his heels, still entranced by the novelty of a fresh visitor. I stopped at the cottage to grab my tumbler out of the kitchen and a six-pack from the fridge in the basement—the pricey stuff from Burton's private stash.

I dragged another Adirondack to the edge of the break-water so we'd all have a seat and a nice view of the Little Peconic Bay, now turning a blue-tinted dark grey, like the gunmetal of Ackerman's forfeited automatic.

"Mr. Ackerman has been sharing his point of view," said Amanda as I sat in my chair. "He said it was a misunder-standing."

"More than one. But who's counting."

I handed him the beers. He looked grateful.

"Okay, Honest Boy," I said, "let's start from the top."

He said as soon as Sullivan cut him loose he headed back to his office in White Plains. Donovan had given him voicemail service so he could leave him messages, but it was discontinued. That was the first hint something was amiss. At the office was the second—a pair of security guards waiting for him with his belongings already packed in boxes and stacked on a handcart. He said he just turned on his heel without a word and led them to his SUV. Then he did more or less the same thing I did when faced with similar circum-stances: he killed a fifth of bourbon.

Despite the resulting hangover he got up early enough the next day to interrupt Marve Judson's morning jog along the wooded lanes of Pound Ridge.

He'd guessed right. Marve knew nothing of the termination. And nothing about the special project that preceded it. Ackerman was pleased at how interested Marve was in his story, which he told in detail as they sat next to the swimming pool drinking coffee served by Marve's wife.

While they were still by the pool Marve called a contact he had with an outside investigation firm and asked them to take on Ackerman as a freelance operative and bill back his fee under the firm's name. Ackerman got the feeling the guy on the other end of the line was a good friend of Marve's, and it wasn't the first time there'd been such an arrangement.

Marve told Ackerman that his responsibility was to Con Globe's Board of Directors, and not to any one board member, even the chairman. That was the kind of thing Marve would say, having a decided bent toward the bombastic and self-righteous. I felt like telling Honest Boy that Marve's dearest responsibility was always to the personal agenda of Marve Judson, but that would have served little purpose.

"So Judson told you to come back out here and talk to me?" I asked.

"Basically."

"You're wasting your time."

"What do you mean?"

"I don't know what's going on any more than you do."

Ackerman shook his head.

"With all due respect Sam, that's kind of a crock. People still talk about your flame-out at Con Globe and all the wild shit you got into after that. You had that towheaded Captain America imprison me on a freaking boat overnight, and then cut me loose without hardly a fare-thee-well. I don't need security training to know that wasn't just fun and games. As fun as it was."

Amanda had been following the conversation intently. She looked at me after Ackerman's last comment as if to say *he's got you there.*

"How's the beer?" I asked.

"It's very good," said Ackerman, graciously.

"About that flame-out, as you call it."

He gave sort of a sympathetic smirk.

"Yeah?"

"The severance agreement dictated that I cut all contact with Con Globe employees, in particular those in middle or senior management, forever. Even the slightest violation of that provision would be very bad for me."

"Me breaking into your house wasn't your doing," said Ackerman. "They can't hold that against you."

"Oh, yes they can. Even if I'm in the right, the legal fight alone would ruin me."

"And we know Sam hates a fight," said Amanda.

"Could've fooled me," said Ackerman.

"So after a long talk with a lawyer friend of mine, I decided to just let it go. Discretion being the better part of valor."

"I never understood what that meant," said Ackerman, "but I get the idea. And it's still a crock. I don't know what sort of vegetable wagon you think I just fell off of."

"Turnip is the standard, I think," said Amanda.

"Anyway, that's my story for Marve Judson," I said. "Too bad if he doesn't like it."

Ackerman looked unhappy.

"Man, you don't make anything easy."

"I think some truffle pâté and a wedge of Fromage d'Affinois would be just the thing right now," said Amanda, standing abruptly and striding off toward her house. We watched her in silence, all the way to her front door.

"Nice set of legs on that one," he said.

"Don't tell her that. Only go to her head."

"Better to keep 'em in the dark."

"Same goes for you. And Marve Judson," I said.

"So there is a real story," said Ackerman. "You know it, but you'll never give it up."

"Maybe you could beat it out of me."

"They didn't tell me you were an ex-fighter. I'da been more careful."

"So now who's in the dark?"

"The little guy, Acquillo. Always the little guy."

I turned my attention back to the Little Peconic Bay. The sky by now had gone a garish crimson and gold, drawn in a swirl pattern atop the western horizon. It felt like fall had already taken hold in this second week of September, the air cool and dry, the fading sunlight having shed the soft summer glow. Every season in the Hamptons had its claim on the heart, but I prized autumn most of all.

Eddie smelled the cheese a hundred yards away and ran over to guide Amanda back to the Adirondacks. As a reward, he got the first wad of the soft cheese, slathered on a slice of pâté. The rest of us got ours in due course. I didn't want to give any more information to Ackerman, and luckily he didn't press it. Instead he set himself to finishing off the six-pack of Burton's expensive beer and Amanda's hors d'oeuvres. Then he padded back to his hulking SUV and disappeared into the night.

"I'm not sure what that was all about," said Amanda when he was securely out of earshot.

"Complexity theory," I said.

"Of course."

"The rapid compounding of variables that causes an orderly system to be suddenly and irrepressibly propelled into chaos."

"In other words, you need to find that girl in a hurry."

"You bet," I said.

"So what're you going to do?"

"Have another half a tumbler of vodka. Which means only half a tumbler tomorrow, unless I want to skip it entirely the day after."

"Or simply adjust the budget parameters," she said.

"Spoken like a banker."

"Not a banker by choice. I aspired to greater things."

"I forgot. You were a science major."

"Biology. I would have thought that was obvious."

"Mostly the flair for anatomy."

"Let's see if you can hold that thought through the next round," she said, scooping up my tumbler and her empty wine bottle to take back to my cottage for reprovisioning.

Not a problem, I thought as I craned my neck to watch her move across the lawn again. That's when an association that should have been obvious leaped to my mind. From behind, Amanda looked a lot like Iku Kinjo. Tall and slender. Moved with the kind of feminine roll of the hips that could distract a stadium full of heterosexuals. Iku's skin tone was darker and redder than most Japanese, though her features were emphatically Asian. Including the coal black eyes that signaled a readiness to either accept your abject submission or rend your flesh into bloody ribbons.

This is where my mind was wandering. She didn't fit with George Donovan. Unless you invoke the canard that opposites attract. Lord knows my skills in the mysteries of love and attraction were pathetically inept, but it just didn't feel right. Iku was a shooting star. Brilliant and incandescent. Lit up the sky wherever she went. Young and self-assured, she didn't need Donovan. If anything, he needed her. As a sign of his progressive business acumen, his drive to introduce modern strategies to a mature industrial company like Consolidated Global Energies.

When Amanda showed up again I asked her opinion.

"Why would a beautiful and accomplished young superstar like Iku Kinjo want to roll around naked in bed with a shallow, albeit wily, old stuffed shirt like George Donovan?"

"Girls do dumb things sometimes," she said without hesitation, settling herself back into her Adirondack, passing me my tumbler on the way down.

"Okay."

"Or she didn't do it. He just says she did."

She raised her wine glass so I could clink it with my tumbler. She didn't look nearly as self-satisfied as she deserved to look.

"From now on you approve every assumption I make about precocious young women. You're obviously knowledgeable on the subject."

"I was never precocious and I'm no longer young. But all women are capable of sexual conduct that can surprise them as much as anyone else. By the same token, all women are prey to false accusation prompted by male fantasy."

"You learn that in biology?"

"At the disco. New York City. Circa 1987."

"Both possibilities provide a motive for her to go to ground," I said. "Which gets me no closer to finding her."

"Don't be so sure about that."

She studied the inside of her glass, swirling the wine around until it was perilously close to cresting over the lip.

"The bad thing that caused her to run could have been something entirely different," she said, finally.

"You're right. I hadn't thought of that."

"Do you think Donovan was surprised by her disappearance?"

"Definitely. He was completely caught off-guard. That partly explains the reckless way he's been handling things. Taking big risks. Panic mode."

"Alerting Marve Judson," she said.

"Yeah. You can't work around a reptile like that. He can sense perfidy through the soles of his feet."

"What do you think Judson will do?" she asked.

"Get ready to meet him. He'll be here within a week."

"You think so?"

"I know him. It's a sure thing."

"I'll pick out an outfit."

"Think Kevlar."

She went back to examining her wine glass. I focused on the Little Peconic. There were two or three sails still visible in the fading light, stark white against the distant shore of the North Fork, heeled over against the westerly funneling through the channels above and below Robins Island. I'd been watching sailboats crisscross the little bay outside my front door my whole life, and only now was I beginning to think about being on one of them. I'd sailed since the birth of memory, on Sunfish and homemade dories and then bigger sloops belonging to friends around town, and ultimately crewed on stately racing yachts for the vapid sops Abby cultivated up in Marblehead. But it wasn't competition I had in mind. Quite the contrary. I imagined ghosting into the outer waters on a lazy southwesterly and anchoring within the embrace of a sheltered harbor, to watch the show in the sky and listen to the splash and flutter of water birds and the ring of hasps against a metal mast.

It wasn't exactly the male fantasy Amanda referred to, but it served to transport my mind through the balance of the evening, allowing me to postpone another confrontation with uncontrollable forces set loose on the world by the usual concoction of ardor, cupidity, ego and fear.

SIX

I WAS HOLDING A PIECE of crown molding over my head when my cell phone rang. I had three finish nails stuck in my mouth and one half-nailed through the molding, which I was about to pull out, unhappy with the coping job I'd done at the corner joint. I had to keep the twelve-foot-long piece of trim jammed in place with my left hand while I slipped the hammer in its holster and fished the cell phone out with my right. The phone's persistent ring tone lent a lunatic accompaniment to the maneuver. I flipped it open and pushed the talk button.

"Wha'," I said into the phone, or something like it as I spat out the nails.

"Drinking on the job?"

"Hey, Jackie. Can I call you back in a minute?"

"What's the matter? You sound strained."

"That's why I need to call you back," I said through my teeth.

As she started to ask another question I flipped the phone shut and stuffed it back in my pocket. My next trick was to dig a small block of soft pine out of my shirt pocket to stick between the hammer head and the expensive molding so I wouldn't ding it when I pulled out the nail. All with one hand. Another lesson on the advisability of coping miter joints properly the first time.

The phone started ringing again.

I pulled the nail and lowered the molding safely to the scaffold a few seconds before my left shoulder and challenged temperament both gave up the fight.

Throwing the phone at the masonry fireplace on the other side of the room would have been the easy thing to do. Instead I answered it.

"Jesus Christ I said I'd call you back."

"Are you alright?" asked Jackie. "You sound terrible."

"From now on I'm leaving this thing in the car."

"You're supposed to have it with you at all times. That's the point. And you can't get mad at me when I'm doing you a favor."

I shook out my shoulders, dropped my jaw and took a deep breath. "I'm not mad. I'm always glad to hear from you, no matter what the circumstances," I said softly.

"Especially when I'm calling with interesting information."

"Especially. What is it?"

"George Donovan is getting ready to do what he said he would do. Maybe. The original severance documents were prepared by the general counsel, a guy named Mason Thigpen. What did you do to him?"

"I'm not sure. I vaguely remember a lot of blood and really big security guards."

"Donovan has yanked your agreement out of Thigpen's office and given it to an outside lawyer, on the basis that the general counsel's interest in this is adverse to the corporation's."

"You lost me at 'yanked.'"

"Outside counsel has been retained to examine your agreement and make the necessary modifications, if corporate management deems it appropriate, to allow you to participate in the ongoing settlement of the intellectual property suit brought by a group of plaintiffs. Most of whom worked for you, by the way, a fact Donovan is telling the board warrants some careful consideration."

"How the hell did you get all this?"

"What the hell do they pay administrative assistants and what the hell gender are they, usually?"

"Can you get a copy of my agreement?" I asked.

"I thought you had a copy. Silly me."

"I did at one point. But it was probably in that car I lost in downtown Bridgeport. Long story."

"I don't want to hear it. My guess is there's a clause that says for consideration you waive all employment claims, including any compensation beyond the amount of the severance, which includes royalties or the proceeds from civil litigation, which would likely include the intellectual property action. All they have to do is rewrite that clause to specify your agreement doesn't include settlement money, and because they went to the trouble to be so specific about every other form of payment, you're in. Of course, somebody could still contest that exclusion, but as you know, everything is contestable by everybody all the time, which is how we in the legal profession like it, thank you very much."

"I can think of people who might want to do that."

"Contest it?" she asked.

"Yeah."

"Not the nice lady who heads up Human Resources. She's all for it."

"You talked to her? Jesus."

"I'm your attorney. I'm allowed. They've been fielding these inquiries full tilt since the settlement got under way. I made it all sound very routine. I didn't push anything, just asked simple questions. Nobody got wiggy. Not to worry."

"I'm worried about this coming unglued."

"I know," she said. "But I couldn't do what you wanted me to do without talking to the people who have the information. Next I'm talking to Tucker, Blenheim, the outside counsel, to see what they have to say."

I'd seen Jackie in action. If she said it was low key, it was low key. And I knew how isolated and overlooked they were in HR. George Donovan probably couldn't find their offices without a map of the building. But Marve Judson was another story. A legitimate threat.

I told Jackie about Ackerman's visit.

"Judson can do that?" she asked. "Hire somebody who's been fired by the big boss?"

"Not exactly. Which is why he's working the fiddle with his buddy's PI firm. But he's making the right calculation. If Donovan found out he'd have to weigh the risk of canning a senior guy like Judson—who wouldn't go quietly—against whatever damage Ackerman might cause by staying in the picture. I'd say pretty minimal as long as I keep my mouth shut, which Donovan trusts me to do, given my vested interest."

"Holy crap that's Byzantine."

I unsnapped my tool belt and lowered it slowly to the floor. Then backed against the wall and slid down until I was sitting on my butt. All around me was the clatter of construction—the snap-pop of pneumatic nailers, the high-pitched whir of circular saws, thumping hammers and the brainless blather of talk radio.

But I wasn't listening, as recollection dislodged my mind and sent it off to some other place. A place of cowed silence, acreages of office space enclosing a vast checkerboard of work stations and cubicles, where the only mechanical sound was the low hum of copiers and fluorescent lights and desk phones trilling like captive birds.

Glass-walled individual offices lined the periphery of the building where I'd worked. Aquariums with the aerators turned off. That's why I lived in a lab office on the ground floor that for some reason had a huge corner window looking out on a broad, green lawn that appeared to extend out to the horizon, though in fact stopped at a band of trees planted to dampen the noise blowing up from Interstate 287.

My official office was eight stories above my head. Same corner location, more toxic atmosphere. In the basement I could stay close to the design engineers and research scientists who produced the intellectual foundation for the products and services applied by the people sitting above. Applications in the service of rapacious machinations that reached full flower on even loftier floors at company head-quarters in Manhattan.

"I've got a little more on Iku Kinjo," said Jackie, regaining my attention. "Not a ton."

"What?"

"She was adopted by a pair of academics. An historian and a sociologist. Lived in Brooklyn, taught at Manhattan College. Lifetime political activists. Both busted in the Chicago riots of '68. Did the pacifist lecture circuit, started a soup kitchen near campus, gave heavily to worthy social ventures. I'd want to meet them if they were still around."

"Dead?"

"Fifteen years ago. Car accident."

"Jesus Christ."

"Also Jewish."

"The parents?"

"Hyman and Naomi Rothstein?"

"Probably."

"Pretty secular household, though, is my guess. Kept Iku's birth name. No bat mitzvah I can dig up. No connection to any synagogues within forty miles of their apartment. In fact, I don't think they were part of a religious community. Probably too radical."

I wondered what Iku thought of the whole thing. The Rothsteins undoubtedly leveled with her from the outset about her origins and identity. Probably showered her with love and support. And prayed, despite their secular ways, for her to adopt their beliefs and proclivities. None of which, I guessed, included corporate management consulting.

"Fifteen years ago. Where was Iku?"

"Fresh out of Princeton and on her way to Harvard Business School, natch, before a fast run up the consulting ladder from Arthur Little, to Bain, to Eisler. We can stipulate the girl's wicked smart."

I could testify to that myself, from direct experience. I'd also say assertive, bordering on aggressive. And direct, which I'd take any day over oblique or subtle or disingenuous. Donovan said she didn't like me, so I guess she didn't. She had a lot of company. Though I always thought she appreciated the way I dished it back at her as fast as she could dish it out, without being patronizing or calling attention to our difference in age and experience. Or gender.

"Maybe it's good her parents didn't live to see her become a running dog of American capitalism," said Jackie, reading my mind.

"How did it happen?"

"Crushed by a semi on the way back from dropping their daughter off at Harvard," she said.

"That'll teach her to go to business school."

"They say Jewish guilt is even worse than Irish Catholic, though my mother could give them a run for their money."

"Not an issue if they weren't religious."

"My mother wouldn't go to Mass. Blamed God for my father's personality."

"We're getting way ahead of ourselves," I said.

"You're right. We don't know the dynamic in the Rothstein household."

"But her roommates at Princeton, or Harvard, might."

There was a brief moment of silence on the other end of the line, followed by a sigh.

"I'll let you know what I find out," she said, and hung up the phone. I turned the phone off before going back to the crown molding. I also tried to turn off the speculation that kept percolating up from the dark hole that was Iku Kinjo's life. I hated obsessing over quandaries made so principally by the absence of serviceable fact. I remembered the process engineer who first hired me, a born troubleshooter, standing in the control room of an oil refinery smashing his fist on the plant manager's desk and hollering, "Data, data, data!"

I made it to the end of the work day without lousing up the job and embarrassing myself, but I was glad to unhook my tool belt and dump it with my pneumatic nailer into the trunk of the Grand Prix. On the way home I turned on the public jazz station, WLIU, and smoked my third cigarette of the day, the definition of a blessing and a curse. I still had to concentrate on keeping the ten-ton Pontiac from drifting into a tree, but that didn't stop Iku Kinjo from jumping into my brain like an irrepressible child, demanding attention for attention's sake.

That's probably why I didn't notice the dark grey Ford Crown Victoria with the wailing electronic siren and flashing blue light on the dashboard until it was halfway up my ass. I reflexively hit the brakes, which made things worse. I braced for impact, but instead the Crown Vic shot out into the oncoming lane, sped by the Grand Prix, and then swung back in front of me. His brake lights flashed on but I was already heading for the shoulder, wondering what the hell I'd done this time.

The driver's door of the unmarked car swung open and Joe Sullivan jumped out. He hiked up his camouflage pants and adjusted his sunglasses as he strode back to my car.

"You going deaf?" he yelled, when I lowered my window. "I been on your tail for five miles."

"Sorry. Preoccupied."

"Thinking about dinner?"

"And maybe a cocktail, just for a change of pace."

We agreed to meet at Paul Hodges's place in Sag Harbor after I showered and scooped up the pup. The Pequot overlooked one of the last commercial marinas on the East End. Lobster boats and day charters, men and women in high rubber boots and wool knit sweaters. Scarred hands and beer bellies, some courtesy of the Pequot's generous operating hours. Hodges had been a fisherman himself, among other things, so he knew the off-time habits of the trade. He ran the place with his daughter Dorothy and a dour stork of a Croatian named Vinko. It wasn't exactly the career Dorothy had planned after graduating from Columbia, but the day-to-day management of the place had been thrust upon her after Hodges fell through a rotting deck. He'd recovered since then, but admitted the months of convalescence had made hanging around the sturdy old sloop he lived on a hard habit to break.

"Dotty grew up workin' the tap and tossing clams in the fryolator. It's in her blood," he'd tell me, trying to convince himself.

Among the many charms of the joint was its liberal policy regarding dogs on the premises: restricted only when the health inspector was scheduled to visit. For his part, Eddie kept a low profile, lying quietly by my feet and suppressing his social instincts.

When I got there Sullivan was already halfway through a pitcher of beer and a mound of fried calamari.

"You know, some of those things get as big as a city bus," I told him, pointing at his plate.

He studied the breaded wad of tentacles stuck to the end of his fork. "Yeah, and the Loch Ness Monster's been munchin' blues offa Jessup's Neck."

Dorothy already had an Absolut on the rocks and a bowl of water for Eddie on their way over. She was wearing gloves that ran all the way to her biceps. They had all the fingers cut out—a sensible practicality. Her hair color was in constant rotation. Tonight it was a simple everyday jet black, drawn and pinned at the back tightly enough to look painted on. Her face, powdered into a lovely funereal pallor, lent a stark backdrop to her lips—tonight red enough to stop traffic out on Noyac Road.

"I hear you serve food here. Principally fish," I said to her as she dropped the vodka in front of me.

"That's what my father claims, though I've never actually seen it come out of the water."

"Really."

"I hate fishing. Never go near a boat."

"Seasick?"

"I feel sorry for the fish. Don't want to know about it. When they show up in the kitchen I pretend they've been manufactured out of protein pulp and formed in little fish molds to look like the real thing."

"There's a way to whet the old appetite," said Sullivan, as he put away the last of the calamari.

"In that spirit, bring me a bacon cheeseburger," I told her. "And a plain one for the dog."

"I know. No bun, just a few fries."

"Too much potato makes him fart."

"And don't think about the cow," said Sullivan.

When she left I asked Sullivan if he'd been able to chase down Robert Dobson. He looked a little offended.

"You gave me his plate number. Believe it or not, the police know how to obtain an ID from just that one little thing. As long as we're able to use the radio and speak without slurring our words."

"Great. Where's he live?"

"Manhattan. Where'd you think?"

"I was hoping out here."

"Manhattan's his official residence. But I thought to myself, maybe that's not his only address."

He leaned into the table. I sat back to give his story a little room.

"This is why they made you a detective," I said.

"I went back to HQ and started searching the tax rolls for a similar name within a fifty-mile radius of Southampton. There're more Dobsons than you might think, though not too many to pick up the phone and call."

"You're kidding."

"The direct approach. Unpopular with today's technology, but cops find it very handy and effective."

"So you found him."

"On the fifth try. His parents have a house in a gated community in Southampton Village, just inside the incorporated limits. On the east side, near the ocean. Five houses in their own private Idaho. They got a guy who sits at the gate all day letting people in and out pretty much as they please, but I guess it makes the owners feel special. I felt special just driving in there, flashing my badge at the hero in the little house and telling him to stick his head back up his ass and open the gate."

"It's the softer touch that gets the results."

"I located the place, saw a Volvo in the driveway, and that was that. I didn't think you'd authorized the Southampton Police to break down the door, put a black hood over the guy's head and drag him to the Pequot."

"Might've expedited things."

"If Ross finds out about half the off-the-books shit I been doing I'll be busted back to patrol in the time it takes to put on the uniform."

As he talked he wrote addresses and phone numbers out on a napkin. He slid it across the table and I stuffed it in my pocket.

"You'd love that."

"Fact is, I would. But the wife is getting used to the pay."

Soon after, Dorothy brought out the burgers and Sullivan's porterhouse steak, which I didn't even know the Pequot served. After that, the place started to fill up in earnest, first with a gaggle of local kids that Dorothy put through a rigorous ID process, then some crews fresh off the day charters, people whose occupation even a blind man could identify if his olfactories were still intact.

"Dotty's got a funny gig for a girl who can't harm a fish," said Sullivan. "The smell in this place is enough to make the fish want to kill themselves."

"Anomalies are essential to the ambience."

"If you're gonna speak French we're done here."

In fact, we weren't done until Eddie, Sullivan and I finished off our meals and another round of drinks, and I snuck enough cash to Dorothy to cover Sullivan's massive consumption, and we debated the prospects of regional teams as we entered the home stretch of the professional baseball season, and Sullivan quieted down a noisy table by gently holding the forearm of the worst offender and whispering something in the guy's ear, and Vinko came out of the kitchen in his greasy whites to get Sullivan's opinion on the porterhouse, and Dorothy tied up the conversation for half an hour with a dissertation on the amazingly contemporary art somebody'd discovered in a tomb inside one of the great pyramids, and Eddie managed to scare the pee out of a young woman who'd been dropping pieces of her meal under the table in an effort to preserve her anorexic body shape, which Eddie keyed in on, and after devouring what was available on the floor, followed the track back toward the girl's lap by way of her naked, parted legs. Since most women aren't accustomed to wet, furry objects thrust unexpectedly between their knees, some screaming was involved.

All in all, a satisfactory evening at the Pequot.

———

Instead of going to work the next day I popped over to Robert Dobson's parents' place. I drove Amanda's shiny red Dodge pickup with the welded-on cargo racks, which was nevertheless far less conspicuous than a 1967 Grand Prix.

First I had to breach the security perimeter at its weakest point: the hut.

"Who you here for?" asked the security guard, a tidy little white guy with dyed brown hair and a thick, straight-cropped moustache.

"The Dobsons."

"Purpose of the visit?"

"Carpentry."

He looked up at me from his clipboard.

"Didn't know they was doin' work," he said.

"Thinkin' about it. The boss sent me over here to appraise the situation."

"They gotta get approval from the association. This place got regs up the ass. Can't do shit unless them I's and T's are crossed."

"That's why I'm here, brother," I said. "I'm the boss's man on T's and I's."

"I'm a T and A man myself."

"I leave that for the weekends."

He went back to the clipboard, on which he wrote something, who knows what. Then he waved me in. I thought about my hike up the hill to Donovan's Greenwich neighborhood. Probably could have saved myself a lot of trouble with a frontal attack. Live and learn.

The houses in the complex were each on about two acres, in a variety of architectural motifs, from standard shingle-style postmodern to stuccoed pseudo-Tudor to amped-up bungalow. There was a curious absence of privet hedges, a standard throughout the Village's estate section. Maybe the developer wrote a hedge ban into the I's and T's.

I found the address Sullivan had given me and parked across the street. The Dobsons had chosen a two-story New England colonial with three dormers protruding from the roof and a colonnaded portico over the front door. The driveway swept past the house in a gentle U-shape that provided two ways in and out. The doors to the three-car garage were closed. A tall white flagpole stood in the middle of the lawn, flagless. The telltales of a professional maintenance crew showed in the edging and tightly trimmed shrubs that lined the drive and hugged the periphery of the house.

Parked up tight to the house was the black Volvo.

I had a cup of Viennese cinnamon coffee from the corner place in the Village and three cigarettes slipped out of the pack on the way out the door that morning. I lit the first one after drinking half the large coffee. Pacing myself. I turned on the public jazz station and pretended to leaf through a file folder opened across the steering wheel. Since a contractor's pickup was the only thing sighted more often in the Hamptons than a third-rate celebrity, I almost felt invisible.

I hadn't evolved the plan any further than this. I hoped something would develop on its own, which it did, soon after I finished the coffee and my second cigarette.

I hadn't seen Dobson leave the house, but I heard the Volvo start up and saw it curve around the driveway. At the street it turned toward the entrance to the complex. I started the pickup and followed as closely as I dared.

I noticed him blow past the hut, so I did the same. He turned north on Old Town Road, which led up to Montauk Highway. It was about nine in the morning, and the low-angled light was mopping up what was left of the mist hanging above the dew-soaked lawns and undeveloped acreage. We'd had a lot of rain in the late summer, so everything was still a dark saturated green, the opulent fecundity of the East End on proud display.

Every other car on Montauk Highway was a black four-door import, but I was able to keep a bead on the Volvo, which was traveling along at an easy pace. We headed east, past a thicket of car dealerships and roadside vegetable stands on the way toward Watermill, notable for the gigantic windmill on the village green and Jackie Swaitkowski's engorged office space.

But we didn't get that far. The Volvo took a sudden right turn into a parking lot serving a small cluster of buildings, one of which housed a Mediterranean café with an authentic aroma of over-roasted beans and an eclectic array of comfy seating options.

I waited in line behind Robert Dobson, my hat pulled down as a meager disguise. He was shorter than me and a lot lighter. His shoulders sloped down from his neck and rolled forward, making a hollow out of his chest. He wore a pink dress shirt, open and untucked, over a white T-shirt, and crumpled off-white chino pants.

He ordered a concoction with an Italian name I couldn't pronounce. So I avoided the embarrassment by pointing at something on the menu. Dobson had to wait longer for them to whip up his order, so I killed time picking out the only wad of pastry in the glass display that wouldn't automatically induce a heart attack.

Dobson snatched a real estate glossy out of a wire rack and, fortuitously, moved to a far corner where he dropped into the kind of nubby overstuffed sofa you used to pick up off the sidewalks of Greenwich Village. I waited until he looked settled in, then sat down next to him.

"Hey, Bobby," I said quietly.

He looked over the top of the magazine, struggling to make sense of the moment. Which didn't take too long.

"You," he said, his face now filled with defiant alarm.

"If you run, I'll catch you for sure this time. And you won't like what happens next."

"You can't do that," he said, looking over my shoulder as if seriously considering a run anyway. I put my hand on his forearm like Sullivan did to calm down the rowdy fishermen at the Pequot. It seemed to have the same oddly terrifying, and consequently quieting, effect.

"There's no reason to get emotional here," I said, in barely audible tones. "I'm just trying to get some information."

"Who are you?" he asked.

"I'm Sam Acquillo. I'm looking for Iku Kinjo. They say she's your girlfriend."

Without taking his eyes off me Dobson reached for his foamy light brown coffee and took a sip. Terror and confusion weren't going to stand in the way of a hot jolt of caffeine. Not at those prices.

"Why are you looking for her?" he asked.

"Why aren't you?"

"Who says I'm not?"

"You don't seem concerned," I said.

"I'm concerned. I'm very concerned."

"I don't think you are."

"What're you, a psychologist?" he asked.

"An engineer. It's a type of psychology."

"Look, I don't know who you are."

"Sam Acquillo. I told you that already."

"But I don't have to talk to you about anything if I don't want to."

I nodded. "That's right. Though I wonder why you wouldn't, if you're concerned about Iku. We should be on the same team."

"Concern for Iku and wanting to find her are two very different things," he spat at me, proud to advance the proposition.

"Really?"

"Oh, come on. You think I don't know what you're trying to do? Even if I knew where she was, and I don't, I wouldn't tell you people."

"You wouldn't?"

Courage of conviction didn't sit that comfortably with Robert Dobson, but as we talked, he warmed to the role.

"Yeah," he said. "So let go of me and let me get back to my coffee or something's going to happen that somebody's not going to be too happy about."

I realized I was still holding his arm. I let go and said, "What something?"

He obviously hadn't thought that through.

"If you don't mind," he said, starting to rise.

I grabbed his shirt sleeve and shoved him back in his seat.

"What do you mean, 'you people.' What people?"

"If you don't know, I'm not going to tell you."

"What the hell does that mean?"

"I'm not stupid. You can tell Angel and his overpaid, glorified goons to go jump in a lake. Or the East River, which is closer," he said, making another attempt at escape, which this time I let him do. Almost.

I followed him out to the parking lot and met him at his Volvo, where he was fumbling with his keys and half-consumed liquid confection.

"I just need to know she's all right," I said to his back. "I don't have to see her or know where she is. Take a picture or a videotape with a current newspaper. That kind of thing."

He spun around.

"Like a kidnap victim?" he asked.

I moved in closer, forcing him to back up into his car's side panel.

"Come on, Bobby, loosen up. Nothing bad can happen from this. Only good. I don't give a shit about why she bugged out, or where she is or where she's going from here. I just need to know she's okay. Then I'm gone from her life forever. And yours."

His face loosened up for a second, then suspicion crept back in again. "That's all you want? Why?" he asked, the first sensible question of the day.

I told him the truth.

"Somebody's paying me to find out. All I need is proof she's alive and unharmed and I'm done."

"If I did, hypothetically, know how to get her that message, what's hypothetically in it for me?"

He went to take a sip of his coffee thing. I took the cup out of his hand before it reached his lips, tossed the coffee and shoved the crumpled cup into my pocket. He looked at me like I'd just pissed on his leg.

"You're not so good at listening," I told him. "Do this and I'm gone. Don't and I'm so far up your ass we'll be sharing sunglasses."

I wanted to feel sorry for him, but I was having a hard time doing it. Maybe it was that whiny, overfunded, soft-palmed, self-reverential air of blasé entitlement. Or maybe not. Maybe I was just in a bad mood.

"I don't know where she is, I swear I don't," he said, an anxious quaver in his voice. "We sort of split up a while ago. Her idea. But I'm sure she's okay. I'd know if she wasn't."

I moved in even closer. Close enough to see the pores on his cheeks and smell the fear on his breath. I gathered up the front of his pink oxford cloth shirt and half lifted him off the ground.

"What are you going to do to me?" he asked, like he thought he already knew.

I immediately felt like a piece of shit. I let go of his shirt, took a few steps back and inhaled a deep breath, shaking the dopey fury out of my head. I searched my memory for mantras designed to quell anger, but I was still too worked up to think of any.

"It's not that important," I said to him.

I pulled a pen out of my jacket pocket and searched around my jeans, eventually coming up with a gas receipt. I walked over and used the Volvo's hood to write my name and phone number on the back. I handed it to him.

"I apologize," I said to him. "I still want to find her, but if you don't want to help me, okay. I don't know for sure, but I think it would be better for Iku if she opened a channel of communication. Give her my number. She'll remember me. She can trust me, though she might not believe that."

Dobson flinched when I stuffed the receipt into his shirt pocket. I left him and went back to Amanda's pickup. But before a half dozen paces I stopped and turned around. Dobson was still leaning against his Volvo, studying the piece of paper I'd given him.

"Who the hell is Angel?" I asked him.

Dobson looked up from the receipt.

"If you don't know, who the hell are you?" he said, and then rolled to his right, catching the handle of the Volvo's door and letting himself in, starting the car and racing off in a cloud of dust, overwhelmed by the moments in life that remind people like him of their own ineffectuality, their brittle love of self.

SEVEN

I SPENT THE REST OF THE DAY at Sonny's beating on leather bags until my legs, wrists and lungs were equally sore. Then I poached myself in the hot tub, which almost put me to sleep. In that somnambulant stupor I was defenseless against visions of Iku Kinjo caught in a fervent embrace with George Donovan, lounging around afterward wrapped in desultory pillow talk.

I felt better after nullifying the hot tub with a long, cold shower. Better than I felt after leaving Robert Dobson.

It was late evening by then. I'd left Eddie's secret entrance open so he could come and go as he pleased. By now, Amanda was likely home diversifying his diet with hors d'oeuvres selected to accompany her first glass of pinot.

So when Robin and Laura from House Hunters of the Hamptons called me on the cell phone I felt free to join them at a place in Southampton suitable to their social aspirations.

I was met at the door by a guy in a white coat and black bow tie. He was a lot taller than me, but about the same weight. He spoke with an accent, though too quickly for me to make it out. All I heard was something like "the ladies has been waiting you to be here." I followed him through the noisy roomful of entrenched City people, the ones who got to stay on after the season because they owned the houses they lived in during the summer. Most of them probably knew each other. None of them knew me. Except for Robin and Laura, who made a ridiculous show of standing and waving me over to their table.

"A rare man to get such greeting," said the maitre d', pulling out my chair with one hand and fiddling with my place setting with the other.

"Medium," I said to him. "Medium rare."

"Don't let him fool you," said Robin. "Red meat all the way."

"Just bring the vodka," said Laura. "There's plenty of time for ordering."

Laura's wavy head of dark brown hair had been recently cropped and inexplicably combed and glued into jagged stalagmites. I'd known her to be the staid and restrained member of the pair, so it caught me by surprise. Robin was still her loud, brassy blonde self, with a lot more lipstick than self control. Judging by Laura's stiff posture, despite the hair and a green drink in a platter-sized martini glass, their respective social styles remained stubbornly unresolved.

"So, things are good?" I asked.

"Been worse," said Laura.

"*Fab*-ulous," said Robin. "We just closed today on the Garrison place. Ox Pasture, don't you know. La-di-da."

"Co-brokers. Discounted commission," said Laura, looking out across the big low-ceilinged room. Scanning for the next prospect. "Some la-di-da."

"She's such a killjoy. It's in the genes."

"Scandinavian."

"Bergman on quaaludes."

"I'm an ant," Laura said to me, pointedly. "Robin's a grasshopper. What can I say."

"So, you called," I said, snatching my vodka off the waiter's tray as he lowered it to the table.

"Somebody asks me for something I put out," said Robin.

"There's a straight line deserving attention," said Laura.

"Can you believe what I have to suffer?" Robin asked me.

"I like your hair," I said to Laura, stopping them both in their tracks. "The ants are going to heave you out of the anthill."

"Is he a goof or what?" asked Robin, fumbling for a cigarette, then realizing they were banned. She folded her arms and sank back in her seat.

"Robin's the one who called you here, but I'm the one who got the goods," said Laura.

"This is not a competition," said Robin.

The waiter, who'd discreetly disappeared for a while, reappeared with pad and pen in hand. Both woman looked defensive, caught unprepared.

The waiter covered the moment by reciting specials and making doodles on his order pad. I focused on the vodka. The women kvetched and bickered over the menu until the suspense became nearly unbearable. I saved the waiter's sanity by ordering a selection of appetizers for the table. That and another round of drinks.

"So you got the goods," I said as the two of them sipped on single malts served neat in tiny brandy snifters. "I'm all ears."

Robin jumped in.

"We found the Japanese girl's rental. Or rather, Laura did."

"Is she still there?" I asked.

"Don't know about that. She wasn't on the lease. We found her through Mr. Dobson, who was. The agent lent me a copy of the file. Out of professional courtesy."

"And for a free dinner at the Silver Spoon," said Robin.

"How do you know Iku was there? Or is there?" I asked.

Robin looked at Laura, eager to tell the story but afraid to grab the floor. Laura made a show of looking nonchalantly around the restaurant.

"Oh, just clever detective work, you could say," she said.

"Clever detective work. She read the file."

"The *police* file. If that isn't detective work I don't know what is."

"Police file?" I said.

"They had a note in the file that the Town cops paid a call on the place one night. Noise complaint," said Robin, unable to resist stealing Laura's thunder. "I think 'noise complaint' and 'group rental' are the same words in the dictionary."

"Synonyms," said Laura.

"Sin's another story," said Robin. "Plenty of that, too."

"The cops usually alert the owners through the rental agent whenever they're called to a property. This is a big issue around here, you probably know. Lots of people want more control on the groups, which is fine with me. Who needs them?"

"People who want to come to the Hamptons and can't afford a kazillion dollar rental," asked Robin.

"So this complaint," I said, wedging my way back into the conversation, "what was it about?"

Laura shrugged.

"No biggie. Some neighbor said they were blasting their stereo out the window. Cops get there, a woman named Iku Kinjo apologizes and immediately turns off the music. Cops leave. No further complaints. Not exactly an earth-shattering event in the history of law enforcement."

"Didn't make the cover of *The New York Times*," said Robin. "Maybe page three."

"Do you have the names of the cops who made the call?" I asked.

They looked at each other, then nodded.

"Sure. It's right in the report. Don't remember their names, but it's in there," said Laura, pulling a big pink envelope out from somewhere under the table and plopping it down on top. "Address, telephone number, owners' names, square footage, number of bedrooms, instructions on cleaning the swimming pool, it's all there."

"Us agents are thorough," said Robin.

"We're anal," said Laura. "You'd be, too, if you had to deal with these owners. You'd think we were renting out their children."

"That'd be easier. Kids are an expense. The house in the Hamptons is an asset."

"You're so cynical."

I slid the envelope off the table and onto my lap, and then sat on it.

"You're both brilliant," I said. "I really appreciate it."

That stopped them faster than the comment about Laura's hair. Robin nodded appreciatively.

"That is the nicest thing I've ever heard you say about us, Sam. Shit, it's the nicest thing I've ever heard you say period."

Laura nodded, too.

"I hate to agree with her, as you know. But it is."

The waiter came to the rescue again with the appetizers. While he hurriedly spread them around the table I ordered the next course, lecturing everyone on the merits of the selected dishes, entirely contrived for the occasion. The women didn't object. In fact, they seemed to like it. I toughed my way through the meal, which I tried to pay for, but Robin had already slipped the waiter her credit card.

After I got out of there I headed to another place part-way up North Sea Road, where I could take a look at the envelope. It was one of the last local hangouts that still looked like it did twenty years ago, when a City person would as soon pop in for a drink as stroll naked through Bedford-Stuy. Though compared to the Pequot, it was like sipping at the Ritz.

"Vodka. Ice. Swizzle stick. Nothing else," I said to the bartender.

"You want a glass with that?"

"No. Bring it in your hands. I'll suck it out with a straw."

Ten years ago this might have escalated into something more serious, but we were both older and a lot smarter, and in no way a lot tougher. So he laughed along with the other jean-jacketed, grey-haired, rosacea-encrusted barflies and went to get my drink.

I opened the envelope and slid the contents out on the bar. I stuck a tiny Maglite in my mouth so I could read the papers under the low, neon-tinted light.

On top was the rental agreement signed by Robert Dobson and the owner, John Churchman. The lease was still in effect. Two years, five thousand a month, utilities, pool maintenance, lawn crew and trash pick-up generously included. From what Robin told me, that was considered quite the bargain, with comparable houses going for sixty K or more for the summer season. She speculated that Churchman discounted the rate to secure the full-time, two-year term. A bird in the hand.

Much more interesting was the police report, a grainy Xerox of a filled-out form. As Robin said, a neighbor's noise complaint led to a visit by two Southampton Town patrol-men, one of whom wrote that the sound levels coming from the Dobson residence were "excessively voluminous."

An apparent resident, a young woman who identified herself as "Ikoo Kent Jew," was waiting for them as they came up the front walk. As Robin reported, she immediately complied with the cops' request to turn down the music, and that was that.

The cop who made out the report remarked on Iku's willingness to cooperate, despite "The young woman's obvious state of advanced intoxication as the result of unidentified substances."

I took a sip of the easily identified substance in front of me on the bar and leafed through the rest of the file. Then I asked the bartender for a pen and wrote down the address of the place on a cocktail napkin.

"What's 'at?" he asked, when I gave him back his pen. "Writin' down a poem?"

"Yeah. An ode to drunken Japanese girls."

"That'd be a haiku," said the guy sitting next to me. "Japanese don't go in for a lot of words."

"This is why I like working behind a bar," said the bartender. "You learn shit every day."

"Do you know where this place is?" I asked him, spinning the napkin around so he could read the address.

He frowned at it for a few moments.

"Vedders Pond, right?" he asked the poetry expert sitting next to me. He studied the napkin.

"Yeah, not even a mile from here. Little shit-ass freshwater pond with a half a dozen places, give or take. Can't build more'n that on the wetlands."

I knew where he meant. I jogged through that area back when I was motivated to jog more than a few miles from my house. The last time I'd passed through I noticed how the original shacks had been upgraded to suit their new status as waterfront property. Robin and Laura were right to say it was a bargain. Waterfront was liquid gold in the Hamptons. They once proposed an inflated price for a house in the shadow of the Village water tower. When the buyer balked they pointed skyward and said, "Hey, check it out. Water view."

———

I decided it was too late and I was too tired to do anything else that night but go home and discuss the day with my dog. And if I got lucky, have a chance to hear Amanda tell me about hers.

I pulled the Grand Prix into its usual parking spot next to the shack at the back of the property, leaving plenty of room for Amanda to zip by in her Audi. Eddie didn't run up to greet me, but otherwise things were normal. On the other hand, he didn't always do that, so it was normal enough.

When I got out of my car I looked toward Amanda's place and was stopped by an unusual shadow pattern on the driveway. I'd been looking in that direction for a few years now, and no matter what my state of sobriety, I knew when it wasn't like it was supposed to be.

I shut the door of the Grand Prix with conviction and rather than heading toward the cottage, crouched down and ran over to a swayback shed at the back of my property. It was hemmed in by a robust assortment of indigenous foliage, which helped cover a move around to the other side, where I saw a bulbous pale blue minivan, half submerged in the brush, and half gleaming in the light of Amanda's post lamp.

In another reckless action, however foresworn, I strode up to the driver's window with my left fist cocked and self-discipline temporarily disarmed.

I looked through the open window and in the dim light saw Marve Judson trying to adjust the radio dial to a more diverting station. "Where's the dog?" I asked.

He jumped violently in his seat and said something like, "Christ, shit, what dog?"

"The dog that runs around my yard. Where is he?"

"I saw a dog run down the basement hatch a few hours ago," he said.

With that Eddie ran back out the basement hatch, finally noticing I was there in the driveway. He jumped up on the side of the minivan and tried to get a look inside, excited by the prospect of fresh company.

That's when the gun came out. Judson must have had it stowed somewhere near the center console. I watched the arch of travel until it was almost level with my head, then grabbed the barrel and snapped the gun and the hand holding it against the window frame. I stuck a few tidy left jabs into Judson's face until he let go. Then I opened the car door and pulled him out.

I hit him again, then got a better grip on the front of his shirt. I dragged him across the lawn, opened the door, and dumped him on the kitchen floor. I ejected the clip and a round from the chamber of the silver .45 right before Amanda swept festively into the kitchen.

"Oh, my God," she said, seeing the gun in my hand.

I used the barrel to point at the guy moaning on the floor.

"Again?" she asked.

"Meet Marve Judson," I said. "I think I've told you about him."

She held up a china plate overflowing with cheese wedges and crudités.

"How does he feel about Fromage d'Affinois?"

"We'll ask him when he regains his faculties."

"Your hand is bleeding."

"Not my blood. Can I open that?" I asked, pointing to the bottle she was holding under her arm.

Eddie stopped for a second to sniff Marve's head, then followed Amanda out to the screened-in porch, where she dropped off the cheese and came back with the bottle held like a club.

"Just in case," she said, as she watched me hoist Marve up on his feet. I fed his face into the kitchen sink, rinsing off the blood and half drowning him, until he shook himself and put up a legitimate effort to fight back. I pulled him up and handed him a dish towel.

"What the hell were you thinking?" I asked him.

"I look after my own," he said, through the soggy towel and his mashed-up face.

"Not too effectively."

Marve was short and wiry and probably five years younger than me. His hair was as thin as he was, but ambitiously bolstered by the kind of hair dye women chuckle over in the ladies' room. He was wearing a safari jacket, which would have been a tip-off even without the bad hair job and the steely set of the jaw. He was the kind of guy who might have been redeemed by a self-deprecating, worldly sense of humor, if he'd only had one.

"I think you broke one of my crowns," he said through the towel.

"One's better than nothing."

"You're supposed to be a degenerate alcoholic."

"Still working on that."

I grabbed him again, this time by the shoulder, and pulled him with me through the kitchen and out to the screened-in porch. Amanda followed with a pair of glasses and a corkscrew, though still looking tense and wary.

I sat Marve on the floor and took the stuffed chair, holding Eddie back from the nearly irresistible allure of an accessible, albeit hostile, human being at his own eye level.

I picked my cell phone out of my pocket and flipped it open.

"I don't know what Honest Boy told you, but I only let one person per year pull a gun on me. The cop on the other end of this phone insists upon it."

A spray of alarm passed behind Judson's eyes.

"It was self-defense," he said.

I continued to punch in Sullivan's number.

"You're not going to talk first?" he asked.

"I don't know, Marve. I'm pretty mad at you. I either call the cops or shoot you and toss your body in the Little Peconic. You pick."

"He's not a very good shot, but you *are* rather close," said Amanda. I kept dialing Sullivan's number.

"Okay, I apologize," said Marve.

"Huh?"

"That's what you want me to do, right? I apologize for the gun."

One of the many things I learned after being ejected from the corporate bubble was just how strong that bubble can be—an impervious, impenetrable membrane. Nothing gets in, nothing comes out. A self-sustaining ecosystem.

Even as Judson imagined himself the rogue agent of mystery and truth, he was ultimately no different from any sweaty schlub locked inside one of thirty thousand cubicles in fluorescent-lit, grey-toned offices around the world.

I wanted to hit him again, and at one time in my life I would have. Instead I tossed Amanda the phone and went back to the kitchen to fill my aluminum tumbler with Absolut and ice. When I got back, Marve was still on the floor, looking suspiciously at Eddie standing over him with slack tongue and wagging tail.

"Don't worry about the dog," I told him. "The only thing that bugs him is talk radio."

"I'm allergic to dogs."

I knelt down across from him and took a pull off my tumbler. Eddie moved in and I scratched his ears.

"So, Marve. What the fuck."

He stopped fiddling with his busted crown.

"Things have been pretty stressful lately at the company," he said, as if that explained it all.

"Yeah? How?"

"Rumors, weird signals, comings and goings. That sort of thing. You can smell it. Especially if it's your job to have your nose in the air."

"Or up somebody's ass."

"I'm responsible to every stakeholder in the Con Globe organization. Lotta asses."

"You like a challenge," I said.

"Change is in the wind. But it's an evil wind."

"Who else have you been spying on? Donovan?"

Judson actually stuck out his lower lip like my daughter used to do when told to finish all the green things on her plate. The association probably saved him from another shot to the face.

"You can't spy on people and threaten them with guns in pursuit of business interests," I said. "You live in a nation that's bigger than Con Globe. Hate to break it to you, but there're laws that supersede the corporate charter."

"All fine and good, Mr. Acquillo, but you violated that charter. You have no standing in this discussion."

I felt a wave of resigned fury wash over me.

"Hey, Amanda, can I just beat this guy to death?"

"That's for you to decide."

"I want to."

"Then I suppose you should."

Before I had my fist two-thirds of the way raised he was yelling through his hands.

"The board thought Donovan was behaving strangely. Unexplained absences, after-hours meetings with people nobody recognized, that kind of thing," he said as quickly as he could. "They directed me to investigate. It's a sacred trust. And presumed to be confidential," he added, then groaned, as if in dismay over the forced admission.

"Boy, there's a startling revelation. The Chairman of the Board having late night meetings. Never heard of that before."

"Oh, yeah. Like you never heard of the Mandate of 1953," said Marve. "You wouldn't think all these shenanigans would have something to do with that?"

He had me there. I wouldn't think anything about it because I didn't know what the hell he was talking about.

"I don't know what the hell you're talking about."

He didn't believe me.

"You were a corporate vice president. Of course you know."

"Pretend I don't and tell me what it is."

"The mandate establishes corporate independence in perpetuity. Donovan's elevation to chairman was contingent on his unqualified allegiance to this decree," Marve snarled into his bloody dish towel.

"No kidding."

Marve huffed wetly through his nose.

"Boy are you out of the loop," he said.

He told me that before the founding family gave up full control they had the board vote on a charter resolution that prohibited the company from ever being purchased as an entity. No more than twenty percent could be sold off in any five-year period and no investor could own more than thirty percent of the voting stock. Every new board member had to sign a pledge to defend this resolution before their election. Some thought Donovan was secretly examining legal tactics for breaking the charter in hopes of driving up the value of his considerable stock holdings.

"The board resolution is only a theory," said Judson. "Not binding until it's tested in court. You didn't know any of this? What a putz."

I had to agree. I was a putz, with no inkling of these corporate convolutions. I've been told that my ultimate downfall at the company was my political naiveté. The comment never bothered me, because one man's naiveté is another's disdain. I don't know which is worse, or more dangerous.

"Even if Donovan's trying to break up the company," I said, "it's got nothing to do with me."

"Oh, sure. That's why he gave Ackerman an ex-officio assignment to spy on you and sent your severance agreement to outside counsel. Can't have anything to do with that."

"My division's long gone."

"Your ex-division is ass deep in a massive intellectual property suit with the company. Nobody knows more about that property than you, except maybe Ozzie Endicott. How is old Ozzie, anyway?"

"I have no idea."

"Really," said Marve, in a way that made clear he didn't believe me. I realized I still had a grip on Judson's shirt, and when I felt the urge to give him a shake I snapped it out of my hand.

"Get lost," I said to him.

He stood up, looking equal parts confused and defiant.

"I don't know what your game is," he said, "but . . ."

I cut off whatever he was about to say.

"My game is carpentry. And that's the only game I'm

interested in. I don't know what George Donovan is up to and I don't care. It's got nothing to do with me. Go back and report that to the board. They already killed me once. Can't do it again. Divine double jeopardy. Just don't come back. You only get one pass. Next time I break your neck and dump you in the lagoon."

I twitched in his direction and he lurched back a few steps, then turned and made a run for it. I whistled for Eddie to stay when he tried to follow Marve out the door. I busied myself sliding the clip back into the .45 and acquainting myself with the gun's general operations. It was a beautiful wood-handled chrome automatic, an expensive limited edition Smith & Wesson.

"What do you think?" asked Amanda, looking over the top of her book.

"That I ought to quit while I'm ahead."

"After you find the Japanese girl."

"That wouldn't be quitting while I was ahead."

"Just try not to get killed," she said. "I'm starting to enjoy it over here. All sorts of interesting people always dropping by."

After a decent wait I went outside with Eddie to look around. All clear. The sky was blue-black and salted with stars. The air was dry but still warm from the early autumn day. We walked out to the street and looked for overembellished SUVs and loopy minivans. Marve was probably gone for now, but I knew I wasn't done with him. Guys like him often display obsessive determination as a stand-in for genuine courage.

The aftershock of adrenaline release was zinging around my nerves again, which helped lift the dreary weight of the past. Con Globe had consumed the central core of my life, the vital arc from young adult into middle age. I'd been gone for years and still didn't know how I felt about the whole thing.

I preferred to concentrate on the present. The immediate present and then maybe a few hours ahead of that. This strategy was now threatened by the arrangement with Donovan and its by-products, like Honest Boy Ackerman, Marve Judson and disturbing photographs of Iku Kinjo.

I'd been living with a long list of feelings in need of repression, in particular disappointment and regret. Now here I was experiencing both. I looked back at my cottage, lit stem to stern. I could just make out the top of Amanda's head bent over a book. An improvised riff of elevating emotion rose in a flourish around my disconcerted heart. It had come late to me, and was hardly a sure thing, but there it was. Heart and home all in one place, in plain view. Who knew.

I whistled for Eddie, who heeded the call, and we strolled slowly back home. I fingered the hard barrel of the .45 automatic and set aside further deliberation. I tucked it all into one of the few empty corners of my brain, stuffing it into a deep cabinet and slamming shut the door, a housekeeping chore at which I've proven myself particularly adept.

EIGHT

I THINK I UNDERSTAND why certain people feel powerful when they point a gun at somebody. People who otherwise feel powerless and afraid. Having been on the receiving end of that a few times, I can attest to its effectiveness, at least for impressing an opponent—or victim. Though personally, I don't think flashing a gun around is anything to be particularly proud of.

So I've made a practice of staying as far away from guns as possible. Which is why I brought Marve Judson's .45 over to Joe Sullivan, who I knew would be at his desk at the Hampton Bays HQ just after the crack of dawn.

Before I could give him the gun I had to get past Janet Orlovsky, the station's first line of defense. I'd have shot her if she hadn't been sitting behind a bulletproof sliding window.

Officer Orlovsky had never thought much of me, even before I'd given her a reason. As more reasons piled up, her attitude dug in.

"Can I help you?" she asked, wanting to do nothing of the kind.

"Is Joe here?"

"State your business."

"Christ, Janet, do we have to do this every time?"

"Your name?"

"It's still Sam Acquillo."

"Do you have an appointment?" she asked.

"Sullivan doesn't make appointments."

"Then you can't see him. Not without an appointment."

"Don't try that on me. I read the same book."

"I can give you the number of our public information officer. If you call him and leave a message, he'll call you back if he can help you."

She started to write his number on a small note pad.

"I've got his cell phone number," I said.

She looked up.

"Who?"

"Sullivan's. And his home phone. And the phone at the desk he's sitting at right now. I can call him and say you won't let me in."

I held up my own cell phone.

"You can't use cell phones in here," she said, using her pen to point at a bulletin board on the other side of the room. It was straining under the weight of public notices, wanted posters, charity appeals and desperate cries for help. And maybe a sign that said no cell phones in the reception area.

"Why the hell not?"

She just looked at me, hoping I'd start down that road. The one ending with her whistling for the boys in the back to come out with night sticks.

I smiled.

"I guess it interferes with secret police frequencies."

She just kept looking.

"Thanks for your help," I said and went outside and called Sullivan on his cell phone.

"Hey Sam, where are you?"

"On the lawn outside HQ. You gotta get me past Cerberus."

"I thought Orlovsky was at the desk."

"Just come out and get me, will you?"

I tried to look cool and laid-back while I waited for him to come out. The sky was wearing its regular morning mist. The September air in the Hamptons was a lot better than the August air, though not quite what you got in October. As that thought crossed my mind a huge flock of Canada geese crossed noisily overhead, getting a head start on the run south. Elongated shadows cast by the rising sun rippled across the fresh-cut grass. I thought of Eddie's usual response, eyes fixed on the sky as he ran random circles hoping to magically coax one of the foolish birds to swoop closer to earth, to come within the arc of an energetic leap.

"Nice day," said Sullivan, striding toward me. "What's up?"

"I've got something for you," I said. "And now that I think of it, it's better to give it to you out here."

He glowered his wary cop glower.

"What are you talking about?"

I put my hands on my head.

"Right hand jacket pocket," I said.

He moved closer and patted my side, then drew out the gun.

"Orlovsky probably saved my life. If I'd pulled this inside half the squad room would still be shooting."

"What's with you and the automatics?" he asked.

"Same source, more or less," I said, lowering my arms. "Corporate security. Honest Boy's boss, to be exact."

I handed him the clip before he had a chance to check for it. He slapped it in and out of the gun, racked the slide and ran through all the other stuff guys did with guns when they knew what to do with them.

"You're going to explain this to me," he said, not a request. "Over here."

I followed him to a beat-up, greyed-out picnic table used more for smoke breaks than picnics.

He listened carefully as I told him about Marve Judson's visit. He didn't know whether to be angry or relieved that I hadn't called him like I'd done with Honest Boy Ackerman. More likely the latter. Inconvenience aside, he'd had enough legal ambiguity.

"What the hell is going on?" he asked.

A question I never get used to asking myself.

"What do you think?"

"Me?" he said. "How would I know?"

"You're a detective. Give me a theory," I said.

He looked up at another flock of geese as he tried to focus his mind. "Everybody's lying," he said, finally.

"How come?"

"Because everybody always lies. I go out on a case, I know that mostly what I'm going to hear is a bunch of lies. Even from people who don't need to lie, who've got nothing to gain by it. It's like a reflex. Low-life crud or corporate big shot, it's no different. People aren't wired to tell the truth."

"That's a cheery thought."

"You know that. What am I telling you for?"

He was right. I knew that. Deception was natural human behavior. Deception and self-deception. Mostly just little omissions or mini fact spins. People were compelled to distort the reality delivered by their senses through the selfish lens of the mind.

"But there's deception, and then there's deception. With a capital D."

"I hear you. With this you got a capital D. This is just what I'm thinking."

"I got to find that girl."

"You do."

"If you could hold on to Marve's gun while I figure out what to do with him, I'd appreciate it."

Sullivan shook his head.

"I can't do that again. Holding these guns proves I'm aware of the commission of crimes that I failed to report. Not good. Ross would have my ass. Especially with you involved."

"Okay," I said, "I'll figure something out."

"Don't throw it in the bay."

"I wouldn't tell you if I did."

Still armed and dangerous, I left Sullivan and headed back up toward North Sea. A mottled grey cloud cover had set in, cooling both the air and my mood. Quixotic pursuits always felt a little more rational under sunny skies.

Vedders Pond was buried deep in North Sea scrub oak, not far from the coastline. I was often surprised by the number of neighborhoods you could cram into a relatively small area and still feel like you were more or less in the country. Even with all the rapacious development, there were occasional stretches of winding North Sea roads bordered only by scraggly local flora and "no trespassing" signs.

Though I once ran these coastal trails, it took me a while to find my way by car. Despite the gloom of the day, the homes lining the little pond looked sharp and freshly landscaped. A big improvement on the past, at least aesthetically.

I was sorry I'd left Eddie at home. He would have enjoyed snarfling around the reedy bogs and shallow creeks that fed the pond, rousting amphibians and complacent water fowl.

Robert Dobson's rental was across the water, so I slowed to get a good look at that side of the house. It was a nominal contemporary with lots of glass filling in the gable ends. There was a large raised deck that sat above the pond. Underneath was a collection of kayaks, canoes and wind-surfing gear. Also a tiny unattended Bobcat backhoe in mid-engagement with a stone retaining wall.

When I got to the other side I saw a Nissan Pathfinder and a rusty dirt bike in the driveway. Real estate agents would describe the front yard as a natural garden, which meant a bunch of weeds and rocks with a scattering of figurines. A brilliantly painted Madonna, nestled inside a half shell, watched over the territory with a cool beneficence.

I walked up to the front door and rang the bell. Twice. Nothing.

I walked around to a side door next to the garage on the basement level. I knocked, but no answer. From there I went up a staircase to the rear deck and peered through the sliding glass doors. I saw a large, unkempt living room open to a kitchen and dining area farther inside the house. There was a huge white brick fireplace that was likely useful in the cold months when all the heat would rise into the cathedral ceiling. Overlooking the living room was a balcony with an open loft, and two doors probably leading to enclosed bedrooms.

I knocked on the glass doors. No movement or sounds coming from inside.

I circumnavigated the house looking for other entrances. Along the way, just out of curiosity, I tried a few windows. All locked. I looked around the neighborhood for busy-bodies. Nothing obvious, but I was within view of at least two other houses. I stopped checking windows.

I went back to the side door next to the garage and casually examined the lock. I knew the brand, inside and out. I knew how to jimmy it without a lot of effort.

The logistics solved, I took a moment to ponder the legalities.

Illegalities, to be technical.

While pondering I went back to the Grand Prix and dug around the trunk for the necessary tools. Sometimes it's easier to focus on specific tasks than general implications.

I found what I needed in my tool kit—a thin, flat piece of steel with a notch cut out of the side. I'd shaped it myself when I was a teenager handling beer procurement for my friend Billy Weeds, whose job was to steal cars in which to drink the beer. It was a symbiotic relationship.

I pulled on a pair of surgical gloves and worked the lock. Then I thought about the gun in my pocket: B&E, bad. Armed B&E, fatal.

"Aw, shit."

I went back to the car and pondered some more. If I got caught in the house, they'd surely search the car.

I looked around the property and saw the obvious way out. In a few seconds I'd secured the gun and was back at the door, giving my skeleton key that last gentle twist. Click.

Inside was a foyer with a staircase that led to the first floor. I took the staircase up to a living room with a big wall of windows. I stepped as quietly as I could, listening for signs of life. Evidence of group living was everywhere: the smell of cooking, dust and lousy hygiene. Dirty dishes on the coffee tables, full ashtrays. Fresh newspapers. A houseful of young slobs. Never my way. Even when living on the brink of annihilation I kept my place reasonably shipshape. My mother's doing.

I searched the kitchen cabinets and counters for paper evidence. I saw a stack of mail. I wrote down the names Robert Dobson, Elaine Brooks, Sybil Shandy and Zelda Fitzgerald. The last on a mailing label stuck to a *New Yorker*. Likely somebody's joke.

No Iku Kinjo.

There were two bedrooms upstairs and a pull-out couch in the loft space. One bedroom betrayed the presence of male and female. As did the common bathroom. The other was empty, but there was a pile of sheets and towels on the floor and some miscellaneous pieces of clothing strewn about. Men's and women's. After browsing through the dresser drawers and closets and looking under the beds, I left. I wasn't about to search beyond that.

I went back downstairs to the basement level and tried the door inside the little foyer. It was locked, but so flimsily it didn't deserve the honor of the skeleton key. I used the key that unlocked my roof rack.

I walked into another common area, like a small lounge you'd see in a suite of dorm rooms, with a sliding glass door that took you under the deck and out to the pond. It was a lot cleaner and better organized than upstairs. The neatniks' refuge. A galley kitchen was at the far end of the room next to a bathroom with a big walk-in shower. There were two other doors, both closed.

The first was the kind of room I fantasized my daughter would like, though I knew how terribly misinformed that fantasy was. The bedspread was drum tight over the single bed, every furniture surface brightly polished and uncluttered. The closet door was open. Inside, a row of skirts, shirts and summer dresses marched left to right in close formation. Pumps, flats, sandals and Nikes were stuffed in a pocketed contraption hung over the back of the door.

I hated to disturb the folded clothes in the dresser, but I'd come this far. I found nothing that identified the renter, and no evidence of a roommate, male or female.

One room left.

The room was also fresh and orderly, almost indistinguishable from the one next door except for the dead girl lying on the single bed clutching the handle of a large carving knife with two hands, the blade buried to the hilt, having passed upward behind her chin through her palate and into her brain.

There was a lot of blood, but otherwise the corpse looked as tidy as the room, formally composed, like a carving on top of a medieval sepulcher.

All of which I absorbed a few minutes after walking into the room. Though I was drawn by more important observations. The jet black hair, the rich, reddish brown complexion, the apparent epicanthus.

The beautiful face of Iku Kinjo.

———

There was never any question about what I had to do next.

I unlocked the front door on my way outside where I flipped open my cell phone and called Sullivan. I disposed of my beloved skeleton key and rubber gloves the same way I'd taken care of the gun. As the phone rang I forced myself to recall everything I'd done in the last half hour.

"Sam Acquillo," said Sullivan, the master of caller ID.

"I need you to get here first," I said.

"Where?" he said the word slowly, already getting the import.

I gave him the address.

"I know Vedders. What are you doing there?"

"Time is important at a murder scene, right?"

"Yeah," he said, again stretching out the word.

"So let's talk when you get here. Bring everything and everybody you got. You're going to need it."

"Shit, Sam. What the fuck."

"Like I said, try to get here ahead of the crowd. I like Will Ervin, but I don't want to explain myself to a beat cop."

"I'm already moving," said Sullivan. "I'll call you from the car."

Time managed to slow enough for me to get a grip on my brain. It wasn't the specific situation I had to worry about. It was all the specific situations that had come before. These things have a tendency to pile up. When the pile gets big enough you attract the interest of law enforcement. It's understandable. All they're doing is working the odds. I'd been able to beat those odds so far, but I knew statistical probability as well as the next engineer with a minor in physics from MIT.

When Sullivan called I described the scene as well as I could.

"And what are you doing there?" he asked again, his tone rhetorical.

"Looking for Robert Dobson. It's his rental. He told me to stop by anytime. I wanted to ask him a few more questions, so I took him up on his offer. When I got here I knocked on the door and thought I heard someone call to come in. The door was unlocked, so I did. I walked around the place calling for whoever I thought had called to me. I thought I heard a sound coming from the lower level, so I went down there and discovered the body."

"You need to get that hearing checked out. Along with your brain. Hearing voices is an indicator."

"Good advice. I've had a history of that sort of thing. Can we talk about the important stuff now?" I asked.

"More important than keeping your ass out of jail?"

"Actually, yeah. Somebody's daughter is dead. This is now your thing, too. We have a situation."

"I hate that word. Situation."

I sat on the ground and lit a cigarette, one of the three I'd brought along for the day. It seemed an appropriate use of rations. My nervous system had been geared up for lurking around Bobby's rental, but not for finding a dead body. Least of all Iku Kinjo.

God forgive me, my reflex thought was of my own daughter, about Iku's age, and in my mind far more vulnerable than the hard-driving management consultant. I willed those thoughts back into their special chamber and forced a more immediate issue to the fore.

George Donovan.

I knew I had to tell him, and the sooner the better. Preferably right at that instant before the world was flooded with cops, voyeurs and reporters. I really didn't want to do it. Not on a cell phone. Even if I could reach him on the first shot, which was unlikely.

Do I leave a message?

I gave myself time to finish the cigarette, then I dialed his number.

"Hello there," he said, to my surprise and regret. "Kind of an awkward time. Can I call you right back?"

"No. We need to talk now. With nobody around."

"I see. Hold on a second."

I could hear the sound of his hand muffling the phone and some indistinct conversation. A minute later he was back.

"You're sounding serious," he said.

"I've got news," I said. "The worst news."

"Oh, God."

I didn't know how he'd want to hear it, so I just told it straight.

"She's been murdered. I found her myself a few minutes ago. In Southampton, just a mile or two from my house. The cops are on the way."

He made a sound that might have been the word "why." So I tried to answer.

"I don't know why, or by who. She was stabbed. Pretty recently. I found her in the house rented by Robert Dobson."

"The boyfriend," said Donovan.

"Maybe her boyfriend. I'm not so sure. Listen, George," I said before he could answer, "I'm sorry. I really am. It's a terrible thing."

Now it was more obvious that he was crying. I just sat there and listened to those unnatural, animal sounds.

"I better go," he finally forced out. "I've got a half dozen people waiting outside my door. Call me tonight when you know more. We have to talk."

Then he hung up.

I heard the first sirens coming in quickly from the south. I lit the second cigarette and leaned up against a tree. As I sat there the cloud cover gave way. The sun lit up the oak trees above my head and splattered puddles of light on the ground, casting a hard glare on the hoods of the flashing police cruisers as they swarmed into the little pond-side neighborhood, its reclusive anonymity a forgotten thing.

NINE

W HEN S ULLIVAN ARRIVED at Robert Dobson's group
rental he sat on the ground next to me and said it was time to
catch Ross up. I knew that. Sullivan was too far out on a limb.
I also needed to preserve some elbow room, especially now.
The situation was way too complicated to get into a war
with the cops.

So I put the call in to Jackie Swaitkowski, who was thrilled
as always to hear we were on deck for a visit with the
Southampton Town Police.

I've always had a deeper respect for law enforcement than
our historical relationship would suggest. I know they have a
hard job. I couldn't do it. I don't have the patience or the presence of mind. Or the focus.

What I've done to reconcile my beliefs with my behavior
is make friends with cops and lawyers, thereby benefiting
from both their wisdom and their largesse. While doing
almost nothing to reciprocate.

An imbalance I most earnestly pledged to rectify, some-day, as I sat with Jackie Swaitkowski in a windowless white room at a banged-up conference table.

Jackie was wearing a men's button-down collar shirt with a bolo tie under a khaki suit, and a pair of cowboy boots. Lonesome lawyer of the high plains.

I was going to ask her if she had Trigger tied up outside, but decided it was better to stay friends, at least until we got through with Ross Semple and Lionel Veckstrom, the Chief of Police and the Chief of Detectives, respectively, who were sitting on the other side of the table.

Both had tried on more than one occasion to carve me up and serve me fricasseed to the wolves. Still, Ross I liked. Veckstrom, not at all.

"You're in here so much we're thinking of naming a new wing in your honor," said Ross, lighting us both a cigarette and passing mine across the table.

"I didn't know you were expanding," I said.

"We're not. But if we were, you'd be on the plaque."

"It'd say 'Asshole Numero Uno of Southampton,'" said Veckstrom.

"Bilingual," said Jackie. "Must be handy with our new population specs."

"You mean population Spics?" said Veckstrom.

Ross blanched.

"I'm impressed that he thinks that would bother us, because it does. Very perceptive," I said to Ross. "Pero él todavía es un pedazo de mierda debajo los pies."

"Speak French and I'll be impressed," said Veckstrom.

"Va se faire foutre," said Jackie.

Veckstrom had been a brilliant detective in Lower Manhattan. He dressed like a dandy, disdained his fellow cops and cracked cases everyone else thought uncrackable.

He stayed on the job while going to law school at night, passed the bar, then inexplicably moved out to the Hamptons and went to work for Ross. It was harder to build a legend out here, but he'd tried hard enough by making me his special project. So far unsuccessfully, but then again, he was what he was. Another virtuoso shit who truly hated me.

"I don't know about the three of you, but I've got other things to do today," said Ross, scrounging around a soft pack of Winstons. "So what say we just get this done without all the parry and thrust."

"No offense, boss," said Veckstrom, "but don't you have to thrust before you can parry?"

Ross's look took the temperature of the room down about forty degrees. Veckstrom threw up his hands and sat back in his chair.

"So, Sam," said Ross, lighting another Winston off the one he already had in his mouth. He shook one out for me. I took it and gave it to Jackie. Ross gave me another one and we all lit up.

"Could you people hang on there for a second while I go get an Aqua-Lung?" said Veckstrom.

"So, Sam," Ross repeated, "what's going on?"

"I've been talking to some of my old friends from Con Globe about getting back in the game. Carpentry's honest work, but, you know, I used to drive a nice car and have a little leeway between hand and mouth."

"Or foot in mouth," said Veckstrom.

"Ross?" said Jackie.

"Shut up," Ross said without looking at Veckstrom, who shrugged and sat back in his chair.

"Back in the day," I went on, "there was this very smart young woman who worked with me on a project for my company. We hit it off, professionally. I liked what she did and how she thought, and decided if I was going to try to get back in, I'd do what she did. Consult. Be a pro from Dover."

"Iku Kinjo," said Jackie, for the record.

"So I went to see her in the City, but they told me she'd basically gone AWOL. Never showed up for work one day, no word since. But they did tell me if I happened to run into her, have her call, yadda-yadda. This piqued my curiosity, of course. And you know how that goes," I said to Ross.

"Unfortunately."

"On a hunch I thought she might be hiding out in the Hamptons, so I started looking around for her. Nothing else to do, why not? Then I got a few leads, tracked down a friend of hers, went to call on him, and here we are."

I sat back, leaving the hand with the cigarette on the table to flick ashes into the ashtray.

"What a crock," said Veckstrom to Jackie.

Jackie looked at Ross.

"Do we always have to endure this charade of hostility?" she asked him.

"No charade," said Veckstrom, convincingly.

"Any time you want, we can settle this outside," said Jackie.

"I'm not afraid of the old rummy."

"I'm not talking about him," she said.

Ross liked that. He smiled and lit new cigarettes for everybody but Veckstrom, who looked half-asphyxiated already.

"Mr. Acquillo and Ms. Swaitkowski are here voluntarily, detective. We're just havin' a good old chat."

Ross liked to affect what he thought was the manner of a pre–*Brown v. Board of Education* Mississippi sheriff, which was unconvincing from an overeducated, lifetime Long Islander.

None of Ross's attempts at theatricality did anything but make him appear exactly as odd and ill-at-ease with social discourse as he truly was.

"I know the drill, boys," I told them. "I'll be available whenever you want to talk. If I think of anything else, I'll call. If I learn anything that might help the case, I'll call. Otherwise, I keep my nose out of it."

"Huh," said Ross.

Veckstrom looked skeptical, as did Jackie, which I hoped the other two didn't notice.

"Okay?" I asked, stubbing out the cigarette and getting out of my chair.

"Just one thing," said Ross, gravely.

I sat back down again. Jackie studied his face, holding her breath.

"What?"

"Tickets to the Police Ball. You have yours yet?" he asked Jackie.

"Christ, Ross. You know I do."

"What about him?"

"Put two more on my tab," said Jackie. "That's the limit before a charge of official misconduct kicks in."

We left Ross and Veckstrom in the interrogation room and cruised through the noisy squad room and back out into the intimidation-free air. I took a deep breath.

"Is Veckstrom a dickless prick or what?" Jackie asked.

"I think that question carries an interior contradiction."

"Does this mean Sullivan's already off the case?"

Joe and Veckstrom were Southampton's only plainclothesmen, Sullivan being the junior partner. There was little love lost within the Detectives Unit.

"Nah. Ross always brings in Veckstrom for our little chats. It's his good cop–dickless cop technique."

"You need to be careful," she told me. "Ross doesn't like it when you lie to him."

"I'm not lying. I'm just not sharing all the facts. I will when I can."

"You're not stopping, are you? How come? You did what Donovan asked you to do."

She was right. That was the deal I insisted on with Donovan—that all I had to do was find Iku, dead or alive. But that was when she was just a memory of an ambitious young kid, compelling in her intelligence but hardly likeable. And then when Donovan talked about her, the memory turned into an abstraction, almost a fiction, as I tried to put the two of them together in my mind. The photo from Eisler's annual report reinforced the illusion that she wasn't quite real, that she was just an artifice conjured by the mind of an aging plutocrat and Randall Dodge's computer wizardry.

It wasn't until I saw her dead, now truly and irrevocably lost, that she became real. Lying there in her own blood, still a kid in my eyes, still ambitious and impatient, desperate to get to the next big thing.

I found a dead overachiever, an orphan, a tragic victim, but I still didn't find her.

"It used to be about money," I told Jackie. "Now it's not."

"What's wrong with money?"

"Money's good," I agreed. "Sometimes."

"If I heard your tape right, you've got some coming from George Donovan."

"I told him about Iku. He wanted me to call later, but I can't right now. We need time to figure out what happened."

"We?"

I tightened her bolotie, then left her outside the station and went back to Oak Point and the Adirondacks on the breakwater at the edge of the lawn. Eddie was glad to be out running around the place again, working out the kinks. I wished Amanda was there to sit with me, but she was busy with her construction projects and had enough on her mind without all this.

So I lay my head against the wooden slats and closed my eyes, feeling the faltering sun of early fall and the shifting winds off the bay. And then, for some strange and miraculous reason, I fell asleep. Something I almost never do in the middle of the day.

I dreamt of skyscrapers and industrial plants, men in suits and women in heels, hard faces and eyes filled with aspiration and dismay. A lost world.

———

Eddie woke me with a single bark. I knew what time it was by the bark's tone and timbre. Dinner time. I opened my eyes and was rewarded with a nice sunset below a lavender sky. And the company of Joe Sullivan, sitting next to me drinking one of Burton's special beers.

"I was happy to let you sleep," said Sullivan. "Just have my beer and go home."

I went into the house to throw water on my face and change my clothes, shaking off the weight of sleep and the lingering dream state. I must have been more tired than I realized. I threw Eddie's food in a bowl and got Sullivan another beer. I filled my tumbler with ice water. For novelty's sake.

When I got back Sullivan asked me how it went with Ross and Veckstrom. I told him everything I could remember. He wrote it down in his case book.

I apologized to him. "If I'd known this was going to happen I wouldn't have involved you at all. You'd be clean," I said.

He waved it off.

"You didn't know. Like you said, we got a new situation here."

He asked me to tell him whatever I knew that I hadn't told Ross and Veckstrom. I did. I owed him that. I only left out theory and conjecture. No point in confusing the facts with all that stuff.

"When do you get the forensics?" I asked him.

"In a day or two. Prints a little before that."

"Maybe that'll settle everything."

"I'm not going to keep you out of this, am I?" he asked.

I shook my head.

"Okay," he said. "Just try to tell me what you're doing. And I'll tell you. Like, for example, after I leave here I'm bringing in Robert Dobson. Easy pickings, since I know where he lives. Now, you tell me what you're doing."

"Having dinner and resting up for insomnia."

"Let me write that down."

"See if Dobson'll give up the other roommates. No reason why he shouldn't. If not, you got the mail. That should do it. And ask him about Angel. Don't know the last name. I'm guessing the connection is back in the City. That's where I'm going tomorrow. See? Full disclosure. My new way."

He looked unconvinced, but found it in himself to politely finish off a few more of Burton's beers.

Between him and Honest Boy Ackerman, I might have to get Burton over here to replenish my supply.

—

Eisler, Johnson's building had the good sense to install a coffee shop right in the lobby. Not exactly a shop, more like a big pushcart and a few bistro tables. The coffee was great, and you could make yourself sick on Danish pastries and stuffed croissants, which I did, mostly to appear like a normal customer rather than the stalker I actually was.

My disguise was one of the suits I'd rescued from my house in Stamford before the demolition. It still fit fine, though the cut was probably dated. Which would only reinforce the look of a middle-aged office rat hiding out with a crossword puzzle and double latte.

I'd picked eleven in the morning to begin the stakeout, and allocated a maximum of two hours. Lingering longer than that might draw the attention of people staring at a bank of security monitors somewhere. I hoped it was enough time. As usual, I didn't have much of a Plan B.

I assumed the crossword puzzle was great cover until I realized I'd have it solved in about a half hour.

"Why is it the last few are always the toughest to get?" I asked the lady sitting to my right, hoping to burnish my act.

"Why do you think they're the last?" she asked, leaving an unsaid but implied "you schmuck" hanging in the air.

"Yeah. I guess you're right," I said, cheered by her observation.

I spent the next hour staring off into space trying to squeeze the name of a river in Russia, six letters long beginning with "Dn", out of my memory. I wrote it down when I saw Jerome Gelb stride by. I tossed the paper in front of my crabby neighbor so she could share my triumph.

Gelb moved very fluidly, a nice City gait capable of gracefully covering a lot of ground in a short time. I was pressed to keep up without looking like I was trying to. I checked my watch once a block to convey hurry—the guilty employee finding himself gone a little too long from the office.

Gelb suddenly stopped and stepped off the curb, looking down the avenue, I assumed to catch a cab. I strode past him and raised my hand. I got lucky when a cab shot out from the cross street and pulled over. I jumped in and we buzzed by Gelb, who glowered at what he rightly thought was a dirty cab snatch. I turned my head away and rubbed my face.

The cabbie looked at me over his shoulder.

"And?" he asked.

"Pull over here on the right, will ya? Behind that van," I said.

"Big ride. A whole block," he said, but did as I asked, cutting across four lanes with a heedless jerk of the steer-ing wheel that anywhere else would have caused a massive pile-up.

"Just wait here," I said.

I had a good view of Gelb, his hand still extended from the end of his long, thin arm. No cabbie could miss it. The next one didn't.

"Okay," I said as they flew by, heading downtown, "follow that cab."

"No shit?"

"No shit."

Gelb's cab was timing the lights well, so we quickly ate up several blocks. As we began to hit the intersections on the yellow, I asked the cabbie to move alongside so we wouldn't get caught at a red.

"You're really following him, aren't you?" said Benny Roscoe, the name I read off his permit.

"I am."

"You a cop?"

"Engineer."

"Then is this legal?" he asked.

"Absolutely. Engineers have all the same authority."

Both cabs stopped at a red light at the next intersection. I slid down in my seat.

"Try not to look over at him," I said. "Let him get a little ahead when the light changes."

"Got it, Kojak."

We settled into the usual rhythm of a cab ride down a Manhattan avenue—hurtling, undulating momentum interrupted by sudden lurching stops, abrupt lane changes, a series of near front-end collisions and generous application of the horn. Throughout Roscoe did a fine job of keeping pace with our quarry without calling undue attention, though he had to push the speed envelope occasionally to take up the slack.

"I'll cover the ticket," I said.

"You got that right."

Down around 23rd Street Gelb cut over to Broadway, then continued south. We had a tense moment when a box truck got between us, but Roscoe managed to cut around on the right, using a wide entrance to a parking garage to cheat into the sidewalk space. No pedestrians were killed in the maneuver.

Gelb took Broadway past the Village and into SoHo. His cab turned onto Spring Street and stopped.

"Go halfway down and let me out," I said, dropping a fifty dollar bill through the security slot, covering both the fare and the unscheduled stunt driving. "Nice work."

"Not a problem. A car chase always breaks up the day."

Gelb was easy to spot, heading west. He crossed Mercer, then walked to the end of the next block, crossing Greene and ducking into a restaurant that took up the whole corner. I gave it a few seconds, then followed him in.

The place featured a U-shaped bar anchoring the center of the room, lit by floor-to-ceiling tinted windows. The booze was on brass racks over the bartenders' heads, the upper strata reachable by a ladder like the one in Donovan's library.

There were also a few stool-high round tables between the bar and the window walls where Gelb was talking with a young woman who'd apparently saved him a seat. I sat at the bar on the other side of the U so I could keep them in direct view. I ordered an Absolut on the rocks to maintain authenticity.

The first fifteen minutes or so involved the usual boring stuff. Ordering food and drink, running to the restroom, settling in. Then it picked up when I saw the woman run her high-heeled foot up the inside of Gelb's calf. She might have seen him grin in response. It looked to me more like a leer, though to be fair, I was sitting much farther away.

The woman leaned closer into the table and started fiddling with a necklace that hung between her breasts. Gelb leaned in as well. He held his drink by the rim of the glass and swirled it around to either melt the ice or send another suggestive message. He didn't have to do it for my sake. My intuitive powers were up to the challenge.

Not knowing when I'd be back, I left a ten dollar bill on the bar. I walked over and set my drink down on their table. Gelb looked up with a jolt.

"Hey, Jerome," I said, "Floyd Patterson again. Mrs. Gelb, I presume?" I added, looking at his ring finger, then his lunch date.

What followed was an awkward silence. For them. For me it was just a silence.

"No, actually," said the woman, putting out her hand, "I'm Marla Cantor. A colleague of Jerome's."

"Oh," I said, happily, "wonderful. Fine firm you folks work for."

"So, Floyd," said Gelb, not quite through his teeth, "what can I do for you this time?"

"That'd be a private matter, Mr. Gelb. I think you'd want

that," I said, keeping my smile as big as a face that almost never smiled would let it.

He grimaced, but judging by the red flush on his cheeks, he was eager to deal quickly with the situation. He made stammering apologies to Marla, who graciously wouldn't hear of it. She said she'd concentrate on her salad and be there when he came back.

We went out to the sidewalk. I led him across the street to a shop that had a huge display window with a sill deep enough to sit on. We were both well dressed enough to loiter there while I asked him a few questions.

"I've consulted with our attorneys, by the way," said Gelb. "They're unaware of any action being taken against Eisler, Johnson."

"That's because there isn't any," I told him.

"I beg your pardon?"

"Shut up and listen. I found Iku Kinjo. Dead. It was very upsetting. When I think about how you talked about her, I get even more upset."

"I wasn't happy with her, but I didn't want her dead, for God's sake."

"Your wife know about Marla?" I asked.

The rosy little patches on his cheeks drained away, turning his skin back to white.

"I resent the implication."

"Don't waste my time with all that. Assume I got the goods."

"You're a private investigator," he said in a hushed breath.

"Doesn't matter what I am. You need to tell me why you think Iku dropped out of sight. And you need to do it in the next five seconds."

I looked at my watch.

"I don't know," he said, rushing out the words. "Honestly, I don't. She just didn't come in one day."

"What kind of a mood was she in?"

"Tense. But who at Eisler isn't? She seemed tired and a little frayed at the edges, but that's also nothing unusual. Our relationship was one hundred percent professional," he said, his eyes twitching toward the joint across the street, as if catching the irony. "So if she was concerned about something at work or in her personal life, I wouldn't know. And that's the honest-to-God truth."

"So she was handling her job."

"Iku? We used to think she dictated memos in her sleep. Everything brilliant, all the time."

"Jealous of her, huh?" I asked.

He smirked.

"Yeah, of her talent. Not what it got her. I want a life outside of work."

"Apparently."

He was a really tall guy, but sitting there on the windowsill in SoHo, he'd begun to shrink. I felt a little bad for him, but not enough to take out the hook. Not yet.

"What was she working on? The big stuff."

"Consolidated Global Energies. You'd know it as Con Globe. Oil-based, refining and petrochemical. Though her regular assignment was the hedge fund, Phillip Craig. And the usual load of small stuff that Eisler likes to pile on to maintain their reputation as the sweatshop of the consultancy trade."

I made the mistake of stopping to think. Gelb took the opening.

"I need to get back to my table," he said.

"Yeah, 'course you do."

He stood up and looked down at me. I leaned back so I wouldn't wrench my neck looking up at him.

"Are you going to talk to my wife?" he asked.

"I don't think so. And if I do, we won't be talking about Marla. Though we could."

"That sounds like blackmail."

I shook my head.

"I'm not threatening you. I'm just looking for some information. And a favor."

"Oh?" he asked.

"Yeah. I want to talk to Angel. I need an introduction."

His eyebrows rose, accentuating the lightbulb shape of his skull.

"Angel Valero?" he asked.

"Yeah. Iku's Angel," I said, hoping I had the right one.

"She consulted for him. Though I wouldn't exactly say he was hers. Even if she did help him get a nice piece of the big oil deal."

He went on to specify which deal. Big indeed.

"So he's with Phillip Craig," I said.

"Officially. Though he rarely leaves his house in the Hamptons. Why would he if he didn't have to?"

I asked him to give Valero a call and tell him I had an opportunity worth listening to. He was welcome to improvise from there as long as he told me the story line. As I escorted him back across the street I said I couldn't promise he'd never hear from me again, but I'd try to leave him alone after I got the introduction. Then I told him to call me on my cell phone, and gave him the number.

I didn't know if he'd follow through, though nothing about him said he wouldn't.

When I handed him back to Marla she shook my hand.

"It's an honor to meet you, Mr. Patterson. I must say retirement from the ring has had a surprising effect."

"Remarkably well-preserved?"

"Remarkably white."

—

Before checking into my hotel I found another bar where I could have a drink and call Amanda. I gave her a cleaned-up version of my meeting with Gelb, skipping minor details like the stakeout, the cab chase and the girlfriend at the SoHo bar. This wouldn't have met Rosaline's standards for full and free disclosure, but it did make for a less tense and sober conversation.

In turn, Amanda told me about her day sanding floors at one of her rehab houses. It sounded like more fun than I'd been having, only dustier.

"It's not nearly so difficult as one would think," she said.

"That's because of the floor guy lobby. They're very powerful."

"I'm finishing it tomorrow."

"Watch out for bubbles and don't walk on it till it's dry," I told her.

"Excellent advice. Think of the trouble you just saved me."

After that I called my daughter and asked her out to dinner. She delighted me by saying yes. So I got myself out of the monkey suit, cleaned up and took her to her favorite place, which was a few blocks from her apartment. We had a meal and a nice talk with not a single discouraging word from either of us. I was so afraid of breaking the spell I hardly said anything on the way back to her place. I just hummed something from Thelonius Monk, who's just about unhummable, and then hugged her again, though not too hard like I did when she was a little girl.

So when I was trying to get to sleep, listening to the street noise leaking in through the old windows, I was elated to mark the second discord-free engagement with my daughter since she reached puberty. I'm sure she wasn't aware of the occasion, though I wanted to think she noticed something as well.

And that even now she could sense my heart soaring high over New York City, leaving a temporarily unencumbered mind behind to fall into sleep.

TEN

I HAD TO SPEND THE NEXT two days in the little shop I built for myself in the basement of the cottage, to catch up on all the work I owed Frank Entwhistle. It was barely adequate to the tasks he'd normally assign: architectural details like mantelpieces, built-in bookcases and corner cabinets, and garden gates. I'd bought all the heavy equipment, like the table saw and lathe, and most of the smaller tools, from tradesmen I worked with on various job sites. The wear on some of those tools meant a fair amount of maintenance and repair, but I didn't mind. In fact, I liked the chance to mix a little mechanical and electrical tinkering into all the sawdust.

I was ambivalent about the construction boom that had been going on in the Hamptons since about the time I wandered back home. Lucky for me, it provided a living. Enough to pay the taxes on the cottage, buy dog food for Eddie, parts for the Grand Prix—not an easy or inexpensive proposition—keep the lights on and fuel oil flowing, and sustain frequent forays to the Pequot.

My new woodcraft career bore some resemblance to the job I once had with the company. Design and fabrication, problem solving, enabling technology and a fair amount of trial and error. The only differences were the pay scale and the level of complexity.

And the management demands. At the company I had about four thousand people working in my division. Half of them were at headquarters in White Plains, the others scattered in field offices and operating plants all over the globe.

Nobody worked for me on Frank's jobs, so I marked that as definite progress.

The equipment I once maintained and repaired was also more elaborate, with some petrochemical plants in the U.S. sprawling over an area the size of a small city. We built even bigger ones for the Saudis, Kuwaitis and Malaysians. All shiny new and run by automated control systems that reduced operating personnel from a few hundred to maybe two dozen. What a world.

The pay was a lot better at my old job, of course, I'd made a startling amount of money before losing most of it to Abby when we got divorced. I don't know what she's done with it because I haven't spoken to her since the last time I saw her. If I can preserve that record till the day I die, it will have been a worthwhile investment.

It'd be nice to say my interest in engineering came from my father, who was a car mechanic his whole life and never designed a flue gas scrubber or optimized a single ammonia plant. For me, every faulty device was a little puzzle that was fun to solve. For him, it was a battle against evil, intransigent machines possessed by demons whose sole purpose was to frustrate his every honest effort.

As I moved into designing the devices themselves, the puzzle became making things that had never been made before. My reward was more than a favorable outcome, it was the thing itself, something I could look at, touch, contemplate in three dimensions. Tangible manifestations of imagination, of dreams.

People think things of substance are where legitimate value lives, where wealth is created. I learned wealth actually comes from manipulating the consequences of having material things. It's the financial side of the house that ultimately matters. Since finance is based more on assumption and belief than empirical reality, it's far closer to the world of imagination than the steel, gears and wiring of a complex process application.

So who am I to beef? It wasn't the company's fault I wanted my imagination to produce something more tangible than a number in the middle of a ledger column.

I don't know where Iku Kinjo stood on this question. I know she had little difficulty absorbing the technical information I threw at her, never looking intimidated or knocked off balance. This was a woman who lived entirely in the world of the immaterial, the theoretical. The consultant's world of genius, smoke and mirrors.

If the young Iku thought my operation could stand as a model for the rest of the company, I'm sure it pained her to admit it, but that was what her research and judgment yielded, and that was what she was going to report. No matter her personal feelings toward me.

Thoughts like this set my mind adrift as I worked alone in the shop. Mostly alone. Eddie would hang around when the power tools were off and I was drawing or noodling out a design. That's why he was down there when I heard a gentle knock on the hatch door. Like the valiant watchdog he was, he looked up half interested. When Burton Lewis came down the stairs it was a different story.

"Quit sucking up," I said, watching Eddie's fawning attentions. "You're already in his will."

"You and your heirs," said Burton.

"The ones we can find."

"That's what DNA is for. How about a beer?"

Despite the best efforts of visiting cops and intruders, I still had some of the good stuff. Burton dug one each out of the basement fridge and pulled a stool over to my drawing table.

Burton was about ten years younger than me, but still managed to look at least as weathered and roughed up, in a boyish, handsome sort of way, if all those things can be present in a single individual. It wasn't because of a hard life, though Burton certainly worked as hard as anyone I knew. His great-grandfather had established one of the notable American fortunes in the early part of the last century and Burton had built it up from there. He was unquestionably a rich guy, though with little interest in pampered indolence.

He once said, "Spending the precious hours of one's life pursuing leisure and entertainment, or obsessed by self-glorifying avocations—what could be more abhorrent? What are you if you aren't contributing to the economic advancement of the community at large? A silly, emasculated contrivance whose sole purpose is the redistribution of someone else's hard-earned treasure."

Before building his tax law business he'd founded a free criminal defense practice that operated out of a storefront in the City. Over the years it continued to expand and command a large portion of his precious hours and concentration. Everyone assumed this was standard noblesse oblige, but the truth was Burton loved the challenge and access to lives lived far closer to the bone than he'd otherwise ever experience. Along the way, he'd made a home for the idealists and misfits of the legal profession, and provided first-class defense to any and all, the less deserving the better.

He was able to work at whatever he wanted to work at, when he wanted to work, but I didn't begrudge him that.

"So," he said, "I'm holding two beers. Why loiter in a wood-shop when the Little Peconic awaits just outside the door?"

On the way to the Adirondacks I started to brief him on current events, which I continued through two more rounds of beer.

He listened carefully throughout, then said, "The promise to modify your severance agreement offers some intriguing possibilities."

"I'll believe it when I see it. Anyway, it's not about that now. It's about the dead girl."

"Not your obligation. You found her. There was no proviso concerning dead or alive," he said.

"What do you know about the Phillip Craig Group?"

"The company reflects the personality of the founder: deranged by ambition and greed. Talented investors, though, I have to say. Creative. Our firm has managed the tax particulars on their major acquisitions. Most of the work had been done for us by their own excellent counsel. Anticipated nearly everything."

"Iku was involved with them on the big oil deal," I said.

"Big is right."

"You know Angel Valero?"

"Nominally. The name comes up in relation to Craig. I see him at fundraisers, the Financial Roundtable. Nothing beyond that."

"Reputation?"

"Deranged by ambition and greed. I thought we covered that."

"We did."

This time of the season most of the big powerboats had emptied out of the Little Peconic Bay. There were still small fishing boats hugging the buoys and rocking in the turbulence above the shoals, and a scattered fleet of sailboats responding to the better wind and lighter traffic. Again, I felt a pull as I watched the sails angled to the wind glide across the green coast of the North Fork.

"Getting out on the boat much?" I asked Burton.

"A cruise or two. Club racing. Enough to satisfy the impulse."

"Is that impulse a lifetime thing?" I asked.

"Begins in utero," said Burton.

"Hm."

We studied the approach and subsequent disorganized tack of a small sloop. Neither of us wanted to break the spell by criticizing the maneuver.

"I need to talk to Angel Valero," I said. "I think I have an introduction, but I need a shtick. Something to get him talking."

Burton always looked slightly in need of a haircut. A thing he drew notice to by frequently using his fingers to comb his hair off his forehead, a futile gesture when sitting at the edge of the breezy Little Peconic Bay.

"Large-scale investments are at once dauntingly complex and simple as it gets," he said. "The complexity is all in the targeting of opportunity, the valuation and subsequent number crunching, the accounting and regulatory contortions, conflicts in corporate structures, tax implications—our bailiwick—and personnel considerations, mostly as it relates to management, though sometimes middle management and unions come into play. To say nothing of core business practices and strategic planning."

"What's the simple part?" I asked.

"The motivation."

"Ambition and greed?"

"Natural economic evolution. The formation and reformation of corporate enterprise, a necessary function of a dynamic free market system. Anyway, people like to buy and sell things, and when those things are worth billions of dollars, it calls for robust capital markets. It also breeds people like Angel Valero."

"A dealmaker." I said.

"Not exactly. Angel operates on the outer fringes of the hedge fund and private equity business. Very aggressive, creative, risk-based. The type who buys a business, usually distressed, at a big discount, reorganizes the company, then rearranges the playing field, changing not only the business model but the market in which it operates."

"You can do that?"

"Angel runs a unit at Craig they all call Special Ops, short for special opportunities, meaning anything you can turn into a huge profit if you have huge capital to invest and a willingness to take the accordant risk. A slot machine maker in country A is bankrupt, partly because country B next door has banned gambling. You buy the slot business, figure out a way to repeal the gambling law, and bingo, if you'll forgive the expression. A bank in the next country is collapsing under defaults because management is made up of second cousins who happen to be the brothers and sisters of the borrowers. You buy the bank at a fire-sale price, broom everyone in management, entice a third party collections operation with giant commissions and have at it. It's a lot harder than it sounds, but people like Angel Valero do it every day."

"Make good money, does he?"

"A few hundred million a year, if you believe the street. I think that's an underestimate. Craig is privately held, and pretty opaque, but the word is Special Ops comprises a tenth of the revenue and forty percent of the profit."

"So Angel will talk to me if I have a lead on an exotic, undervalued financial opportunity." I gestured toward the driveway. "Like a 1967 Pontiac Grand Prix."

"An asset to tantalize the cagiest investor."

For some reason Eddie brought us a slimy piece of driftwood that he'd pulled from one of the tidal pools next to the beach. He dropped it in front of Burton and stood poised to chase it like he usually did with normal things like oak limbs and tennis balls.

Burton obliged and we watched Eddie do his soaring wonder dog routine off the breakwater.

"Sorry about that," I said to Burton, watching him wipe his hands on his khaki duck hunters.

"Interesting departure."

"That's what he wants you to think."

Eddie's toss-the-beach-debris game and a few more beers occupied the rest of the productive day. We wandered down some desultory conversational paths, some relating to the dismal prospects of any baseball franchise arrayed against the Yankees. Burton caught me up on the garden renovations at his estate over near the ocean, and his success at tiling the master bathroom. Years ago he'd set himself the challenge of mastering—or at least making an honest go of—the construction trades, an area of common interest that first brought us together. As with most things Burton did, it was misinterpreted as a way to get in touch with working-class sensibilities. Burton just liked to build stuff, and uncover wonderful new experiences, like meeting the dry cleaner or using an ATM card at the grocery store.

"By the way," he said to me as I walked him back to his car, "Angel worked as a professional wrestler while earning his MBA. His nom de guerre was 'The Brainiac.' Word is physical intimidation features largely in his negotiating repertoire."

While I watched Burton drive off in his late-seventies Ford Country Squire, an automotive atavism as illogical as the Grand Prix, Eddie trotted up to me with another hunk of driftwood, more slickened with saliva than brine. I reached down to take it, but he moved out of the way and headed for Amanda's place.

"Good luck with that one," I called to him, but he continued undeterred, head upright and tail under sail, happy in his eccentricities.

—

For all I know Eddie and Amanda spent the rest of the evening tossing and retrieving smelly chunks of petrified wood. Neither of them interrupted me as I sat at the pine table on the screened-in porch scribbling on a yellow legal pad. This was a habit of mine left over from my trouble-shooting career. Writing things down helped me think, if only by holding certain thoughts immobile as suppositions to validate or upend.

Deep into the night, I was still underlining and pointing arrows at one of these suppositions when a thought occurred to me. I picked up the phone.

"Wha'," said Jackie.

"If you're stoned I can call you back."

"Asleep. What time is it?"

"Bedtime. If you live in the next time zone."

"Christ."

"Is your computer still on?" I asked her.

"My computer's at the office. My old computer that I hardly ever use is on the porch disintegrating in the salt air."

"Can you use it to get on the Internet?"

"Oh, you heard about the Internet? Did you also hear that you, too, could access this modern marvel simply by buying your own fucking computer?"

"Start 'er up. I'll hold," I said, lighting a cigarette and settling into a more comfortable chair.

She said a few more things I couldn't make out, I guess intentionally. About ten minutes later she came back on the line.

"Finding the thing under all the stuff on my desk was the biggest challenge," she said. "Started right up. Good old HP."

"See what you can find on Jerome Gelb, an employee of Eisler, Johnson."

"Iku's place."

"Former place, according to Gelb."

I knew enough not to interrupt her when I could hear the tap-tap of the keyboard, so I let her work in silence.

"He's a senior partner," she said, several minutes later. "Way up the food chain. Specialist in strategic mergers and acquisitions within global heavy industry. Ran Eisler offices in Zurich, Mumbai, Tehran—I didn't know you could have an office in Tehran—Caracas and Tokyo, for ten years, before returning to New York to head up their International Energy Practice. A graduate of Wharton, he's married with two children, his hobby is foreign languages, and his favorite quote is 'If you snooze, you lose.' I wonder how you say that in Farsi."

"No mention of Marla Cantor," I said.

"Who's that?"

"His girlfriend."

"Oh."

"How're you on American literature?" I asked.

"Excellent, Bub. I was an English major."

"See if you can get Zelda Fitzgerald's address and phone number."

She was quiet on the end of the line.

"Sorry, Sam. I focused on the early nineteenth century. Mostly Romantics. Like me."

"Just look. I think she's here on Long Island. Maybe in the City."

I could hear the patter of Jackie's fingers on the keys, frantic little bursts alternating with cautious deliberation. In my mind's eye I could see her staring, more like glowering, at the screen. Coaxing the computer to give up the goods.

"Holy cow, there she is," she said, after about ten minutes. "In Amagansett."

"You have her address?"

"She's a big donor to the East Hampton Library."

"And why not?"

"It just says 'Zelda Fitzgerald of Amagansett.' Let me see if I can get closer than that."

I could almost hear the baying of hounds as Jackie mounted the chase. Even dragged out of a deep sleep, she was helpless in the face of her own inquisitiveness.

"Unless there's more than one Zelda Fitzgerald on the East End, I've got her address. Phone's unlisted. I could try the wireless directory."

"You could?"

"Oh, please."

When I was a kid, Amagansett, on the east side of East Hampton, seemed as far away as Chicago. Later it was a stop on the way to Montauk, where my father and I hired out to the sport fishermen, a part-time trade he brought me into out of some peculiar sense of paternal obligation. I didn't like the work or the clients, but I liked being out on the water with the captains and crew.

"I can't find a phone number," said Jackie. "Maybe Zelda doesn't have a phone."

"It could be in Scott's name."

"I'm assuming this is connected to Iku Kinjo," she said.

"It is."

"Keep Sullivan in the loop," she said. "Even the guesses."

"I will. You should go to bed. It's way too late to be messing around on the computer."

"Unbelievable."

I'd been messing around myself for the last five or six hours with little in the way of drink to keep me company. This left me strangely sober and awake, a condition I corrected with a sturdy nightcap. My mood lately had been drifting alarmingly toward unaccustomed moderation. I should keep an eye on that, I thought to myself as I fell back on the daybed, flicked out the light and looked at the big blue moon staring brilliantly above the black horizon.

—

I tried to get Sullivan the next morning but he was up island visiting the DA. So I left a message on his office answering machine. I told him about Jerome Gelb and Marla Cantor. And Angel Valero. I told him I got Angel's name from Bobby Dobson. Then I told him I was on my way to Zelda's house in Amagansett, but if he could call me with any news I'd be grateful. I didn't know if they monitored his voice mail at the station, so I didn't mention forensics, but he'd know what I meant.

I'd decided to head over to Zelda's since I still hadn't worked out my approach to Angel Valero. It was a Friday in late September, so there was a better than even chance she'd be in the City. Jackie'd told me there were a dozen Zelda Fitzgeralds in Manhattan alone. More specifics would have to wait.

Anyway, it was a good day for a drive. I had Eddie with me, who was having a hard time deciding which window to stick his head out of. I tried to focus him by shutting the two in the back, but he barked at me until I opened them again.

"Next time you drive. See how you like it."

He stared at me, considering the offer.

"Not until you learn the stick shift."

The calendar said it was fall, but it still looked and felt like summer. A few of the trees, mostly unhealthy maples, had begun to turn red and yellow, but the rest were still green. The clearest sign of the change in seasons was the traffic on Montauk Highway, still heavy but moving. I took the back roads anyway, partly out of habit and partly to catch the views off Scuttle Hole Road, the white fences, barns, vineyards and potato fields. And to give Eddie a chance to yelp at the show horses, none of whom were inclined to retort.

According to the map, Zelda's house was equidistant between the beach and downtown Amagansett, which was essentially a short row of shops to either side of Montauk Highway, which I passed before dropping down toward the ocean. The houses lining the streets were mostly standard Hamptons shingle-style cottages of a certain vintage. Out in the fields beyond were clusters of newly developed attempts at postmodernism, and the occasional all-out mansion. The really serious stuff was at the end of white-pebbled driveways, standing like citadels behind towering fortifications of privet and arborvitae.

Knowing this, I was interested to see the number for Zelda's place beside a drive made up of two parallel bands of sand, with a strip of grass in between, that disappeared around a curve a hundred yards into a stand of scrub oak and evergreen.

The Grand Prix wasn't the world's best off-road vehicle, so I took it very slowly. I pulled Eddie back from the window and raised it so he couldn't jump out. I was afraid of creatures lurking in the woods whose scent might prove irresistible.

As I approached the house, I was braced for Jay Gatsby. What I got was Brothers Grimm.

The cottage looked like it had been built inside a pair of gigantic holly trees. The front door was in the middle of the gable end, with a pair of windows to either side, and a Palladian half-circle above. It was stucco imbedded with wide slabs of wavy planks of thickly painted wood. The front stoop, a single rounded chunk of grey stone, was only a few inches high. In fact, it looked like the house was set directly on the ground, a possibility given its vintage, which I guessed to be late 1800s. The driveway ended under a pergola, which was doing a poor job of sheltering a leaf-splattered Nissan Altima.

I left Eddie in the car and did my best to wield the ten-ton brass door knocker. The door was snapped open by a very tall young woman in a kimono. Her features were unnaturally small for her size, probably exaggerated by the cut of her dark black hair, which curved down from a center part to form two sharp points just below her chin. The color of her eyes was at that moment a mystery, covered as they were by tiny black sunglasses.

"I saw you coming," she said. "I don't usually stand by the door."

"Zelda Fitzgerald?"

"And who would be asking?"

"Sam Acquillo. I was a friend of Iku Kinjo."

Her sloped shoulders fell a few degrees forward.

"It's horrible," she said.

"I'm sorry."

She leaned against the doorjamb, taking the weight off one long leg. "How did you say you knew Iku?" she asked.

"I didn't. I knew her from work."

She stood up straight again and reached for the door.

"Not a client, I hope," she said, her voice gaining a notch in volume.

"Not Angel, if that's what you mean," I said.

"Fucking Angel is how we put it."

She started to close the door. I put my hand out to stop her.

"I'm the one who found her."

She let go of the door and leaned back on the jamb, and studied me. At least I think she did. It was hard to tell with her eyes blacked out.

"It's malarkey, you know," she said, after a pause.

"What is?" I asked.

"Suicide. Would never happen."

"That's what they're saying?"

"Possible suicide. It was on the news this morning."

News to me.

"What do you think?" I asked. "If not suicide."

"I have a kettle boiling. You drink tea?"

"Under duress."

"Come in anyway. Maybe I can find some coffee."

She fell back into the house and I followed her. The style of the interior carried through the general motif. I was glad she was leading the way. The woodwork was so dark I could barely see where I was going as we moved through the front hall, which was dominated by a stubby grandfather clock and the stuffed head of a black bear. The ceiling might have been seven feet high, probably less. Zelda almost had to crouch to get through the doors. In the kitchen things lightened up considerably, helped along by a wall-length window made of maybe fifty individual panes of glass. The kitchen was packed into a tight space, but sparkling clean and organized.

The smell from a thick, blue-grey spice plant, I guessed thyme, filled the air. A fat little tea kettle whistled on the stove, as advertised.

"I used to drink coffee," said Zelda, "until my father died of cardiac arrest one morning at breakfast. The sight of him sitting there in disbelief sticks with a person."

She scooped up the kettle and dumped the steaming water into a mug. It smelled great.

"I'm sold," I said. "Give me one of those."

"It's Hibiscus Paradise. Irresistible aroma."

"Apparently."

After handing me a mug, she leaned up against the counter and clinked around hers with a spoon. She still wore the black-dot sunglasses. The kimono told about as much as any kimono about the shape underneath. The V at her neck took a pretty severe plunge, but I was trying hard not to look. I was only able to judge the shape of her shoulders, which were wide and angular, like a swimmer's. The fingers that held the mug were also long and thin.

"I only knew Iku on the job," I said to her. "I'm glad to know she had friends. Had a life outside."

Zelda clinked the mug a few more times.

"How did you know she was a friend of mine?"

I picked a *New Yorker* off the counter.

"You get these at Bobby's house."

She pursed her lips.

"Quite the long shot," she said.

"With a name like yours?"

"My great-grandparents owned a place out here two doors down from Gerald and Sara Murphy. My mother married a pretty drunk named Mike Fitzgerald. You can guess the rest."

She told the tale like she'd told it a thousand times, which she probably had.

"Lucky for you Tallulah Bankhead preferred Atlantic Beach."

Something like a smirk formed across her narrow lips.

"Funny," she said. "No, honestly. Very funny. What did you say you did?"

"I didn't. But I used to be an engineer. Iku advised the company I worked for. How'd you know her?"

"Robert, the dear heart. He brought her home like he'd found a wet puppy by the side of the road. Not exactly wet. Wrecked would be more like it."

I clinked my own mug a little. Getting into the groove of Zelda's kitchen.

"Where was home?"

She pointed at me with the handle of her spoon.

"You don't think it was suicide either, do you? And you're not an engineer, are you?"

"I am. And I'm not a cop. And no, I don't think it was suicide."

"You think somebody killed her," said Zelda.

"I do."

"And you are, again?"

"Sam Acquillo."

"Should I be expecting a call from the police?"

"Probably."

"I thought so," she said, half to herself. "From the moment I saw you walking toward the door. You were intense."

She put her foot up on the rung of a kitchen chair, and in so doing allowed the kimono to part across her leg. It was a very long, very slender leg that I could follow almost as far as it went. The way she covered up when she noticed me looking made looking feel that much worse.

"I hope you find him quick," she said, pretending what had happened hadn't happened. "We can't have people out there killing our brilliant and beautiful."

"So where was home? Vedders Pond?"

"You engineers are very persistent," she said. "Dogged even."

"If you like dogged, I got some in the car."

"Yes. That was our place, on the pond. Robert, Elaine and I. Robert has rented it every summer since college to get away from his parents and we chipped in. Others would come and go, and help spread the burden. Like Elaine's brother this summer, with his unfortunate girlfriend."

"Sybil Shandy?"

She nodded.

"The hostess at Roger's," she said "You probably know her."

"If I could afford to eat at Roger's. And Iku?"

"She joined the party this summer."

"As Bobby's girlfriend?"

She looked startled. Then she smiled an actual smile.

"Is that what I should tell the cops?" she asked.

"Is it the truth?"

"Does it matter?" she asked.

"Yeah, it matters. Your friend's dead. Not coming back. It matters how that happened."

She pushed herself off the kitchen counter and leaned over the table, supporting herself with her palms flat on the cherrywood surface.

"I loved Iku. She was a superstar. A shooting star. Robert, Elaine and I had all lived together since our junior year in Florence. We wore each other like comfy old clothes.

Too comfy. Iku lit up the world. Our little world. Having her around was the best thing that could have happened to us. Don't lecture me on what it means to lose her."

She seemed to be trying to stare me down.

I leaned across the table myself, meeting her halfway. "Fair enough," I said. "So who killed her?"

She finally took off her black sunglasses, revealing a set of brilliant cobalt blue eyes.

"She loved all of us," she said. "Why not try the ones she hated? The people she worked with. Clients and colleagues. She loathed them all."

"Not all of them. Me she merely disliked."

Zelda had something to say about that, but was interrupted by the shrill twitter of my cell phone. It took a few moments to remember how to answer the thing.

"Hey, Acquillo, good news," said Jerome Gelb. "I'm leaving my wife. And I owe it all to you. I thought you should know right away."

"Mazel tov. Though I told you I'd keep Marla to myself."

"Sure, so you can keep a gun at my head. Not anymore, *compadre*."

"So how'd you get my name?"

"I got a call from Mason Thigpen."

"How is the little craphead?" I asked.

"Talkative. He told me who you are and what you are."

"An altruist?"

"A violent sociopath. He called to warn me about you. He said his security team was investigating your activities. They sound like some pretty tough customers."

"The toughest."

"But you know what?" he said. "I don't care. I'm in way too good a mood. Before you know it, I'm going to be a free man. Of course, it'll cost a fortune."

"Yeah, but what cost freedom?"

"By the way, I also called Angel Valero to warn him, too. I gave him your name. He was very appreciative."

"Who's talkative now?"

"Ah, it's a great day. I'm going to take some time off to smell the roses. You should think about doing that yourself."

"All I smell is Hibiscus Paradise," I said.

"Hey, Acquillo, one more thing."

"What's that?"

"Fuck you," he shouted, then hung up.

I flicked the phone shut and stuffed it in my pocket.

"Sorry about that," I said to Zelda.

"It's hard to imagine the other side of *that* conversation."

"It is for me, too, and I was listening to it."

Zelda looked eager to rid herself and her Hobbit hole of my presence, and I couldn't blame her. I made it easy by stumbling through the dark toward the front door without being asked. Though there was one question in serious need of answering.

"So did Iku actually have a boyfriend?"

She seemed to enjoy the question. Though now that I could see her eyes it seemed I knew even less about what she was thinking. So her smile might have been genuine, or I might have just thought it was in the dim light of the foyer.

"I don't know," she said. "What do you think?"

—

On the way back to North Sea I was jarred again by the ring of my cell phone.

"You want to talk to me?" said a voice so deep I thought it was synthesized.

"Depends on who you are."

"Angel Valero. You want to talk to me?"

"Yes. I want to talk to you."

He gave me an address on Dune Drive in Southampton.

"Five o'clock. I'll be down at the pool," he said, then hung up.

"Doesn't anybody say goodbye anymore?" I asked Eddie, but he couldn't hear me with his head out the window, trolling the breeze for bugs and the streets for miniature French poodles to roust from their coddled complacency.

ELEVEN

I KILLED THE REST OF THE DAY walking around the docks of Sag Harbor looking at sailboats. With the likelihood of my buying one on par with a flight to the rings of Saturn, I'd never narrowed my preferences. Big boats, little boats, racers, cruisers, ketches, sloops, schooners and yawls, it was all the same to me. Equally desirable and equally out of reach.

But a thought struck me one day when I was working in my shop. What if I just built one myself? How hard would that be?

Impossible. Though maybe I could restore some miserable old derelict dredged off the bottom of the sea, or salvaged off the rocks after a hurricane. In that case, I'd need to get a little focus, clarify my priorities. This meant careful research of the type I was doing in Sag Harbor, walking around and looking at boats, with Eddie on a leash to avoid municipal sanctions and spare the resident waterfowl.

The process was easier than I thought it would be. The only boats I really liked were akin to Hodges's Gulf Star—forty-something-foot, beat-up old live-aboards.

I didn't want to race, I didn't want to sail around the world. I wanted to sit with Eddie in the cockpit in a quiet harbor. I wanted to grill off the transom and listen to Miles Davis. And drink my vodka ration and smoke my Camel ration, then sail to another quiet harbor and drink whatever vodka was left over from all the dumb rationing. If I wanted, I could bring Amanda along and she could drink wine. There were any number of other things we could do on a boat if we put our minds to it.

This is a want, I said to myself. I want something. It had been so long since I'd felt that sensation it was hard at first to identify. But there it was. An unrequited yearning for an entirely unnecessary object of desire.

While still in the thrall, I drove Eddie back to Oak Point, where I let him out so he could wait in the backyard for Amanda to get home. Then I headed back toward the ocean.

On the way I called Sullivan, but his phone kicked me into his voice mail again. So I left another message, sticking to the facts, leaving out all speculation, conjecture and phantom sailboats.

Dune Drive was as good as its name, a curvy, two-lane road running parallel to the dunes and the shoreline. Scattered atop the dunes were oceanfront houses built mostly in the late twentieth century, a catalog of architectural triumph and catastrophe. The pampered landscaping had flourished in recent years, making it harder to see the houses, but Angel's place was easy to spot. You'd probably find it in a magazine or academic text described in terms to inflame the imagination of design students and critics, but to me it was just a three-dimensional rectangle on stilts.

There was a square white gate with an intercom stuck to the gatepost. I pushed the button.

"Mr. Acquillo?" asked an accented voice a few registers above Valero's.

"Yup."

As the gates swung in I half expected the guy to say, "Enter ye, if thou darest."

The cobblestone drive curved around plantings of dune grass and wild roses and formed a large parking area in front of the gleaming white staircase leading to the first floor of the house. Across the parking area, partly filled with the customary Jaguars, Porsches and Mercedes Benzes, was a white picket fence. Farther back were two smaller versions of the main house. Guest house and pool house by my astute reckoning.

When I got out of the car a woman in a minute, buff-colored bikini and a pair of Roman-style sandals with wide ribbons laced up her calves passed through a gate and strolled over to my car.

"You're on time," she said. "That's rare these days."

"Precision is an engineer's curse."

"A poetic engineer. Follow me," she said, pivoting and heading back to the gate. It wasn't the hardest thing anyone's asked me to do.

Inside the gate she picked up a Siamese cat that was trying to twine itself around her ankles.

"Meet Opium," she said, holding the cat out so I could scratch its ears.

"She's such a greeter."

Holding the cat under one arm, she continued the trip down a curvaceous path paved with grey bricks and lined with cultivated tufts of grass and purple and yellow flowers.

"No trouble finding the place?" she asked.

"I just looked for a big gift box."

"A gift from Angel to himself," she said.

When we got to our destination I could see why he'd said "down at the pool." It was settled into a hollow inside the dunes, open to the ocean on one end and encircled by more grey pavers and yellow and purple flowers. There were enough white chaise lounges and deck chairs to seat a pool party, but only two were filled—another girl and a giant, barrel-chested, pot-bellied guy, both wearing only bikini bottoms and baseball caps.

I rounded the pool following my guide. Angel watched us approach through a pair of dark green aviator's glasses. I stood next to his chaise and waited.

"You're Acquillo?" he finally asked, not offering his hand.

"Sam Acquillo. You can call me Sam."

"You can call me annoyed."

He put his hands on the armrests of the chaise and lugged himself to his feet. He was about the height of Zelda Fitzgerald and outweighed her by several orders of magnitude. He stood slightly too close to me for comfort, but I held my ground. His breath smelled of the red wine he and the girl were drinking out of little plastic bowls. When he plucked his off the armrest he saw me notice.

"It's the pool. Can't have glass anywhere near. You like Shiraz?"

I looked up at the sky.

"It's too light out for wine. How 'bout a gin and tonic?"

He pointed at the woman who led me in and jerked his head at a pink bamboo dry bar wheeled up to the side of the pool.

"Jesse, get the man his daylight drink."

He took the pressure off my personal space and pulled over a couple of chairs and a round side table. I took the one that kept the girls in view. What the heck.

"This Gelb. You know him?" he asked, settling his bulk into the painted rattan chair.

"Only to coerce."

"He says you want to make a run at me."

He sliced the air with a slab of hand, as if to underscore the preposterousness of the idea.

"I don't know what that means," I said. "I just want to talk to you about Iku Kinjo. You were an important client. You might be able to shed some light."

As with Zelda Fitzgerald, his sunglasses did a lot to contain his thoughts. But there was something said in the long pause in the conversation.

"She's dead. What other light do you need?"

"The illuminating kind," I said.

"That's redundant," said Jesse, now in a chaise of her own, reading a weathered copy of *The Agony and the Ecstasy*.

Angel ignored her.

"What's your part in this?" he asked.

"Finder of the body."

He made a grunt deep enough to be felt through the grey pavers.

"There's no legal standing in that."

"Since when did legalities trouble you?" I asked, taking a second sip from my drink. The first tasted like pure, lime-flavored gin. Jesse wasn't much of a bartender.

Angel pointed at me. "How's that mouth of yours served you so far? In life?"

"Intermittently."

"I'll bet."

"So, any thoughts on what happened to Iku? If what I hear is correct, you had a close working relationship. They're suggesting now it might be suicide. Any sign she was pre-occupied? Or depressed?"

"No. But I am. By this conversation."

"You're a sensitive guy, Angel. I'll try to soften the edges for you."

Jesse was sitting behind him, so he couldn't see the intimation of a grin pass over her face. I kept my gaze fixed on him so I wouldn't give her away.

"Like you said, I had a working relationship with the woman. I didn't know anything about her personal life. It's all business with those Eisler people. It's a mentality. Just get it done. Straight down the middle. Hired brains. No life, no heart."

"So, nothing suspicious right before she died?" I asked.

He slid down in his chair and downed his bowl of Shiraz. He wiped his mouth with the back of his forearm.

"Even if there was, I wouldn't know. I was in Europe at the end of the summer. No reason to talk to her. For that matter, no reason to talk to you. So why am I?"

"Because you're a people person?"

I think Jesse liked this one, too. But it went right by the topless girl. In fact, she never looked up the entire time I was there. Can't please everybody.

Angel took off his baseball cap and wiped his forehead. The move dumped out a large ball of wavy black hair. It took him a few moments to get it all stuffed back under the hat again.

"Gelb told me you were locked up in a loony bin for a while," he said. "I'm understanding now how that could be the case. Because you got to be fucking crazy to talk to me like that."

"I don't suppose you'd want to tell me about the last deal you two were working on."

As if realizing there were other people within earshot, Angel twisted around in his chair and looked over at Jesse.

"Can you believe this shit?" he asked her.

She held up her book.

"Not paying attention, darling," she said.

"Whether somebody killed Iku Kinjo or she did it herself, there's a reason it happened," I said. "Given your close association, I'd think you'd be curious about that. I'm curious that you're not."

He leaned as forward in his chair as the medicine ball of a stomach would let him.

"Why all the curiosity?" he asked.

"I was looking for her. Until I find out why she's dead, I haven't really found her."

He sat back in his chair again and put his hands on the armrests, preparing to haul himself to his feet.

"I got something to show you."

He got up and waved for me to follow. We walked over to another gate in the white fence, one leading out to a patio area with round wrought-iron tables and chairs, umbrellas and a view of the ocean through a cut in the dunes. He opened the gate and ushered me through. I walked out on the patio and looked at the ocean, which was relatively calm and blue in the fading light of the sun coming in over our shoulders from the west. It threw our shadows out from our feet, which should have told me Angel was a little too close behind.

It was an embrace to take your breath away. Literally. I looked down at his arms crossed over my chest, one hand holding the other wrist, and the contours of his arm muscles swelling with the effort. The pressure increased steadily and rapidly, until I felt my ribs about to collapse. I gathered what breath I could and held it while straining against the relentless compression.

"You fuck with me," he whispered in my ear, "and it'll be the last fucking crazy thing you do."

I think he said a few more threatening things, but I don't remember. I was preoccupied by the blood being squeezed up into my head and the popping sensation behind my eyes. It wasn't the ideal state of mind for working out a defensive strategy, but I had the advantage of panic and desperation.

I hadn't troubled to dress up for the visit, so all I had on my feet was a pair of worn-out Timberlands. Worn, but with a good enough heel to dig into Valero's toes where they stuck out of his sandals. This had less effect on his grip than I hoped, though he stopped talking and started growling in my ear.

I used the other heel to kick him in the shins, forcing him to look down to see where he'd placed his feet. This gave me the chance to tap him in the face with the back of my head. I caught him in the mouth, cutting my scalp on his teeth, but the move loosened up his bear hug. I probably should have stopped with the head butts, given my neurological issues, but it was the only weapon I had available. And it was working. The growling stopped and his breath was coming faster, more seriously as he tried to twist clear of my hammering skull.

With all the butting and Valero's maneuvering, I'd been able to turn a little to the right, which caused my hand, pressed into my side, to come in contact with the impressive package Angel had stuffed into his swimsuit. He had a split second to ponder the wisdom of allowing this configuration to evolve before a slight bend in my elbow allowed me to have both polyester-covered testicles firmly in hand.

This was a first for me, and I imagine for Angel as well.

I'd spent the last several years swinging a hammer and throwing around bundles of lumber. So my grip was probably as good as ever. I gave those boys of Valero's a pretty lusty squeeze.

He must have thrown his head back to bellow, because when I butted him again I caught the edge of his chin. He lost the hold when he tried to grab my wrist. I didn't give him another chance. I spun out of the hug and danced back out of his reach, on my toes with my fists up where they belonged.

I didn't know how a guy my size would do against a human bull, but I was done wrestling.

Angel was leaning forward, gripping himself around the midriff. I stepped in and planted a right jab in his face, snapping his head back, which made a nice target for the following left. He was still upright, but wavering. So I threw another neat combination. This seemed to have little effect, but before he could get his big arms up to protect his face I shot a right straight into his mouth. I was very happy to see this drop his ass down on the patio, where I was even happier to see it stay.

"I never cuddle on the first date," I told him.

By now he'd let go of his balls and was holding his face.

"You're a dead man," he said into his hands.

"We all get there eventually," I said as I circled back around to the gate, keeping my eyes on him the whole time.

Jesse opened it for me.

"Well," she said, matter-of-factly.

"Thanks for the drink. Next time I'll take it with tonic."

"I'm sure there'll be a next time."

I took one more glance at the blonde before walking up the grey path to the outer gate, where Opium was sitting licking her ass, and out to where the Grand Prix stood staring down the German performance cars scattered around Valero's driveway.

When I got to Dune Drive I tried to take a full breath, with little success. I didn't think anything was broken, but I'd bruised ribs before and knew I was in for a long hurt.

The visit hadn't turned out exactly as planned. All I'd done was make an enemy, in record time, out of a wealthy and ruthless son of a bitch. I'd fully exposed my own intentions without learning a thing about his, or about anything else for that matter, and ruined any chance for future discussion or cooperation. And all I had to show for it was a sore chest and a cut on the head.

"Brilliant," I said, pulling a smashed cigarette out of my shirt pocket, seeing if a little jolt of carcinogen would do something for the aching ribs and eroding self-regard.

—

That night I finally got through to Joe Sullivan. I'd called him at home on my cell phone from a table at the Pequot. He'd been tied up with the DA for a few days, and his wife, whom I'd never met, was none too delighted by my intrusion. He used a clever ploy to hustle me off the phone—the promise of a full forensics briefing, delivered at the crime scene.

Mollified, I went back to *The Wealth of Nations*, a single, abridged volume I'd bought from the library when they were clearing out their stock.

"The root of all evil?" I asked Dorothy Hodges, holding up the book.

"Not to me, and I'll ignore the stereotyping," she said, dropping my drink on the table as gracefully as you could with three-inch-long black fingernails.

"I've got *Das Kapital* back at the cottage. I'm going to put them in the middle of the room and let them fight it out."

"They did that already. Smith won."

"They taught you that at Columbia?"

"Marx belongs in the fantasy–science fiction section. Lovely dreams." She used one of the black daggers at the end of her fingers to scratch her head through greased orange hair. It wasn't my favorite Dorothy look, though it was hard to pin down what was, since it changed almost by the day.

"Maybe I won't bother reading either of them and you can just explain it to me," I said.

"Easy. People yearn for community, but they're biologically hierarchical. Trouble is, hierarchy's defined in two ways. Brawn and brains. Brains run the kitchen, but they need brawn at the front of the house. It's a natural symbiosis. And the rest of us have to eat whatever they dish out."

"The Pequot Theory of Economic Interdependency?"

"Money doesn't suck. Not having money sucks. Using money for stupid things sucks."

"Like the time you bought tropicalbirds.com at fifty bucks a share?" said her father, sliding a chair into the conversation. "Don't get me wrong. Dotty's a hell of a stock picker."

"Not really," said Dorothy, though clearly pleased with the compliment. "I'm just a mid-cap index kind of a girl with a taste for the occasional social-conscience buy. Which do very well, by the way, most of the time."

"There's so much about the world I don't understand," I said with deepest sincerity.

"You don't think we could live on what comes out of the till, do you?" Hodges asked me as we watched Dorothy disappear back into the kitchen. "A restaurant's a cash business. If you play it right, you get to hold the suppliers' money just long enough to put it to work without pissing 'em off. Dotty's been floating the delta since she was in high school."

Back when I was married and had a regular paying job I handled all the family finances. My wife Abby resented this, and from this remove I can see why. It was an implicit insult to her financial acumen, entirely untested and perfunctorily rejected. I wasn't a bad money manager but I wasn't exactly Warren Buffett, or Angel Valero. I was exactly like my father. Afraid to let the money out of my sight and have it all taken away like in the Depression, thirty years before I was born.

So what did I do? Lost it all anyway.

"You can't know everything, Sam," said Hodges. "That's what we have trust for. To fool us into giving ourselves over to specialists who know more about something than we'll ever know even in a thousand years."

"You can trust Dorothy."

"That's what we have children for."

—

On the way home I called and left a message for George Donovan. I told him Mason Thigpen and the people at Eisler, Johnson were aware I was nosing around about Iku Kinjo. They had no reason to suspect anything but the obvious— that finding her body had drawn me into the case. I said I thought things were going to heat up, but there was no need to worry as long as he played it tight to the vest, something he surely knew how to do.

I was glad to leave a message. If I reached him directly I didn't know what he'd say. This really wasn't up to him anymore, and while his secret would die with me, I didn't need the interference.

When I got to the cottage I found Amanda and Eddie sleeping on the screened-in porch. Eddie was on the braided rug and Amanda was face down on the daybed, still dressed and snoring. Likely a performance piece meant to undermine my tendency to idolize.

I poured my nightcap ration and sat at the pine table to

watch her snore. Seeing that I'd abrogated my rightful place, Eddie jumped up on the daybed and lay next to her, settling himself down with a puff of breath through his long snout.

I went back to Adam Smith, thinking I ought to write a book like this of my own. Call it *The Wealth of Undeserved Blessings*.

TWELVE

JOE SULLIVAN WAS WAITING for me on the front walk that led up to Bobby Dobson's group rental on Vedders Pond. It was only seven-thirty in the morning, but the day was already heavy with humidity. Unusual for September, but the weather had been nothing but unusual lately, so we were used to it. Sullivan wore olive drab safari shorts and heavy hiking boots, a black shirt with a half dozen pockets, a black Yankees cap and sunglasses. And a black leather shoulder harness securing his regulation Smith & Wesson .38.

The perfect plainclothes disguise. Who'd ever guess he was a cop?

He had a headset around his neck with a cord leading to a little black box hitched to his belt.

I had the coffee. A Viennese cinnamon for me and a double latte for him. So much for working-class sensibilities.

"You're recording this?" I asked him.

"Digital, baby. Cheaper than a steno."

"I've got one of those. Amazing things. Tell me when to keep my voice down."

"You're here as a witness. Totally legit. I cleared it with Ross."

I followed him to the front door where he told the recorder we were cutting the yellow tape and entering the building. Just inside was the living room, now cleared of newspapers and magazines and covered in multicolored fingerprint powder. Also strewn about were little yellow cones with black numbers.

"Riverhead's been busy," I said.

That was where the Suffolk County forensics lab was headquartered. According to Sullivan, they were twitchy with paranoia after blowing a famous case, bringing on a huge lawsuit and a savaging on *60 Minutes*. Ross was one of the few officials who stood up for them in the press, earning the DA's fury and the lab's permanent devotion.

"Is this suicide thing their idea?" I asked.

Sullivan scoffed and flicked off the recorder.

"Veckstrom. The paper said it was 'an anonymous police official,' but who else would say the killing looked like a classic jingo thing."

"*Jigai*. Ritual suicide practiced by Japanese women."

"Practiced, huh? Not many chances to get it right."

Sullivan picked out a comfy spot on the sofa and peeled the plastic lid off his latte. He pulled his case book out of his pocket and flipped through the pages while he listened to me talk.

"The problem is, *jigai* involves slitting the throat, severing the jugular and bleeding out," I said. "This knife was shoved straight up into her skull. Even Veckstrom should know that details matter in these things."

"That's what Ross told me, the only other guy in

Southampton who knows about this shit. Though the press leak might've been his idea in the first place. Not bad if the perp thinks we're barking down the wrong trail."

"So you think it's a wrong trail."

Sullivan looked up from his case book.

"Riverhead thinks it's the wrong trail. The knife was jammed up through the soft tissue of her palate, then into her brain. Very accurate. Or very lucky. Especially given the girl's blood alcohol level, which was a point above sloshed. There were also defensive marks on her throat, so the fatal thrust wasn't the first try."

"I didn't see that," I said.

"You wouldn't with all the blood."

"None of which was on the bed. That I did see."

"That's because the body was moved there from somewhere else," said Sullivan. "They thought somewhere in the house, because it happened shortly after death. And they were right. There's a blood trail from the patio under the deck to the bedroom. Good cleanup job, but God Himself can't escape luminol."

"Or Herself."

Sullivan scowled at me and flipped off the recorder.

"I can never tell if you're serious."

"Assume I'm not, as a rule of thumb."

He talked some more about the crime scene, sharing some of the assumptions and conclusions Riverhead had come to based on forensic science, a subject I never tired of. Though my curiosity always led back to the more complex and less easily divined part of the equation, the people.

"So what was Bobby Dobson's opinion of all this?"

He studied me unhappily.

"That would be confidential information concerning an official homicide investigation." He flipped off the recorder.

"Do I need to tell you how happy my wife would be if I blew my pension?"

"Very?"

"Sharing forensic reports is one thing. Revealing confidential statements from potential suspects another."

"You don't have to if you don't want to," I said.

His face fell a little.

"Not saying that." He went back to his book. "I'm recalling from my notes, but I think I got the main points." He cleared his throat. "Dobson stated that the victim had been staying full time at the share since about mid-August. He claimed to know nothing about her motivation for leaving her employment other than what he called burnout, though he wanted it clear that this was his opinion and nothing about this was ever expressed to him by the victim or anybody else. Dobson was the only renter who was in the City during the week. He said the others had summer gigs out here. Carl Brooks and Sybil Shandy at Roger's, and the other Brooks, Elaine, at the Varick Gallery."

"What about Zelda? Zelda Fitzgerald?"

He looked through his book.

"Nothing on Fitzgerald. He did say others would come and go during the summer, though he couldn't remember all their names. I got a note to go back at that if we need to."

"Okay."

Sullivan leaned back on the sofa, dropping his boots on the coffee table and taking a sip from his latte.

"Damn, that's great shit," he said. "Almost makes you stop hating yuppies."

"Speaking of which."

"Right. Dobson said the victim would spend the week basically hiding out in her room. He'd see her on weekends and try to get her to go out and get a little fresh air. Have a little fun. Sometimes successfully."

"So they were dating."

Sullivan shook his head at me.

"Couldn't quite get that one nailed down. He said they were sort of seeing each other. But the way forensics tells the tale, if they were getting it on, it wasn't here."

"So you got some good prints?" I asked.

Sullivan took another sip of his latte before flipping ahead in his case book.

"We have prints from the victim, Iku Kinjo, of course," he read. "And Robert Dobson, the principle leaseholder, which we got off a soda can during the interrogation. Also Carl Brooks and Sybil Shandy—IAFIS had the prints off a lewdness charge. We got a copy of their file. Nice mug shots. Then we have Unknowns A, B and C."

He looked at the recorder to make sure it wasn't running.

"Remarkably, the only prints from the witness who discovered the body were a perfect set on the front door."

"Witness efficiency is definitely on the uptick."

He put the recorder back on.

"Any ideas on the mystery guests?" he asked.

"Elaine Brooks, Carl's sister, and Zelda Fitzgerald are two. My guess is the owner's number three."

Sullivan went back to his case book.

"John Churchman. Lives on a boat at Hawk Pond. Inherited the house from his parents, who built it in 1972."

"There's an accountant in town with that name. He has an office next to Harbor Bank."

"That'd be him. He's been cooperative, so it shouldn't be hard to get elimination prints."

I looked around.

"So everybody's prints showed up in the common areas."

"Correct again. Be a surprise if they didn't. Let's go upstairs and see what other nifty things we found."

Before he could stand I asked him where everybody was when Iku was killed. He sat back into the sofa.

"According to Dobson, Carl Brooks had returned to the City as planned after Labor Day. As did Elaine Brooks, who works at the Varick Gallery's other place on the East Side. Sybil Shandy is still at Roger's till Christmas, when they close for the season, but left the rental when Carl moved out. She's got a place above the restaurant."

"You're talking to her?" I asked.

"She's on the list."

"So Bobby and Iku had the place to themselves."

"At least on the weekends. During the week she was by herself. Can we go now?"

I followed him up the staircase to the balcony that led to the bedroom doors. He waved me into the first room.

"Here we have Robert Dobson," said Sullivan, "as identified in testimony and corroborated by careful investigation." He held up a Dopp kit with the name Robert K. Dobson in gold leaf on the side. "This is his bedroom, which he apparently shared with Unknown A."

"Not Iku."

"Unless she wore surgical gloves. Knowing what goes on in these group rentals, I wouldn't be surprised."

"Who's next door?" I asked.

"Carl and Sybil, the drunks pulled naked out of a fountain in Las Vegas two years ago."

"I thought that was Zelda's trick."

He looked at his book.

"I told you. Nothing here about a Zelda."

"Look in the evidence room for a *New Yorker* magazine with her name on the label. The prints will match one of the unknowns. When you're ready to confirm with the actual girl, I've got her address."

He frowned down at his book as he jotted down the tip.

"They shoulda seen that already."

"What about Elaine?" I said. "Did Dobson say he was living with Elaine?"

He flipped through some more pages.

"Quote: 'Elaine and I have been off and on for years. But we've always been friends. You wouldn't understand.' I love that shit. You wouldn't understand, you dumb fucking Ivy League–deprived cop."

"Condescension's on the Princeton curriculum."

He flicked the backs of his fingers under his chin. "Fungu to Princeton."

"Any other prints in Dobson's room?"

"Just him and A. We checked the sheets, too, by the way, and got all the usual goodies. Also not the victim's."

I walked back onto the balcony and looked down at the living room, trying to see the players arrayed on the broken-in furniture. I tried to imagine who was sitting with whom. I shut my eyes and listened for their conversation, but I didn't know enough to hear.

"To the basement?" Sullivan asked.

"Sure."

On the way down we stopped at the kitchen so he could show me where a set of carving knives was stored in a wooden block on the counter. A set of five.

"Japanese," he said. "Similar handle design as the murder weapon. Very sharp. The lab is tracking down the source."

We moved on from there, stopping a few times so he could explain the little yellow cones that marked where forensics had picked up a sample or spotted something they wanted to come back and recheck. He told me they needed a warrant each time they did that, but it was almost impossible to get everything on a single pass.

"So Bobby's cooperative," I said.

"Not bad. His old man's been up my ass a bit, but the DA's been up his. It's nice to have that broad on my side for a change."

We went down to the basement, which was technically at ground level at the back end of the house. More colorful fingerprint powder and little yellow cones.

Iku's room looked even more forlorn without her body lying on the bed. The disarray of the search and investigation showed around the edges. There was still an impression on the bed from the weight of her body.

"They searched the hell out of this room," said Sullivan. "Nothing probative to write home about. One set of prints. Hers."

I couldn't help wishing I'd poked around a little myself before calling in the cops. It was an unworthy thought—unfair to Iku and the cops, but I couldn't help it. I was bugged by a strong sense of absence, that something was missing.

"Gadgets," I said.

"Huh?"

"Where're the gadgets? Cell phones, laptops, iPods."

Sullivan rested his hand on my shoulder.

"At the evidence lab, Sam. We don't know what them things do, us hick cops, but we knows we gotta get 'em to the lab."

I turned and looked at him.

"What was on the computer? Did you get her email?"

He still wanted to be insulted.

"Weren't no computers. Jes' an old cell phone. Don't happen to have that report yet, but when I do you'll be the first we tells."

"Really? Great. I appreciate it."

I quieted him back down with a grip on his meaty shoulder. He shook his head.

I walked deeper into the room, with my hands in my pockets as he'd instructed me earlier. On impulse, I tried to look behind a dresser, the only large piece of furniture in the room.

"Can I touch that?" I asked, pointing to the dresser.

He handed me a set of surgical gloves. I squeezed them on and pulled the dresser toward me. Stuffed down between the dresser and the wall was a green cable. I pulled it free.

"What's this?" I said.

Sullivan stood next to me and bent over to look.

"That's not a phone cord?" he asked.

"It's a Cat 5. A phone jack is smaller. Cat 5s are used for Internet connections."

"I'm sure it's in the report," he said. "We do know something about this shit."

I reminded him that only one of us had a computer with broadband access and an email account, and a PDA. And it wasn't me. He looked a little less defensive, but concerned. I went back to looking around the room.

"Two closets?" I asked.

He pointed to one of the doors.

"That one goes to the bedroom next door."

"Prints on the handle?"

"Just on the other side. Unknowns A and B. Shall we look?"

We went back out to the hall so we could go into the other room without touching anything.

"Unknowns A and B are all over the place. Since B was also found in tucked-away places, we're guessing that's the one who owns the room. But that's an inadmissibly wild-ass guess."

"You could ask Bobby."

"We did. He said he never came down here, so he didn't know. The print evidence more or less proves that."

"Don't forget the rubber gloves theory."

"I don't forget anything. And I don't believe anything I can't see with my own eyes, and even then I'm suspicious."

"What about C?"

"C is scattered about the house. The only one you find on the furnace and water heater, along with the usual unknowns found nowhere else."

"The owner and maintenance mechanics."

"You think?"

He took me out to the patio under the deck where they found the blood trace, and showed me how it led back to the bedroom. Reluctant as I was to bring up the concept of jimmied locks, I asked if the patio door had been forced or messed with in any way.

"Nope. No evidence of that anywhere. It's some skill to pick a lock, let alone leave no trace of doing it. Takes a real mechanical whiz," he said, looking at me pointedly.

I put up my hands.

"It's beyond me."

We walked the blood path a few more times, me asking questions, him answering as well as he could and jotting down things to check out later. He turned on the recorder a few times to get my official statement on the disposition of the body, the condition of the house, all the stuff he already knew but had to ask to cover him for the warrant that got us back inside.

I wanted to feel more enlightened after walking around the death-impregnated place, but all I felt was confused and disoriented. It made me wish again that I hadn't found her. Maybe I would have been able to think more clearly if the image of young promise rendered silent and supine wasn't filling my mind's eye.

We were back outside and about to get into our cars when I remembered another obvious question.

"You said Dobson was in the City during the week. What does he do?"

"Wall Street, of course," said Sullivan.

"Like what?"

"Some administrative job."

"Where?"

He sighed and fished out his case book again, with a look that said this was the last time.

"Eisler, Johnson Consulting, Inc.," he said. "He's a help desk administrator, though not much help to me so far."

THIRTEEN

IT HAD BEEN A WHILE NOW since I first awoke on the screened-in porch of my parents' cottage, fresh out of rehab and expectations. I'm a little surprised I survived that first year, so indifferent was I to the basic essentials of life. It's a testament, I guess, to the gene code my parents bestowed on me, their penchant for grim forbearance, their heedless endurance.

Most people are too polite to ask me why I flamed out on the upward arc of my career, why I demolished my marriage and laid waste any future professional prospects. The fact is, I'm not sure why. Or, I'm not ready to understand why. I know it's supposed to be a big deal to me, this thing that happened. I don't deny that, but I'm not sure any good can come from dissecting my motivations, plumbing the depths of my soul, my essential being, to root out fundamental, underlying causes.

All I can say is I used to wake in the morning feeling a rich blend of panic and hollow despair. Now I'm merely undecided.

Another improvement is waking up next to Amanda. I remember Abby as The Lump. Amanda's more like The Volcano. At rest, and then, suddenly, not.

I left her in the big bed in the new room at the back of the house and went to make coffee. Eddie ignored me from the shearling-covered bean bag Amanda gave him to use in the kitchen, the one room in the house without over-stuffed furniture.

I'd pulled Eddie out of a pound where all he had to lie on was concrete. Before that, according to the rescue people, he'd been living in the scrub oak north of Westhampton, not exactly four-star accommodations. You wonder how a dog like that can develop such a taste for upholstery.

When Amanda wandered into the kitchen a few minutes later he jumped up and acted like royalty had come to call, assuming Her Majesty liked having a set of paws stuck in her midriff and a wet nose in the kisser.

The air was cool and the lawn was sodden with dew, but I wanted to get all I could out of the last warm months. I passed out sweatshirts and pants and filled Amanda's arms with worn but stalwart blankets. I brought china mugs and coffee in a big white thermos.

Once settled into the Adirondacks at the edge of the breakwater, we were in a good position to watch the sun slowly turn the Peconic from silver grey to dark blue as it cleared the air of mist and turned the sails across the bay into tiny white blades against the shadowy horizon.

Eddie sat next to my chair and leaned against my leg. I used one hand to hold the mug, the other to scratch a spot near the end of his nose, an attention he found tirelessly agreeable.

"You're thinking about the Japanese girl," said Amanda.

"I'm thinking about computers."

"Why you don't have one?" she asked.

"Why Iku didn't have one. Makes no sense. At the company her laptop was like an appendage. And that was at the dawn of email, before wireless broadband and whatever else you people are addicted to."

"You people? You mean the general population of non-Luddites?"

"Donovan told me the last contact he had with her was an email. There was a Cat 5 connection in Iku's room. We used Cat 5 to run cabling for distributed control systems. The only purpose it has in a house is broadband Internet."

"If you get that email you can check the IP address and confirm it came from the rental," she said.

"I can?"

"Not you, darling. Somebody who knows what an IP address is. Me, for example."

There was a lot I didn't know about household technology. But I knew Iku Kinjo couldn't have survived without it.

"We need to find her computer," I said.

"We do. After another cup of coffee."

———

Before going back down to my shop I checked in with Sullivan. He told me the investigators had noted the broadband connection at a built-in desk in the kitchen, but missed the one in Iku's bedroom.

"We did get her cell phone records. Incoming and outgoing by the boatload until May 30."

"Then what?"

"Then nothing," he said. "She cancelled the service. I guess she'd said all she wanted to say for the year."

"She used someone else's phone?" I asked.

"Probably a disposable. Untraceable."

"I didn't know there was such a thing," I said.

"It's what Ross calls a directional indicator."

"Jesse would say that's redundant."

"Who's Jesse?"

"One of Valero's assistants," I said. "A bikini specialist."

"Bikinis are redundant?"

"Sometimes."

In our ongoing spirit of collaboration I told him my plans for the evening, which were highly dependent on Amanda scoring a reservation on short notice at Roger's.

"I could see me putting that one through expenses," said Sullivan.

"I'll let you know what I learn."

"Find out if their fries come with ketchup."

———

I told Amanda the key to successful undercover operations was to blend into the environment. Since Roger's was often patronized by beautiful women in revealing evening wear, it was clear what had to be done.

Luckily, Amanda was always game for a challenge.

"Great looking nightgown. But what are you wearing to dinner?" I asked when I picked her up.

"You need to carry my lipstick. As you can see, no pockets."

"No nothing."

We took her Audi Avant. The Grand Prix had a lot more room to spread out, but for some reason you always left the passenger compartment covered in dog hair.

Roger's was in an eighteenth-century house set about twenty feet in from the edge of Montauk Highway and about two miles east of Bridgehampton. It had been a restaurant for over sixty years, and after destroying the lives of several owners had settled in nicely with Roger Estay, a chef from Baltimore who'd come to the Hamptons hoping to recover from a nervous breakdown by exposing himself to dire financial risk.

Roger consistently dished out the best food and most breathtaking checks on the East End.

Amanda hadn't only nailed down a reservation, it was for the best table in the joint. The one on the outside patio under the spreading arms of an antique copper beech. We were led to it by a blonde woman in a tubular silk dress that she shouldn't have been able to walk in. Three good-looking young men wearing white shirts, black pants and expressions you often see on devoted evangelists were waiting for us when we reached the table.

"Pulled strings?" I asked her, quietly.

"Threw money."

Before the blonde had a chance to pass us off to the choir-boys I asked her if she was Sylvia Shandy.

It took her aback.

"I am," she said, with an up-speak lilt suggesting she might not be Sylvia Shandy if that was the safer answer.

I put out my hand, which she shook with the same reservations.

"I'm Sam Acquillo. This is Amanda Anselma. I was a friend of Iku Kinjo."

She dropped my hand like it last held Iku's corpse.

"Jesus what an awful thing," she said. "I'm sorry."

Sylvia was either a bottle blonde or a champion tanner. Even in the low light her coloring looked mismatched, though she herself looked pretty good. Small proportionate features, large wide-set brown eyes with lashes you could comb your hair with. Her fingers were long and slender, ringless, with fingernails painted a pearlized white.

"Do you get a break?" I asked. "I'd like to talk a little about Iku."

She shook her wrist until a watch attached to a loose silver chain worked its way into view.

"Maybe in an hour," she said. "Though I don't know what I can tell you. I hardly knew the girl."

"I know," I said. "If you could just give me a few minutes."

She smiled an artificial smile.

"Maybe a minute." She stood back as the waiters passed out menus. "Most people start with the coquilles, but I'm big on the ceviche. Roger says it tastes like a Jamaican sunrise."

As we watched Sylvia vamp through the patio tables back into the restaurant, Amanda asked, "Do you put that dress on or have it applied?"

"Let's get one and find out."

With nothing else to do, we focused on ordering food and explaining to the waiters why a chunk of fruit has no more business in a glass of vodka than a Jamaican sunrise in Vladivostok. The menu looked like it was hand-lettered, which must have been hard work, because they gave up before adding in the prices. It was nominally in English, though I only recognized about half the words.

"My mother told me never eat anything I can't pronounce," said Amanda.

"Probably saved you from a diet of ceviche and coquilles St. Jacques."

The lighting out on the lawn, mostly from strings of little pin lights draped around tree limbs and stretched overhead, made everybody look better than they deserved, which meant Amanda looked ridiculously great. Her bountiful auburn hair, parted in the middle, cascaded over her shoulders and the liquid satin of her dark blue dress.

"What," she said, catching me staring.

"You look ridiculously great."

"Even if I'm not blonde and shrink-wrapped in polyester?"

"Even if you were," I said. "You can't help it."

"I think we're talking 'eyes of the beholder.'"

"The beholding comes later. Don't get ahead of yourself."

By mutual consent, we launched into a game called "blissful ignorance." The object was to talk only about things we knew nothing about, which meant we couldn't talk about our work, our past, our social, economic or political views or how many games the Yankees were out of first place. This is harder than you think, but virtually guarantees the avoidance of painful, emotionally challenging conversation. Since both parties are blissfully ignorant of the subject at hand, you spend a lot of time speculating on things, like how often Buddhist monks wash their robes or the chemical composition of Neptune's atmosphere.

Post-game fact-checking was entirely permissible, though I never did. "The basic geopolitical unit of local Texas government has got to be the county. The place is too damn big to organize around municipalities," I offered up.

"Is that why it's legal to shoot people in broad daylight, provided it's a fair fight?"

Thus contentedly engaged, we were slightly disappointed when Sylvia catwalked back across the patio to our table.

"Hey, guys," she said. "I gotta few. Can I sit?"

Amanda waved her into an empty seat.

"Before you get all interested in what I have to say you should know a guy just came in who actually knew Iku, like intimately."

"Really," I said. "Big guy?"

"Yeah. Angel Valero. Ya know him?"

"Intimately."

"Love your hair, by the way," Sylvia said to Amanda. "I could manage the color, but it's hard to get thick outta Clairol."

"Did Angel ever visit Iku?"

"Hell no. She made us swear we wouldn't tell anybody she was there. She just talked about him all the time. Called him the Evil Troll. Or just plain Fucking Angel Valero. Can't support that opinion one way or the other. Not the friendliest guy in the world, but he's a good tipper."

"So what did you think of Iku?" I asked.

She looked like she was calibrating the politics of her answer.

"Work bitch. Not like a bitch bitch, but a fiend for the job. You know what I mean. The City's crawling with them. Stress bunnies, Carl calls 'em. So wired up they can't stop hopping around. Not my cup of tea, to be honest with you. Who doesn't like money, but really, what's the point?"

"Any talk about why she started staying at the house full time? Any kind of trouble?"

"Was it a personal crisis?" Amanda asked.

Sylvia nodded immediately.

"Exactly. She was going through some kind of personal crisis. You read about it all the time. Your symptoms are," she ticked off on her fingers, "lots of crying, usually locked up in the bedroom, extra drinking and not only at night, playing your favorite depressing songs at a high volume and less care with regular hygiene, though that girl always looked great no matter how fucked up she might have felt, as annoying as that is."

"What was the problem?" I asked. "Boyfriend or job?"

She looked at me as if I'd just drooled down the front of my silk shirt.

"It always has to be about guys?" she asked, insulted on behalf of the sisterhood. "Okay, it was probably about a guy, but I told you, I hardly knew the girl, so I wouldn't know. Angel might, like I said."

"Not Robert Dobson? He's not the guy, is he?"

This was amusing to her.

"Bobby? You're joking, right? I'd've pegged him for a fruit-cake if I hadn't heard him and Elaine thumpin' and gruntin' every morning, waking me up after an hour of sleep."

I called a waiter over to order another Absolut on the rocks. I always found an empty glass distracting and wanted my full attention on Sylvia.

"Let me get this straight," I said. "Elaine was, is, Bobby's girlfriend. Not Iku."

"Duh."

"Bobby didn't know Iku from Princeton?"

"I don't know," she said. "Maybe."

"So who introduced her to the rental?"

Sylvia looked around the outdoor seating area, then back at us.

"Ms. Hot Pants, who do you think?"

I must have looked confused.

"Elaine, Carl's sister," she said.

"I'm not getting this," I admitted.

She shook her wrist, catching the wayward watch with her other hand.

"Sorry. Gotta run. Stephan is probably pissed about me leaving him with the floor."

"Iku just showed up one day with Elaine?" I asked, trying to keep a grip on Sylvia's attention.

She shook her head.

"One night. The two of them drunker'n shit. They got to the house right after Carl and I got off. Lots of falling down and giggling and all that shit that looks so lame and stupid to people who aren't so lucky as to be drunk. Bobby was already in bed, but Zelda was there, pissed off as all hell. Freak job that she is. I'm sorry, that was mean. You can't blame the girl. Nobody likes getting rousted by a pair of drunks. She really let Elaine have it. Called her a total tramp. I really got to go."

She abruptly stood up from her seat, smoothing the fabric of her dress back down the tops of her thighs.

"Thanks for talking," I said.

"Not a problem."

"One thing, real quick. Did Iku have a computer?"

She looked incredulous.

"Are you kidding me? Lived on her laptop. That's another thing I don't understand. Why you don't go blind after a while."

Amanda and I watched again as she wound through the tables and back into the elegant old building.

"When I was a kid we had other ways of going blind," I said.

"The march of progress."

We spent the rest of the evening pretending to be nourished by the teaspoon-sized portions of unpronounceable but admittedly tasty food. The staggering cost was partly explained by the effort put into arranging things on the plate. Much of this involved a form of construction, using a wad of mashed potatoes, for example, to support a golf ball–sized scoop of tenderloin sprinkled with inedible green twigs. At the Pequot, you got a lot more food on a plate half the size. In fact, you routinely ate most of your meal as it spilled onto the vinyl placemats.

Yet I can honestly say that Roger's did a better job on the salads. The foundation greens resembled nothing I'd seen before, but I liked the way they stood up to the tangy salad dressing and digestible flowers, and the colorless, chopped-up stems of who-knows-what. The salads at the Pequot, by comparison, were solid slabs of exhausted iceberg lettuce floating in a vinegar soup, though most of the Pequot's customers were too captivated by the ambience to notice.

The dessert choices showed up on a big platter. I was glad because this meant I didn't have to ask for a French-English dictionary to make a decision. All the choices were out there in plain view.

After Amanda picked something, I asked if they had ice cream.

"Yes, sir. Pine sorbet and chocolate raspberry truffle. Handmade."

"Bring me some anyway. One scoop each, with a foot or two in between."

"You're a craftsman," said Amanda. "Ever make ice cream by hand?"

"If it involves a table saw, I'll give it a try."

We ordered a few cognacs to help us over the final throes of the meal. Amanda asked for the check, but I'd already slipped a wad of bills to the waiter. She had a lot more money than I did, but I had an archaic, dug-in notion that self-respect meant paying your own way. I'd let her pick up the next tab at the Pequot.

On the way out we passed Angel Valero's table. I can't say he was happy to see me. He looked around the restaurant in protest over its failure to properly exclude.

I was pleased to see that the powder dabbed on his cheek had barely disguised a yellow and purple bruise. But I was more distracted by his dinner companion.

"Hey, Jerome. Where's Marla?"

Gelb half stood, but Angel reached out, and without taking his eyes off me, touched his forearm. Gelb sat back in his chair.

I was about to ask Valero how the soprano lessons were coming, but a better part of me took possession.

"You're like a bad penny, Acquillo," said Gelb. "Always turning up and spoiling my mood."

"I thought your mood was unassailable."

"That's because you'd rather talk than think, pal," said Valero.

"And what should I be thinking about?" I asked.

"Who to put in your will," said Gelb, which drew a sharp look from Valero.

I had Amanda gripped lightly by the elbow and could feel her tense up.

"I miss the happy Gelb," I said. "Had a better sense of humor."

"You just don't know what's funny."

This put Amanda over the brink. She pulled my hand off her elbow and took me by the sleeve, dragging me through the restaurant and out to the parking lot.

"You keep frightening me," she said,

"Me?"

"You talk about sharing, but all you do is withhold. And you think I don't notice."

We ran into Sylvia again before making it out the front door. She blessed us with her ersatz smile.

"How was everything?" she asked, deeply interested.

"Everything was the most," said Amanda.

"Don't you know," said Sylvia, pleased, I think.

On the way back to Oak Point we cracked the windows just enough to let a little wind into the car. Amanda slid down in the seat, kicked off her shoes and allowed the hem of her dress to float on the breeze. I commented on the result, keen on changing the direction of the conversation.

"Fashion is becoming painful," she said.

"You get out of practice hanging around construction sites."

"I should try hostessing."

"Sylvia envy?"

"Just her youth."

"Wasted as usual," I said.

I'm practiced at ignoring bitter reality and allowing myself to live in various states of denial. But outright self-delusion has never been my strong suit. Which was too bad, because I really wanted to convince myself that the evening had enriched all of my operating theories.

"You haven't told me about those men," said Amanda.

I did the best I could, filling in at least some of the details of my dealings with both of them. It was a heavily censured report, but more than she enjoyed hearing.

"The big guy was Angel Valero. Iku's client. Former client, I guess, technically."

"Sylvia mentioned him."

"She did."

"He looked like he wanted to mash you up into an Italian meatball."

"Franco-Italian meatball," I said. "The kind of thing only Roger Estay would know how to make."

"*Boulettes de boeuf à l'Acquíllo*. An acquired taste."

"One of his girlfriends liked me. I liked her, too. But not as much as you," I added quickly.

"How many girlfriends did he have?" she asked.

"Two I could see. I wasn't invited into the house."

"And what about Gelb?"

"He was Iku's boss at Eisler, Johnson."

"So they have that in common," she said.

"At least."

The rest of the night wasn't very notable. I know because I got to see most of it. It was one of those nights where I had to settle for lying down as still as possible with my eyes forced shut. Jackie Swaitkowski once said that insomnia was like trying to sleep with a rock band in the bedroom. Only all the noise was in your head.

I finally did the only thing I knew how to do in those situations. I got up and poured a drink and lit a cigarette, promising myself to deduct it from the next day's budget, and settled in at the table on the screened-in porch. I stared at the Little Peconic Bay with questions roiling my brain. I'd invested a lot of time trying to wring answers from that edgy little body of water, with no success. But I continued to hold out hope until about 7:30 in the morning, when I gave up and called Joe Sullivan.

"If you had Iku Kinjo's computer, what would you normally look for?" I asked.

"I'd look for the report from forensics. They do all the looking."

"Can I talk to them?" I asked.

"You can talk to me. I can talk to them."

"I don't know what questions to ask."

"Yeah, you do. You just don't want to share."

He was right. It was a bad habit.

"I'd want to know everything she ever wrote relating to Bobby Dobson and Angel Valero. I'd want to see private logs, journals, love letters, confidential memos and photographs. Financial spreadsheets. To-do lists. Shopping lists."

"That's all? How come you don't want to read all her email? Inbox, sent, deleted and saved. What about a full record of her Internet habits? Websites visited. Click-throughs. Searches. Social networking sites. Chat rooms. Blogs read and responded to. Rants. How about iTunes and YouTube downloads? How come you don't want the whole fucking hard drive?"

"Because I don't know what any of those things are."

It got quiet on the other end of the line.

"You might think about catching up with the contemporary world there, MIT," he said finally.

"You're right. Though I did get a cell phone. Did you know you can call people from your car or when you're sitting on the can?"

"People like the victim run their whole lives on the computer, and forensics can get it all. The public thinks they can delete what they want, hide what they write or do online, but they can't. It's all available. No secrets. No privacy, and nobody seems to care but the people who make a career whining about it."

"So where is it?" I asked.

"What?"

"The computer."

"Stupid," he said.

"What's stupid?"

"I am. For not realizing that was an Ethernet connection in the girl's room. Or asking anybody about it. I oughta know better."

Sullivan was one of those intelligent people who grew up in a world that assumed otherwise, based entirely on your relatives, your neighborhood, your choice of profession. It used to annoy me, but I'd since developed a tactful way of overcoming his inferiority complex.

"Pretty stupid. But I've seen stupider," I told him.

"Thanks, Sam. That makes it better."

"So where do you think it is?" I said.

"Vedders Pond. I've already called in the divers."

"That's where I'd start. But if you find it, there's a bigger question."

"What?" he asked.

"Who put it there?"

FOURTEEN

I REMEMBER THOSE SCIENCE CLASS analogies of the sun as a basketball and the earth as a pea. It's the same for the Hamptons and New York City. We have more room out here, but the City is a whole lot bigger.

To say people in the Hamptons have mixed feelings about the colossus next door would be to understate the matter by an appropriately vast degree. Even for people who work in town and live here when they can. No matter what you want to believe, the Hamptons are an adjunct of the Big City—an appendage. We're in her orbit, her gravitational pull, and utterly in her thrall.

Which is one of the reasons I like driving into town. To see the big girl in all her arrogant glory. The only question was how I drove—or more precisely, in what.

"You're thinking of taking the Audi, aren't you," said Amanda.

"Why would I think that?" I lied.

"I'll drive the pickup."

"Nah. I'll drive the pickup. If you need to haul a few tons of stuff, you can use the Grand Prix," I said.

So I ended up in Amanda's little red truck, with Eddie next to me in the passenger seat, heading into New York City. It was a compromise, admittedly. It wasn't easy for me to accept help from anyone, least of all my rich girlfriend. But driving the Grand Prix over the lunar landscapes of Manhattan was getting to be a hit-or-miss proposition, and I could do without the added stress.

I'd booked a hotel in Tribeca that allowed dogs. "Pet friendly" is how they put it, which sounded more like a predilection than a policy. The ad in the *Times* noted that the hotel bar featured the widest selection of vodkas in New York City. Providence like this demanded a reservation.

I had the rough edges of a plan. I'd drive in before rush hour, settle Eddie into the room, take my daughter out to dinner, then figure out the rest of the plan while testing the legitimacy of the bar's claim.

I executed everything but the figuring out part.

The best I could do was wake up early enough to walk Eddie, bring him back to the room and haul myself up to the West Side in time to catch Bobby Dobson getting ready for work.

As I pushed the button on the panel outside his building, I was still waiting for a bolt of inspiration.

"Who's there?" said a male voice over the scratchy intercom.

"It's Jerome," I said, my inflection pitched to Westchester by way of Brighton Beach. "We need to talk. Let me in."

Seconds trudged by. Then the door buzzed.

I took the elevator to his floor, still wondering how I was going to beat the inevitable peephole in the door. But my luck and Dobson's stupidity caused him to open his door when I was only a few paces away, allowing me to shoulder my way into the apartment before he knew what hit him.

What hit him actually was the door, hard enough to knock him off his feet, which I really didn't mean to do. This left me standing over him as Elaine Brooks stepped into the hallway wearing only a terry cloth bathrobe, which in the excitement she'd neglected to tie closed.

I squatted next to Dobson.

"You're not going to believe this," I said, "but I'm here to help you."

"I'm calling the cops," he said, leaning on his elbows.

"You can do that, but that'll force me to tell them how you've been lying about Iku Kinjo."

"Bobby?" said Elaine from down the hall, now more properly pulled together.

"It's okay, baby," he said, still looking up at me, "we're just talking here."

"It doesn't look that way to me," she said.

"All I want to do is talk," I said to Bobby. "Honestly. We keep getting off on the wrong foot. My fault. I want to make it up to you. If you'd rather fight me, I'll have to fight back. I'd hate that. And so would you."

He slowly got to his feet, feeling around a red spot on his cheek. He waved me into an area that served as a combination living room and kitchenette, where he cracked ice cubes out of a tray to put on his face. All the while Elaine was whispering at him furiously, to which he responded with semi-articulate grunts.

Feeling stupid standing alone in the living room, I went over to the kitchen and introduced myself to Elaine. She was examining Bobby's cheek, which had again caused her to lose control of her bathrobe. Her body was plenty nice to look at, but I was embarrassed for both of us. I looked away as I offered my hand.

"Sam Acquillo, miss," I said. "I'm really sorry to bother you."

She clutched her robe to her neck, which helped a little, and offered her free hand.

"You got a weird way of showing it."

"You're right. I'm sorry. It's Iku's murder," I added. "Makes me a little crazy."

Elaine took the bait.

"Oh my God, is that horrible or what?" she said.

I saw Bobby let out an inaudible sigh.

Looking over at the gigantic coffeemaker on the kitchen counter, I said, "Can we sit down? Have some coffee?"

Their sitting area was mostly office space, with a tiny loveseat and two swivel chairs, a desk with a PC and bookcases with swayback shelves crammed with stacks of paper and miscellaneous clutter.

They plopped down in the loveseat and I took one of the swivel chairs. Now that I was familiar with Elaine's more essential qualities, I studied her face. It was broad, large featured and pretty in the way old-fashioned writers called handsome. Her hair was dark brown, her chin square and her eyes, also brown, wide-set. There were dimples in her cheeks deep enough to grow crops and her smile was an orthodontist's billboard.

Bobby was still his nervous, pale little self.

"So, Elaine, you guys knew Iku at Princeton, right?" I asked.

Her expression, seasoned with vague alarm, stayed in place.

"She was a Fast Track," she said.

"A what?"

"A Fast Track," said Bobby. "YIT. Yuppie-in-training. Mover and shaker. If you can't help my career, get the fuck out of my way. I was in Economics with her. Awesome focus."

"But very cute," said Elaine.

Bobby blanched. Not a big blanch. A very slight, barely

noticeable blanch. "She was a babe. With a mysterious kind of look. Different," he said. "But she didn't seem to care about herself. You never saw her outside class. I think she skipped the social part."

"So how did she end up staying at your place?" I asked.

Elaine looked to Bobby to answer.

"I ran into her at the Playhouse," he said. "I didn't know her that well, like I said, but enough to chat it up. She was looking for a place to stay. We had an extra room. She paid the whole freight for the summer through to Christmas. So that was that."

I swiveled back and forth in my chair, feeling the painful lack of a coffee cup in my hand. It made me a little irritable.

"When are you going to stop lying to me?" I asked.

Bobby stared, unsure.

"The thing is, man," I said, "you're not that good at it. All this does is aggravate the person you're lying to. With me, it doesn't mean much, even though I hit you with the door—not intentionally. But it means a lot to the cops, who are not as loving as I am. Worse for you, the cops are friends of mine. If I say you're dirty, you're dirty. They'll escort you to a session at the cleaners—a good washing and drying. Do you hear what I'm saying to you? Do you understand?"

"That's very threatening language," said Elaine.

"No, it's not. It's informative. Iku didn't just want a place to party for the summer, she wanted a hideout. You made it appear, to some people at least, that you were romantically involved with her, which clearly you weren't. How come? Unless you wanted to give her some cover."

Elaine was studying my face while I talked, intent on grasping what I was saying. When I stopped, she turned her attention to Bobby, with the same concentration. Assessing point and counterpoint.

"You ever been to a place where people are hooking up?" Bobby asked. "Probably not. It's a fluid dynamic. If Iku wanted to hide out, that was her business. And as far as me being her boyfriend, I can't help what people think. I'm Elaine's boyfriend. I think," he added, looking at her. She nodded her head at me, with a look I can only describe as chipper.

"He better be," she said. "Or I'll kill him."

I looked at Elaine.

"You knew Iku was Eisler, Johnson's golden girl," I said. "Must have been a teeny bit weird for Bobby to have somebody with a pass card to the top floor sleeping in the basement."

I let the awkward silence fill the room.

"You said she was a worker bee," Elaine said to Bobby.

"She did a little consulting for Angel Valero," he said, answering her, but still looking at me. "This guy thinks that matters."

Realizing she might have breached their unified front, Elaine snapped back into character. "I don't know anything about business stuff," she said. "I just sell art."

"That's right," I said. "You're only in it for the culture."

She smiled, still holding her ground.

"What difference does it make who introduced who to who?" asked Bobby. "We ran into Iku, had a few drinks, invited her to rent one of the empty bedrooms. So what? What's your point?"

"Who else beside Iku was on the Internet?" I asked.

"Who wasn't," said Elaine.

Bobby liked her answer.

"We also talked on telephones. Again, what's your point?"

I didn't exactly know what Sullivan wanted to keep confidential, but I was backed into a corner. So I said it.

"Iku's computer wasn't recovered. It's missing."

Scorn flashed across Bobby's face.

"Those cops could fuck up a wet dream."

I tried to imagine how Joe Sullivan would have answered that.

"So, you think they lost it? Dropped it down a hole on the way to the car?"

He shrugged. "Who knows. Their problem."

Bobby looked like he was teetering between outrage and terror. I gave him a shove.

"No," I said, "yours. As soon as I throw you to those cops you hold in such contempt."

He stared at me, scraping together his meager shreds of courage.

"This's got nothing to do with me," he said.

"Give me the computer and I won't tell Joe Sullivan you were withholding evidence. I'll say I found it in the woods."

"I don't know what you're talking about. The only computer I have is over there." He nodded toward an overflowing desk. "And you won't find it very interesting, unless you love financial analyses. I should let you take it home with you as punishment."

The computer was the only thing in the apartment that looked new, which was made more apparent by its disheveled surroundings.

"So, no theories," I said.

"About what?" said Bobby.

"The computer. Where it went."

"The killer took it. It doesn't take a genius to figure that out."

"Really? So the killer cared about what was on it. Is that what you think?"

Bobby didn't like that.

"That's not what I'm saying. Maybe he just wanted it."

"Pretty selective thief. Did you report anything else stolen?"

"We didn't report anything," said Elaine. "They won't let us back in the house."

Bobby liked that more. He looked proud of his girlfriend. He jumped to his feet. "Listen, we gotta get ready for work," he said, and walked out of the room.

Elaine stood up and said, "Well?"

I shrugged and got up to follow her, but on the way to the door she turned and used her shoulder to wedge me against the wall. The maneuver caused more revealing disruption to her bathrobe, which by now was getting to be old hat.

"What makes you think we won't have you arrested? Or worse?" she asked in a low voice.

"You would have done it by now if you thought you could," I said.

"Don't be so sure, Mr. Samuel," she said, in an even lower voice. She gripped my forearm below my rolled up cuffs and squeezed.

"Mr. Sam. My mother thought 'Samuel' was too formal. Putting on airs."

I pushed the rest of the way past her and got out of the apartment, down the elevator and out to the street where I'd left Eddie to guard Amanda's pickup. He was barking out the window at a passing Pomeranian, who could have cared less.

I was eager to get away from that unsettling apartment but I needed to give Eddie a chance to sniff the crazy City smells and pee on interesting new things. A few blocks down the street I spotted another parking space and stopped.

It was still early, so after Eddie did his thing we were through the Queens-Midtown Tunnel and halfway down the Island before the sun got above the smoky horizon. It was good to be driving counter to the commute, though I felt a little guilty as I watched opposing traffic creeping toward another day of boredom and triumph and everything in between. I knew for sure that would never again be me.

As I drove along the Long Island Expressway, most of my mind was wondering around the life and death of Iku Kinjo and all the people who might have aided in one or the other. One little part of me was keeping track of the other cars on the highway until the persistent presence of a large black SUV in the rearview mirror made itself abundantly clear.

I instantly regretted leaving the Grand Prix at home. It wasn't much of a car by modern standards, until you wanted sudden excessive acceleration on the open highway. Something the little red pickup could only do in its microprocessor-driven mechanical dreams.

So I took the opposite tack. I waited until I was approaching an exit ramp. Then I slipped up into the far left lane, with the SUV following me, and let off the accelerator, slowing the pickup to about forty-five miles an hour. This being the Long Island Expressway, where hurtling speed was the norm, order quickly deteriorated. Cars piled up behind the SUV, tailgating and beeping and otherwise expressing outrage, finally forcing the SUV to shift over to the right lane and pass.

I watched it race ahead, followed by the pent-up demand. As everyone roared by, I took the exit.

I drove the garish strip streets of Nassau County in a roughly westerly direction until I saw a sign for an on-ramp for the LIE. As further insurance, I stopped to get a cup of coffee and gave Eddie a chance to explore the native terrain. He never understood the point of a leash, and he looked at me disapprovingly whenever I pulled him back from a possible hazard, as if to say, "What do you think, I'm stupid?"

I just couldn't take the chance he'd spot some exotic Nassau County creature, like a house cat or raccoon, and then we'd be off to the races.

When I got back to where I'd parked the pickup, Honest Boy Ackerman was sitting in the driver's seat. The engine was running and the doors were locked. He opened the window a crack.

"What do you think," he said, "I'm stupid?"

"Not entirely. You going to take my truck?"

"Only if you start hitting me."

"I'm not going to hit you."

"How do I know that?" he asked.

"I can't punch through safety glass."

That alarmed him.

"I'm not getting out if you're going to hit me."

I pulled out my cell phone, which Fate had directed me to put in my pocket before I got out of the truck. The same Fate who forgot to tell me not to leave my keys on the floor mat.

"Does 9-1-1 work on cell phones?" I asked as I poked at the keypad.

"Aw, Christ, don't do that."

I studied him through the window.

"What's the deal, Honest Boy?"

"I just want to talk."

I held up the cell phone.

"That's what these are for," I said. "In polite society we don't stalk or steal the trucks of people we want to talk to."

He huffed.

"Polite? Coming from you?"

"Actually, I can punch through safety glass."

"You can?"

"It's my girlfriend's truck. It'd be hard to explain. But I'll do it if you don't get out of there in the next ten seconds."

I gripped the door handle with my right hand, pulled back my left fist with the index finger in the air and said,

"One."

"Don't, don't," he said, ducking down his head and opening the door.

I let him out. Eddie jumped up and down, wagging his tail with the joy every new encounter brought. I still wanted to pop Ackerman one, as a matter of principle. Instead I leaned across and felt around the ignition for the keys. There were none.

I grabbed him by the jacket.

"Switch it off."

Self-satisfaction galloped across his face.

"You don't know how, Big-Time Engineer?"

I shook him.

"Switch it off."

He pulled a little plastic cylinder out of his pocket. At one end was a button, which he pushed. The engine stopped. Then he pushed the button, and it started again.

"Over a hundred yard range," he said.

I took it out of his hand, killed the engine and reached past him to open the hood. It was easy to see the fresh wiring running from a proverbial black box into the electronic ignition. I yanked it out.

"Cool, huh?" said Ackerman.

I wanted to smack him with it, but he looked like a kid more excited about making a bomb than sorry for blowing up the basement.

"What are you doing?" I asked.

He shrugged.

"I want to talk to you. I was about to wave you over when you started playing stall ball."

"You just happened to follow me out of Manhattan. Coincidence."

He smirked.

"Hell, no. I've been following you since we first met. Took you long enough to notice."

"That doesn't make me happy," I said.

"'Course not. Why would it?"

"Fucking Judson."

"That's what I want to talk about. Fucking Judson. I'm sick of living like a mushroom. Kept in the dark and fed on bullshit."

"I don't get it."

"I've been following you, but I haven't been reporting anything back. Not exactly. I make it up. Like when you went to visit Angel Valero, I said you were sitting in a bar in the Village. Judson's always willing to believe you're sitting in a bar."

"How come?" I asked.

"You drink a lot."

"How come you're not reporting the truth?"

He ran a hand over his slicked-back hair, then over his face, stopping to rub his mouth. An extravagant gesture of ambivalence.

"I don't know, Marve's okay, I guess. He told me we're a team. It's just hard to play on a team when you don't know what the game is. I got a brain, obviously," he added, pointing to the tangle of multicolored wires in my hand, "but all he wants from me is muscle, which in your case is a little ridiculous, I think you'd agree."

"So, what're you proposing?" I asked.

"I just want to know what's going on. Tell me and I'll go away forever. Tell Judson to take this job and fuck himself with it."

While we were talking, Eddie had leaped up into the pickup and was lying down on the seat, bored with the whole thing.

I wasn't sure what to say, so I just looked at Ackerman's pale, sweaty face and downturned, close-set eyes, fleshy cheeks and boneless chin.

"Okay, here's what I know," he said, as if that's what I wanted him to say. "Somebody whacked Iku Kinjo, the consulting babe from Eisler, Johnson, and you found the body. The cops grilled your ass but cut you loose, so you're not a suspect. For a change. Since then, you've been working people who knew her, so I'm figuring you want to find the whacker. What I don't know is why Judson's so damn interested. Nobody else at Con Globe seems to give a shit. Though maybe they should. Who knows what the Jap girl was up to. Except for senior management, which doesn't include Judson, no matter what he thinks."

"Japanese-African-American. A little respect, please."

He tossed his head, like he was shaking a bug out of his ear. "Sorry. You're right. Tragic thing."

I dug a restaurant receipt out of my pocket and wrote the Pequot's address on the back.

"Meet me here tonight at seven-thirty. We'll talk. Meanwhile, stay out of my rearview mirror."

He nodded as he studied the receipt.

"Absolutely. You'll never see a thing. I'm a ghost."

He backed up, waving his hands in front of him, conjuring his shield of invisibility. I watched him until he'd turned and waddled furtively—if such a thing is possible—across the parking lot and around the other side of the coffee shop.

"Sun Tzu," I said to Eddie. "Friends close, enemies closer. If you're not sure, take 'em out to dinner."

He perked up at the word "dinner," so I tossed him the last of the Big Dog biscuits I'd brought along and got underway. When I reached the highway, I called Sullivan.

"I have Elaine Brooks's fingerprints," I told him.

"On what?"

"My arm. If that's too technical a challenge, I also have her china coffee cup."

"I'll take the cup."

Traffic thinned as I cleared Nassau County and the western reaches of Suffolk. The day had started out grey and dispirited, but lightened up considerably as we crossed the pine barrens, still partially charred from a big fire several years before. Fresh green growth clustered around acres of burnt stalks that would likely stand until the next fire.

When I was a kid my father would try to search out ways around the two-lane tedium of the Sunrise Highway, then the standard route out to the South Fork, by heading north, inevitably plunging us into the pine barrens. I knew this was a fruitless strategy, having actually looked at a road map, something my father was determined never to do. In those days that area was so devoid of life I'd imagine we were sailing over a dark sea on the way to the Hampton Islands.

According to my sister, the trip in and out of the City was a regular thing, though I barely remember my father's apartment in the Bronx. She thinks I blocked it out. If so, all the better.

What I did remember was more than enough.

FIFTEEN

I HAD TO WAIT ALMOST an hour at the coffee shop for Sullivan to show up. I killed the time reading a book Randall gave me called something like *Computers for Aging Morons*. The subject had come up way too often lately to ignore. The content wasn't that challenging, but the terminology had changed a lot in the last ten years. At least it was a decent distraction from all the noisy coffee drinkers.

Randall's book made me feel like a monk leafing through the *Kama Sutra*. "You can do that?" I kept asking myself, in amazement.

"Welcome to the twenty-first century," said Sullivan, dropping down into the seat across the table.

"I could've used one of these back in the day," I said, holding up the book. "Would've saved a lot of time."

Sullivan scoffed.

"The more of this shit people have, the less time they got."

"The law of unintended consequences."

"Oh, it's intended all right. Get everybody strung out on something that costs you more every year. Worse'n crack."

I slapped the book shut.

"Whew," I said. "That was close."

He pointed at my coffee.

"Is that the cup?"

"It's in the truck."

I got up from the table, forcing him to follow. We scooped up Eddie and found the pickup.

"While I got you in a good mood," I said, after giving him the cup, "I'm hoping you can let Honest Boy Ackerman back into town."

The storm clouds behind his eyes darkened another shade.

"That chump."

I told him about the encounter up island and the subsequent conversation.

"And you believe him?" he asked.

"I don't know. But I can't see the harm. I don't have to tell him anything I don't want to."

He just walked away, shrugging his meaty shoulders.

"Come to dinner with us," I called to him. "At the Pequot. Seven-thirty. You and Honest Boy can catch up on old times."

I think I heard him say something like, "Yeah, maybe. We'll see," but I wasn't sure. Though I felt a gentle stir in the vibe currents left in his wake, telling me to secure a big enough table for the three of us and the inevitable incursions of the proprietor and his idiosyncratic daughter.

———

I killed the rest of the day in my shop trying to stay ahead of the projects I'd promised Frank, and had to hustle over to Sag Harbor so I wouldn't be late to meet Ackerman for dinner.

I was afraid to leave him alone with the regular Pequot clientele without an introduction.

The parking lot was full of pickups and ragged Japanese compacts, but no black SUVs. I let Eddie clear the lot of invisible antagonists, then lead the way into the restaurant. While he hit up the usual suckers for clams and French fries I grabbed a table next to the kitchen. Save Hodges a few steps.

"Did you know they flavor this stuff now? Lemon, orange, raspberry," said Dorothy as she dropped my Absolut in front of me. "The salesman just talked my father into buying a case of each."

"I thought you had a shotgun behind the bar."

"That's for mortal threats."

"Exactly."

I told her to bring an extra menu for a guy recently canned from the security department at my old company. She stood there waiting for me to flesh out the story, but after thinking about it, I didn't know how.

"It's involved," I told her.

"It always is," she said, taking a final half-hearted wipe at the table and going back behind the bar.

Eddie greeted Honest Boy at the door, delighted with a newfound relationship: "Cool, this guy is, like, everywhere!"

For his part, Honest Boy looked somewhere between repelled and vaguely alarmed. The Pequot often had that effect on people. Once they got to know the place, the repulsion wore off.

"I didn't know they let dogs into restaurants," he said as he pulled up a chair.

"Eddie rejects those artificial social barriers."

"I thought it was the health department," he said, looking around the joint.

"You'll have to take that up with them."

"Judson said you had mental problems," said Honest Boy, half to himself, then realizing what he'd said, quickly added, "Not that I think that."

Dorothy arrived in time to hear.

"I don't believe you," she said to him.

"He has to tell the truth. His name's Honest Boy."

Dorothy looked impressed, not an easy thing to achieve.

"Get out of here."

"That's the handle. Honestly," he said, for the fourteen millionth time. She reached out to shake. He looked at her hand, taken aback by the fingerless glove that went up well past her elbow. Then he took it, tentatively.

"Glad to meet you, Honest Boy. I'm Dissembling Dorothy. Not officially. What're you drinking?"

"She's the official bartender," I said.

"Any imported beers?"

Dorothy continued to look at him like he hadn't said anything. He looked to me for help.

"From as far away as Wisconsin," I told him.

"Sounds just right," he said, smiling at Dorothy's back as she strode through the double doors into the kitchen, black leotard–covered hips in full swing.

"Unusual girl," he said.

"I think she likes you."

"That'd be a first."

"Keep your insecurities to yourself. She'll smell it on you like a dog smells fear."

"Sometimes it's hard to imagine you ran Technical Services and Support from almost nothing to, what, a billion dollar enterprise?" said Honest Boy, eager to change the subject.

"A billion point two," I said.

"Not that I'm criticizing. I've spent a lot of time with the big dicks that run Con Globe. Bunch of uptight, self-serving, humorless pricks."

"Pricks or dicks. You have to make up your mind."

"It's no wonder they're afraid of you."

I laughed at him. It surprised both of us. I don't laugh a lot. Not built for it.

"As the fox fears the rabbit," I said.

He smiled broadly.

"Right. Like I said, it's no wonder they're afraid of you. Crazy like a fox."

Dorothy showed up with a mug and a can of Budweiser, which she poured for Honest Boy, something I'd never seen her do before. He thanked her warmly. Before things got out of hand, Eddie intervened, whining for French fries and his regular bowl of water.

"Okay, handsome, keep your fur on," she said to him.

"What kind of dog is this, again?" Honest Boy asked, scratching Eddie's head.

"A Zen retriever," said Dorothy. "Knows where the stick is going before you throw it."

"Make a good bird dog," said Honest Boy.

"Not if you ask the birds," she said. "You want anything to eat? We got imported burgers and local fish. With imported tartar sauce and imported French fries."

"*Pommes frites*, my mother called them," I added. "She was French-Canadian."

"You people obviously know what works here and what doesn't," he said. "You decide."

"He wants the fish," I said to Dorothy. She nodded, of a mind.

"I'll take a burger," I called to her as she headed back to the kitchen. The front door opened loudly enough to cause Honest Boy to turn around and look. A half dozen smelly crew off one of the sportfishing boats crowded through the narrow entrance, leading with their beer bellies, coats open and baseball hats turned to the back, proud of their hard-won, rugged ignorance.

No one else in the place took much notice, but I caught Honest Boy tapping his chest under his left arm.

When Dorothy came out of the kitchen they started to chant "Dot-ty, Dot-ty!" and only stopped when she told them to shut the hell up, which they did, immediately. Though not soon enough to evade the notice of Paul Hodges, who followed his daughter out of the kitchen, wiping his hands on his off-white apron, his eyes bristling with irritation.

"Goddammit, Pierre, I told you," he yelled at the lead meatball, "you're allowed to be drunk when you leave. Not when you come in." Pierre looked sheepish.

"We're not drunk, Mr. Hodges," he said. "Jez happy from the catch today. She'z big, like the customer tips."

Hodges looked over at me.

"I'm not responsible for every Canuck who comes into the place," I said to him as I slid my chair around the table and grabbed Honest Boy by the throat, reaching my other hand into his sport jacket and plucking a little snub-nose out of its shoulder holster. I slid it into my jeans pocket.

"Hey."

"House rules," I said. "I'll give it back when we leave."

The boat crew settled down after Dorothy passed out drinks and took orders. Eddie sat next to their table trying to get in on the action, but she shooed him back over to us.

"Judson didn't tell you anything, did he?" asked Honest Boy, when things finally settled down.

"He told me about the Mandate of '53, meant to keep Con Globe independent in perpetuity. He implied that members of the board thought Donovan wanted to break the mandate. That's pretty much it, none of which has anything to do with me."

Honest Boy sat back, looking self-satisfied.

"I knew you'd say that," he said.

Before I could respond Dorothy and Vinko came out with our meals. Honest Boy studied the slice of lemon sitting atop the white mass on his plate.

"So what sort of fish is this again?" he asked.

"North Sea fin tail," said Dorothy. "Caught off Hog's Neck, right here in Noyac Bay."

"Really," said Honest Boy, looking suspiciously at his plate.

"Why'd you say that?" I asked him.

"I like to know what I'm eating."

"Why'd you say 'I knew you'd say that'?"

"'Cause I knew you would," he said.

"Say what?"

He took a bite of the fish and smiled approvingly.

"I'll have to get some of this when I'm home."

"That'd be a neat trick. Did Judson tell you something different?"

Honest Boy scoffed.

"I told you what he told me. Nothing." He pointed his fork at me. "You can belittle me all you want, but I'm a trained investigator. I'm actually capable of finding things out on my own."

"Okay, that's fine. I still don't know what the hell you're talking about."

Sensing a slight upper hand, Honest Boy took his time with the next mouthful of fish. I pretended I didn't mind. Dorothy came over to ask about the food, which led to a discussion of North Sea fin tail, which Dorothy insisted was far flakier than talapia, a close relative. So it took a while to get back to the conversation.

"Marve's convinced that you're involved with Donovan's plot to void the Mandate of '53. An opinion shared by Mason Thigpen, who by the way Marve reports to, officially, not the full Board of Directors like he wants you to think. Marve says there's no other reason why you'd go from ultimate corporate dead man to Donovan's pet project. Why else would he hire outside counsel to examine your severance agreement?"

"I haven't talked to anyone from TSS since I left. And I didn't know anything about that mandate until I heard it from Marve."

"Have you heard about the big patent settlement? Don't insult me with a denial. Just keep the straight face. You're good at that."

My ex-wife used to say the same thing about me, though in less complimentary terms.

"How many people are talking about this?" I asked.

"Don't worry, very few."

I knew I shouldn't be surprised that some version of the recent connection between me and Donovan had surfaced, however far-fetched. In fact, it was probably a good thing they'd jumped to conclusions. People are always more inclined to concoct a myth than bother with the facts.

"So what's your stake in this?" I asked. "And don't insult me by saying it's only curiosity."

He smiled.

"I was telling the truth. There's a lot I still don't know. But there's more to it than that. If I'm right about what I do know, I know which side to be on."

"Who said there're sides?"

"Oh, there're sides all right. More than two. I just want to be on the one that sees to it that Con Globe is blown to smithereens and scattered on the wind. When I got fired it struck me like a revelation from God. I hate the bastards who run that place. I have for a long time, I just didn't know it. Including George Donovan. But if he's going to be the agent of their destruction, he's my friend. Him and anybody he brings in to help do the deed. And there's nobody on the face of the earth better suited to that role than the guy I'm sitting across from right now. So here's to you," he said, raising his beer, "and to hell with Consolidated Global Energies."

Honest Boy's triumphant defiance was dampened by the timely arrival of Joe Sullivan, which also quieted down the noisy fishing crew.

He sat next me and across from Ackerman. Neither tried to shake hands. They stared at each other until Eddie stuck his nose in Sullivan's lap, disrupting his concentration.

"Hey, Joe," Honest Boy finally said, "long time no see."

"Not long enough."

Ackerman looked over at me. I shrugged.

"Wait'll he has a beer. It mellows him right out."

Which it did. That and the next two. And the usual distractions from the Hodges family and the general flow of the evening. Dorothy in particular made her presence felt, hanging around the table and salting the conversation with an occasional non-sequitur. After a while, Sullivan and Ackerman were chatting up a storm, like a couple of regular barflies ensnared by their own random nonsense.

As a signal that things had truly degraded, Paul Hodges brought out a tray full of shots with a bowl of lemon slices. After a lot of yelling and cracking of shot glasses on the pine tables, some civility returned, though less articulate.

By now Eddie was sound asleep with his head resting on the bar rail and Dorothy was sitting in Honest Boy's lap, fussing with the thin remnants of hair at his temples and seeming to listen to his tales of undercover adventures in the Third World. Her father was over with the fishermen, arm-wrestling and tossing gutting knives at a knot in the pine paneling above the neon Bud sign. Sullivan eventually fell asleep, snoring a duet with Eddie, leaving me alone with a bucket of ice and a bottle of Absolut Citron, which I forced down as a favor to the local vodka distributor, an enterprise worthy of conditional support.

—

This is how I left them. I had to roust Eddie with a gentle nudge of my boot. He stood up, shook out his coat, and followed without complaint. Outside it was cool and clear. The moon was struggling up from the horizon, a bloated red and nearly round. I watched Eddie lope across the parking lot, stopping to pee on the oversized tires of Ackerman's SUV, and then over to the Grand Prix.

I let him in the car and headed back to Oak Point. As we negotiated the hilly curves of Noyac Road on the way home from Sag Harbor a set of headlights came up fast from behind and filled the rearview mirror. My first thought was Ackerman, but the lights were too low to the ground to be an SUV. I rarely pushed the big old car much past the speed limit whenever curves were involved, often frustrating the carloads of overachievers pouring in from East Hampton and Sag Harbor on the way back to the City. So I could hardly blame the tailgaters. I kicked it up a little, but then the car behind me tucked up even closer, until the headlights nearly disappeared under the Pontiac's massive trunk.

Since that was all the thanks I got, I dropped back to the speed limit. He could sit there and stew until I turned off, or take his chances passing around a curve, which is all there was on Noyac Road.

He backed off a little, then pulled in close again, even closer than before. I sighed. Intimidation of any kind never sat that well with me, though lately I'd been striving mightily to control how I handled it. With calm forbearance. Maturity and reserve. An almost pacifistic turning of the other cheek. This is how I strove, not always successfully.

I waited until we hit a short straight patch of road and yanked the steering wheel to the left, putting the Grand Prix into the empty oncoming lane. Then I slammed on the brakes. The car behind shot by on the right. It was a new Mustang, black, the color of choice among automotive intimidators. I pulled the Grand Prix back into the proper lane and fought another little battle with myself.

When I was younger I'd be inclined to bring the four-mile-long nose of the Grand Prix up to about two inches off the Mustang's rear bumper and keep it there all the way to the guy's house, where I'd either let him slink back into his real life as a frustrated, ineffectual asshole or wait for him to get out of the car so I could stick my fist down his throat.

But I was older now, more mature. I regretted a lot of things I'd done, however satisfying they might have seemed at the time. I understood now I'd been merely acting out of my own sense of offended righteousness, that my anger wasn't actually directed at the apparent object of antagonism, but rather an expression of my manifold disappointments and thwarted expectations.

While I was congratulating myself for evolving to a higher level of self-awareness, the Mustang driver stood on his brakes and slammed a hard left, gunning the rear wheels into an impressive power spin that had him flying past me in the opposite direction before I half realized what he was doing.

That's when I thought this might not be an ordinary asshole. And probably not that ineffectual.

"Aw, shit," I said out loud. I gripped Eddie's collar and pushed him down into the foot well of the front passenger seat, downshifted into second and stuck the accelerator to the floor. The ten-ton hunk of Detroit iron leaped forward like a cat, the nearly bottomless torque suddenly awake and engaged.

I didn't know the handling characteristics of the new Mustang, but I guessed they were better than what I had available. The Grand Prix wasn't what you'd call a European touring car. All it knew how to do was accelerate rapidly in a straight line. I figured it would take a few seconds for the Mustang to pull another 180 to get back in pursuit. So I tightened my grip on the ugly plastic steering wheel and held on hard as I experimented with the limits of the big car's suspension system.

I'd done what I could with beefy after-market shocks and modern tires, though you can't do much about the ballistic energy of all that unbalanced weight being flung through hairpin turns.

I was mostly worried about Eddie. I hoped he didn't think this was a cool new game and jump back on the seat to take it all in. As I held a death grip on the steering wheel I reached through the centrifugal force to stroke his head and ask him to stay where he was like a good boy.

The Mustang was back on my rear bumper in less than five minutes. I could hear the throaty roar of the fuel-injected V8 above the wind noise, and the solid scream of tires over macadam, sticky and secure to the road.

Then I heard a strange little metallic pop, and saw a spider web blossom across my windshield. At first I thought, great, what a time to get hit by a rock. But when the second web opened up I knew what it was.

I hung the next right, hurtling down a primitive sand road toward the Little Peconic Bay. I knew the neighborhood well, having jogged through there a hundred times in the last few years. The Mustang was still hard on my tail, but he was holding his fire. The headlights bouncing in my rearview told why—the closer we got to the bay the more the road resembled an amusement park ride. I tightened my seat belt, slouched as low as I could into the leather-covered bucket seat and fought to control the steering wheel.

Somehow I started to open up some air between me and the Mustang. Though sprung like a drunken goose, the sheer mass of the old Pontiac held it closer to the earth than the new Mustang. As long as the struts, springs and tie-rod ends could withstand the punishment. To say nothing of the driver.

The curves were getting tighter, and as the gap opened up I could see the chaotic dance of the Mustang's headlights lighting up the woods. It gave me an idea.

After careening like a psychotic porpoise through a particularly tight turn, I shut off the lights, eased up on the accelerator, jammed the transmission into first and stepped hard on the emergency break. The rear wheels locked up, sending the front end into a barely controllable frenzy, which actually helped to slow and eventually stop the big car. I checked again to make sure Eddie was wedged down in the passenger seat foot well, banged the shifter into reverse and floored it.

The concussion knocked the breath out of me, as if a fist the size of a Volkswagen had hit me in the back. Or more like a new Ford Mustang as it exploded into the vast, heavy-metal trunk of the Grand Prix.

The sound was more startling than the impact—a subterranean thud mixed with the wet spray of glass and the scream of rending sheet metal.

It was a jarring moment for me and Eddie, but a lot worse for the guys in the Mustang.

From the crouched position I took before the crash I reached for Eddie, feeling around for injuries. His ears were back, and when he jumped up on the seat his tail was down, but otherwise he seemed okay. He barked out a single, emphatic bark, which I knew meant, "What the fuck was that about?"

I dug a small flashlight out of the glove compartment and pushed open my door, shutting it quickly behind me to keep Eddie in the car. I stayed low and tried to adjust my eyes to the darkness—the Mustang's headlights having followed the rest of the front end into oblivion. Its windshield was also blown out, so I could clearly see the driver sitting behind the wheel. His head was resting on the top of the deflating airbag, his face hidden behind a mask of blood. Another guy was more out than in, his body flopped across the mangled hood, twisted into a shape that could only be comfortable if you were past feeling it.

Panning around with the flashlight, I saw an automatic nestled in the accordion folds of the Grand Prix's freshly compressed trunk. I picked up a stick, slipped it in the barrel and plucked it free of the mangled metal. I dropped it into my jacket pocket and went to take a closer look at the driver.

My entire rib cage, front to back, felt worked over, but the adrenaline kept me alert. I opened the door of the Mustang and shot the flashlight in the driver's face. His eyes blinked open.

While I kept him in the light, I fumbled around my jacket for the cell phone to call 911. I told the dispatcher to call Joe Sullivan, who was probably only halfway to Hampton Bays by then. I could only give a rough description of the location, but when I asked if anyone had reported a loud explosion in the area, she had our exact position.

"Please don't leave the scene of the accident before the officers arrive," she said.

"No danger of that."

I heard a faint sound from the driver. I reached in and gently pulled away the empty airbag. Tiny crystals of glass rained down, pattering against the dashboard and steering wheel. Some remained, glimmering like jeweled studs on the guy's brown sport coat and black turtleneck.

"Don't move," I said to him.

His eyes stretched open so that the whites encircled the pupils, made even more stark by the blood streaming down his face. I moved in closer to look for the gusher, which I found—a deep slice an inch below his receding hairline. I pulled a crumpled paper towel out of my back pocket and stuck it on the wound.

"Who you working for?" I asked conversationally, like I was asking who he bet on to win the Eastern Conference playoffs.

The injured man closed his eyes, then opened them again, and seemed to smile.

"*El Cerberus,*" I heard him say, the words wet with blood.

"Cerberus? You're kidding."

"*¿Muertos chiste?*" he whispered.

Do dead men joke?

"Why try to kill me? What the hell did I do?" I asked.

He leaned his head back on the seat and smiled again. I smelled the sticky sweet smell of alcohol in the car, though I assumed the man's tranquility had more to do with shock.

I went back to the Grand Prix and got a roll of duct tape out of the glove compartment. I used it to tape some more paper towel to the guy's head. Then I walked around the other side of his car for a closer look at his buddy. What I found wasn't the kind of thing you'd want to study too closely. Likely he was doing the shooting, while leaning out the window, which is why he'd unsnapped his seat belt. Proves there's never a good reason to neglect proper safety procedures.

I went back to the driver, who was now staring out of the destroyed windshield and looking a little less comfortable.

"How you doing?" I asked him.

"Just a little headache. I stop drinking coffee last week. Doctor say it's bad for my heart. It's bad for my head when I stop, I want to tell him."

"So, this Cerberus. Who's he?"

He turned his head toward me.

"Is that how you say in English? You know who he is. I'm declaring the fifth amendment."

He spent the next few minutes coughing up globs of oily blood.

"Good command of the U.S. Constitution," I told him.

He nodded.

"The fifth is a good amendment. In Venezuela the only right you plead for is your life. You think the ambulance is coming? I'm not feeling too good."

"It's coming. They'll get here as soon as they can."

He nodded again.

"Good doctors here, too. Even if they're all from India. The U.S. likes to hire Indians. And *Indios* from Venezuela, like me. Pretty soon Yankees won't know how to do anything."

"Except beat the Red Sox."

I sat watching his breath slow almost to a stop. I couldn't move him, even though I knew he was going into shock. The way his arms lay limp against his body said he might be paralyzed. Maybe temporarily, and one false move would make it permanent. On the other hand, he did try to kill me, somewhat attenuating my sympathy.

"Were you supposed to scare me or kill me?" I asked when his eyes opened again and he looked over at me. "And if so, why?"

"Make it look like an accident. It was Marcello who lost his cool and start off with the gun. Dumb *gordo*."

"Hey, no disrespecting the dead."

"Marcello dead?" he asked, genuinely surprised, even though the evidence was only a few feet away.

"Yeah. Sorry, man. Went out the window."

He rocked his head back and forth where it lay against the headrest.

"That's, like, not what I want to hear."

"You might be dead yourself. Why don't you help out your soul and tell me what this was all about?"

"What're you, a priest?" he asked.

"No, an engineer. We only take confessions based on solid data."

"Whatever. You one crazy fucking engineer," he said, which turned out to be his last words. I felt a little bad about that, since he probably would have preferred to thank his mother, bless his children and plea for mercy from the Holy Mother, but that's timing for you.

Ten minutes later the ambulance roared on to the scene, but all they got to do was certify that the two guys in the Mustang were dead, then wait around for the cops, detectives and forensics people to show up.

Joe Sullivan got there first.

"I'm sure there's an explanation," he said, dropping out of his Ford Bronco and adjusting his sport jacket over the unofficial cannon he kept in a shoulder harness underneath.

"Is this an accident or an act of self-defense?" I asked him.

"Oh, Christ."

"I've got the gun, holes in the glass and, with luck, a slug in the dashboard. I'd really rather stick to the truth this time, as strange as that sounds."

"What's the motive?"

"If we knew that we'd be done here."

"What do they say?" he asked, looking over at the Mustang.

"I don't know. They're dead."

"Terrific. Ross'll be up your ass a mile."

"Good. A little more interest by local law enforcement would be a nice change. Present company excluded."

Sullivan shot his flashlight in my face.

"Are you hurt or anything?"

"I'm fine, but I need to get Eddie checked out."

As if to punctuate the thought, a bark came from inside the crumpled Grand Prix.

"Ross'll want me to bring you in."

"Me and Jackie'll be there tomorrow. Have him warm up the ashtray."

I flipped open my cell phone and called Amanda. I didn't give her a lot of details, though the word "accident" was enough to get her out of the bathtub. While I waited for her to come get me, I called a vet I knew in the Village. He said he'd meet me at his clinic.

"Oh my God, are you hurt?" Amanda demanded as she burst out of her station wagon, her eyes fixed in horror at the unnatural mating of a souped-up Mustang and the ass-end of the Grand Prix.

"I'm fine. A lot better than my car."

"Where's Eddie?" she said, near hysteria.

"He's fine, too. But I want to take him over to Eng's for a look over. He said he'd meet us there," I said.

"What about you? Don't you need a look over?"

"You can do that. Later."

I got her out of there before she could see all the human carnage, though I gave her the straight story on the way to Dr. Eng's. Amanda was an adult. No point in hiding anything.

"Don't think I'm foolish for being concerned," she said.

I squeezed her thigh, then left it at that.

As promised, James Eng was at his clinic when we arrived. He opened the door to let Eddie run in, as he always did. The only dog in the known universe who liked going to the vet.

"This is why I agreed to do this," said Eng, as Eddie jumped up and got his ears scratched. "Just to soak in the adulation."

I described the night's activities as well as I could as we wound though the hall to one of the examination rooms. Eng felt around Eddie's body, checked his eyes, ears, nose and throat and let him lick his face.

"I don't even let my own dog do that."

After about ten minutes of this, Eng shrugged.

"I could do some x-rays, or hold him here for observation, but I don't think it's necessary," he said. "The only condition he's presenting is one of an exceptionally healthy animal."

"It's all the rotten crap he eats off the beach," I said. "Builds up the immunities."

"You're not far wrong," said Eng. "Eddie lived on his own for the first years of his life. You joke, but when I see a healthy stray, I see highly successful genes. What doesn't kill you, makes you strong. Literally."

"If that's true, I'm going to live forever," I said, and then tried to pay him, or at least thank him for the extra trouble, which he'd have none of.

"Go on, get out of here. And take your mutt. I'm always open for the good ones. Just don't tell anybody, it'll ruin my practice."

After Eng lifted him off the table, Eddie did a little spin and wagged his tail, like this was the most wonderful moment of his life. I couldn't stand much more of that, so I took Eng at his word and got the hell out of there.

"Eddie Van Halen, superstar," said Amanda.

"He's going to be insufferable."

She thought it was my turn to get examined, but I felt fine except for a little soreness in my neck and the upper part of my back, which only bothered me when I took a breath. She pressed the issue until I was forced to propose a compromise.

"If we stop at the bar on Main Street and have a few drinks, will that satisfy you?"

I was still a little nervous about leaving Eddie alone in the car, but he seemed happy enough curled up in the back. It was almost closing time, though I knew bars well enough to know you could always linger through the cleanup. They usually like having a few people sitting there, talking quietly, while winding down the night. It makes me feel like a kind of mascot.

"You're an impossible man," said Amanda to kick off the conversation.

"Thank you, dear."

"If you die of internal bleeding, it's not on my conscience."

"Just don't get distracted by it. I need your concentration."

"You think there's a connection between the dead Japanese girl and what just happened?" Amanda asked.

"What do you think?"

"I think there is."

"So do I."

In an effort to ward off Amanda's near-frantic look of concern over my physical state, I got us talking about the good old days at Con Globe.

As I remembered, Iku's task was basic strategic planning, helping the corporation balance its portfolio of products and services—deciding which to invest in, which to milk, which to jettison. It's a good consultant's gig, to analyze the situation presumably free of biases, preconceptions or vested interests.

All she cared about was her report—a clinical analysis of the corporation's financial and organizational health.

As long as she had the support of top management, she didn't have to care if anyone liked her or endorsed her methodologies. She didn't have to joke with colleagues, jolly along administrators or wish anyone a happy birthday. She didn't care if you held the door for her or checked out her ass when you passed her in the hall. The job titles, perks and prerogatives, career ambitions, petty politics, personal dreams and paranoid fantasies of the company's employees were no more important to her than the mindless behavior of a swarm of ants engulfing an orange peel on the sidewalk.

"Angel was interested in Con Globe," said Amanda. "That's the overlap."

"A bold and trenchant analysis," I said.

"Thank you."

"No less so for my having considered it already."

"Certainly not."

"But Con Globe ain't nobody's target. The corporate charter won't allow it."

"Piffle," she said.

"That's Burton's word."

"Used advisedly. Burton would tell you that corporate charters are as substantial as cheesecloth, and not nearly so aromatic."

"That's because he doesn't know Arlis Cuthright."

"Who?" she asked.

"Donovan's wife. Her family owns the largest block of Con Globe voting stock. Not enough to control, but enough to wreak havoc. She doesn't care about the subtleties of corporate law. All she knows is Daddy wanted the company to stay intact in perpetuity, and bolstered by her interests in half a dozen other companies, she wouldn't hesitate to tear Con Globe to pieces to preserve its independence. Most people think these big corporate decisions are based on calculation and greed. In fact, it's mostly heart and soul. Raw emotion."

"And greed," said Amanda.

"And greed. Which is sort of my point. Marve Judson said some of the board members thought Donovan was trying to unravel the corporate charter. But why would he do that? What financial benefit could possibly justify a direct confrontation with most of the board, the executive committee and the controlling shareholders, who are controlled by his own wife? To say nothing of the legal implications and all the lousy press. Who in their right mind would do that?"

"Who said he was in his right mind? He was, after all, screwing his management consultant."

"You say Donovan's a fool in love, but does he have to be a fool?"

She took a sip of her pinot to help her readjust from scold to honored adviser.

"No," she said. "He could string her along with delusions of financial conquest, if that was her game. Men have been known to do that sort of thing."

"Can't accuse me of that."

"No, dear. Certainly not."

"Or Donovan's brain had simply migrated to his dick, just like any other poor idiot."

"Rich idiot."

I wondered, was that it? Was it that easy? Angel and Iku make a run at Donovan with a standard honey trap. They think they'll be able to seduce, manipulate or extort him into breaking the charter, then set up a sale, before which Angel would have Phillip Craig take a big position, and subsequently they'd turn a gigantic profit. The ultimate special opportunity, and one that perfectly fit his modus operandi. Not just calling the play, but making it happen.

Iku's angle? Money. Plain old money. And the rush of

victory, like one she probably got from the oil deal. It's impossible to overestimate how good something that big feels when you're on the winning side.

Although she probably felt less victorious than Angel, at least financially. All she got from the deal was a paycheck, albeit a fat one, for her trouble. Nothing else would be possible without huge exposure to insider trading.

Was the Con Globe gambit a chance to make good on all that?

I shared all these thoughts with Amanda, whose focus had shifted toward a more fundamental question.

"What does all that have to do with people trying to kill you?"

Until that night, no one had ever tried to run me off the road and shoot me. At least not at the same time. It didn't seem like much of a coincidence.

"I don't know," I said.

They finally threw us out of the joint, politely enough. Eddie was still alive when we got back to the car—and filled with his usual élan. I let him bark and run back and forth between the two lowered back windows all the way to Oak Point. Amanda held her thick hair to the nape of her neck and rode along in a fugue state of resigned indulgence.

I drove past my cottage and directly to Amanda's house, bypassing anyone who might be waiting for me with a gun. I just wasn't in the mood.

I walked Eddie around Amanda's yard on the end of a rope, and after a foolishly tense search of her house, settled us in for the night.

Only Amanda and Eddie got fully settled. I stayed up and killed a dusty half-full bottle of Maker's Mark from her sadly under-stocked liquor cabinet and brooded in front of the fireplace.

Ordinarily I'd attribute the wakefulness to nerves. But despite the fearful carnage of the evening, I was more angry than frightened. I'm always offended by the arrogance of people who think killing other people is a legitimate undertaking. I wonder, how do you get up in the morning and think to yourself, "Gotta do some errands, wash the car, and if I can fit it in, permanently snuff the lights out of someone's beloved husband, brother, mother, sister, son"? I've never considered myself more deserving of life than the next guy, probably less, but at least take a second to think about it.

Altruism didn't come naturally to me, but it was easier to apply this line of reasoning to Iku Kinjo than to myself. No willful murder is justified, but hers felt less an act of butchery than a surgical elimination. A tactical execution.

Maybe that's all it was, a simple transaction. A line item on the profit and loss statement. Case closed. Meeting over. The ultimate hard stop.

SIXTEEN

THE NEXT MORNING my case for avoiding a physical exam was compromised by my inability to move without wincing or crying out in pain.

It was those damn ribs, pre-softened by Angel Valero.

So the first part of the day was spent in the tender care of a house-sized Jamaican trauma doctor named Markham Fairchild, whose bedside charm barely compensated for an obvious lack of sympathy.

"I tell you no more bangs to de head, and what do you do?" he said, looking down at me as they slid me into a thumping MRI.

"I didn't bang my head. Just the rest of me."

"Let me and dis machine be the judge of that."

A few hours later I was back with Amanda in her pickup with a bellyful of lectures and a pocketful of prescription painkillers, none of which I intended to use.

"Can't take the side effects. Rather have the pain."

"Then give them to me," said Amanda. "Fair compensation for all the chauffeuring."

Our next stop was the Southampton Town Police, who were politely withholding the APB in anticipation of my prompt arrival.

Officer Orlovsky was way off her regular game. She called Ross without an argument and said please when she asked us to wait in the reception area. I whispered my amazement into Amanda's ear.

"She's got a crush on you, obviously," she whispered back. "Doesn't want to let on to me."

The thought made me want to run back to the car and eat a handful of Markham's pills.

Ross called for me the moment Jackie came through the door. She nodded at Amanda and glowered at me.

"Would you ask Ross if I can have a couple private moments with my client before we sit down?" she asked Orlovsky. "We haven't had a chance to talk."

"Sure thing, hon," said Orlovsky, smiling graciously at Jackie, assuming common cause. "Take the interview room, down the hall, second right. I'll tell the Chief."

She buzzed us through the door, leaving Amanda out in reception with the public safety posters and dog-eared copies of *Cop Station Quarterly.*

Jackie wore black stretchy slacks, an iridescent green silk blouse opened one button too many and a camel hair sport coat that I swear had tails like an antique tux. I wanted to chase down the sadist who sold it to her and get her money back.

"Looking good, Jackie," I said, as we pulled chairs up to a small conference table.

"You're supposed to call me at the moment of catastrophe, not the next morning."

"You'd only just yell at me for waking you up."

"I'm yelling at you now."

"Here's the headline: Two guys tried to run me off the road and shoot me. Instead, they ran into the back of the Grand Prix and killed themselves. I recovered the gun and at least one of the bullets, which I gave to Joe Sullivan. There are no witnesses I know of, and yes, I'd been drinking heavily, but I always drink heavily, and no, I wasn't drunk."

"Breathalyzer?"

"Nope. Joe got there in time," I said.

"Anything else you want to tell me?"

I told her everything I'd done in the last twenty-four hours, as thoroughly as my memory would allow. She huffed through the entire thing.

"I was going to brief you as soon as I had a chance," I said. "I didn't think we'd have to work against a deadline."

"Deadline. Nice choice of words," said Jackie.

"What matters is what I think now. I think it's all connected to the maneuverings over Con Globe. I think all sorts of interested parties, including Angel Valero and nominally Phillip Craig, Eisler, Johnson, and insiders like Marve Judson and Mason Thigpen, are licking their greedy chops over the possibilities. An aberration in George Donovan's behavior lit the fuse. Uninteresting to the casual observer, shocking, or inviting, to the insider. And somewhere in all the fog and fury some bastard thought killing Iku Kinjo was a good idea."

"So it's all connected," said Jackie.

I huffed this time.

"Of course it's connected. Occam's razor. The most obvious interpretation is almost always the right one."

"Almost."

I huffed some more.

"Okay. I used the word 'almost.' A concession to relativism. A polite qualification meant to dress up a naked absolute.

What do you want, a philosophical debate or an assessment of the situation? Either one's okay with me."

"How about a quieter voice?"

I realized I'd reared up off my chair and was half pitched across the table. Nerves.

"Sorry," I said, settling back down.

"I'm on your side," said Jackie.

"I know you are."

"I would be even if you didn't pay me."

"And what have I paid you so far?" I asked.

"A dollar. I've invested it wisely."

"Keep up the good work. There're more dollars where that came from."

"I'll inform my broker."

"I can't let this stand," I said.

"Our compensation arrangement?"

"Iku's murder. There's an assumption in the air that it'll never get solved. You can smell it. The stink of inevitability. They've already conceded defeat with barely a fight."

"Who's 'they'?" Jackie asked.

"The collective 'they.' Cops, associates, reporters, friends—ostensibly—prosecutors. I've seen it before. Iku Kinjo becomes a casualty of war. An unidentified soldier in the battle between the difficult and the expedient."

"Not Joe Sullivan."

"No. Not Joe," I said.

"And I think it's a little early to start judging."

"Probably is. We allowed to smoke in here?"

She made that face that was part grin, part smirk.

"You haven't asked me about my trip to Princeton," she said.

"You went there?"

"I assume all this condemnation doesn't apply to me. The person who drove all the way to the middle of New Jersey in response to a single harebrained request from a guy who the next second forgot all about it."

"I didn't forget. I thought you forgot."

She milked her triumph. I waited it out.

"Okay," I said. "What did you find out."

"Princeton is a beautiful place. People are always pissing on New Jersey, but parts of it are like paradise."

"I feel that way about the Bronx."

"Harder sell."

"You learned some things at Princeton," I said.

"I did. I don't know how much bearing it'll have on our chat with Ross," she said.

"Give me a headline."

"Your group renters were a bunch of art majors."

"Iku?"

She laughed.

"Hell, no. Double major in economics and political science. Magna cum laude. No sports, no sororities, no clubs. Her extracurriculars were all curricula."

"How'd you find this out?"

"Like I always do. I traded sex for information."

"Now you tell me."

"I found a guy in the alumni office who knew Bobby Dobson. He knew another guy in the office where they keep student transcripts. We formed a love triangle. At least in their dreams."

"Why would an artso like Bobby hang around with a grind like Iku Kinjo?" I asked.

"He didn't. He hung around with her roommates."

I could tell by her face that we were about to play the guessing game.

"How 'bout we skip all that and you just tell me, in the interest of time."

She shook her head.

"Ross'll wait."

"Elaine Brooks and Zelda Fitzgerald," I said.

"You are such a pain in the ass."

"Lucky guess."

"Student housing had a computer program that matched incoming freshmen with their opposites. Diversity training 101. They were together through sophomore year, though by then Elaine was hanging out with Bobby in his off-campus apartment. Then Bobby, Elaine and Zelda went to Florence for their junior year. They shared a villa in the hills above the city with a few kids from the University of Bologna who were enrolled in the same program. Senior year the three of them got a country place in Hopewell, New Jersey, an easy commute to Princeton."

"Recapturing the thrill of Tuscany?" I asked.

"Or togetherness. According to the boys at Princeton, Elaine, Zelda and Bobby ran as a pack. Inseparable. Iku had dropped out of the clique by now, either because of her academic schedule, or because she and Zelda were on the outs, or both."

"On the outs? How come?"

"If you believe Bobby's dear friend back at Princeton, Zelda was the jealous type. Especially when it came to Bobby and Elaine."

"Or maybe just another rift between the arts and sciences," I said.

"Maybe."

"Meanwhile, Elaine ends up in an art gallery and Bobby works the help desk at Eisler, Johnson. Thy art, where goest thou?"

"Up his nose, probably. While Elaine was getting her art history MBA at Columbia, Bobby was working the bar at CBGB and studying a famous Columbian agricultural product. Intensely enough to wind up in a rehab tank in Connecticut."

"I think I know that place."

"Bobby's disappointed parents paid the fare with the proviso that Bobby make something of his life, like get into the financial trades like his daddy did and stop all this artistic foolishness. Hence the MSc in computer science and the IT department at Eisler, Johnson."

"And Elaine's still his girlfriend?" I asked.

"Yes. According to What's-his-name at Princeton, whose card is in my pocket, but am I going to call him? Not likely."

"Is cruelty in the service of the truth actually cruel or merely expedient?"

"I let him kiss me. Better men have earned less."

"Elaine," I said, "was she a particularly committed girlfriend to Bobby, or did she, you know . . ."

"Did she play the field? Definitely."

"What's-his-name confirmed that?" I asked.

"He called her omnivorous. Claimed personal experience, but that doesn't undermine the testimony. It was universally believed that she and Zelda were as much an item as she and Bobby, but again, no empirical evidence."

Jackie said Elaine's relationship with Bobby was assumed to be a safe haven from whence occasional forays were made. No evidence that this was reciprocal, nor that it wasn't.

"All this from only two guys?"

"You remember the college social scene? Everybody's business is everybody's?"

"I never socialized, but I'll take your word for it."

A phone mounted on the wall of the interview room rang and made us both jump. Jackie answered and heard Ross tell her the leadership of the Southampton Town Police Force bore waiting with the patience of Job, but that even Job had his limits.

"We're on our way," she said.

When I stood up, she put her hand on my shoulder and gently pushed me back down.

"Before we go, do you remember Oswald Endicott?" she asked me. "He was the Director of Finance for TSS. His office was next to yours."

"I remember Ozzie. Hard to forget now that his name keeps popping up. Not a bad guy. Worked like a bastard. Was always leaning over his file cabinet. Good at what he did. Loved surprise audits, which happened to us a lot, especially near the end."

"Any reason why he'd refuse to cooperate with Tucker, Blenheim?"

"Who're they?"

She stiffened.

"The outside counsel Donovan retained to look at your severance. Christ, Sam, you're paying me way too much to ignore everything I tell you."

"I'm not paying you anything."

"Apparently Ozzie wouldn't answer his phone, or the door, when they sent an associate up to Connecticut to interview him."

I tried to get a better picture of Ozzie in my mind. What I saw was a disheveled workaholic. Obsessed with detail and precision. But joyfully so, because it came to him so easily. The perfect guy for the job, which is why I rarely thought about him, because he rarely gave me any trouble.

"What's Ozzie got to do with this?" I asked.

"He's also refused to cooperate with the intellectual property suit. Something Tucker didn't know when they got your case to look at. When Mason Thigpen found out they were trying to talk to him they got a wrist slap and an order to back-off-in-no-uncertain-terms. Makes it a little hard for Tucker to do their job, since nobody would know more about your division's numbers than your Director of Finance. So they were curious. They asked me if you had any ideas."

None. I was still trying to remember if Ozzie had a wife and kids, where he lived or what he did on the weekend. Since I never asked about the personal life of anyone I worked with, this wasn't surprising. But like Jackie said, and Marve Judson before her, he did sit in an office next to mine, and I spent a lot of time with him managing our divisional P&L.

Another call from Ross propelled us out of the room and into the arms of Officer Orlovsky, who herded us all the way to the little conference room that Ross and his detectives used to browbeat, manipulate and cajole unwary souls into abject self-incrimination. I'd been in that room a few times before and couldn't say I was glad to be back.

On the way we walked through the squad room with all the cops and administrative people staring at me like they'd never seen me before. I wanted to lean into one of those portly desk jockeys and say "boo!," but I knew that wouldn't sit well with Ross, the guy who always seemed to have my future well-being in the palm of his capricious little hand.

I was relieved to see Ross alone this time. Mercifully, Veckstrom was out on assignment. This cleared the way for the three of us to cloud up the room without all the hacking commentary.

"Hey, Sam," said Ross, "long time no interrogate."

"Not an interrogation, Chief," said Jackie, dropping the fifty-pound feed bag she used as a purse on the table, "a courtesy interview. Agreed to voluntarily."

Ross took off his glasses and used both hands to rub his face hard enough to cause red marks to form on his cheeks.

"I love a lawyer with a sense of humor," he said.

"There're people you probably love, Ross, but none of them are lawyers," I said, pulling our regular ashtray out of a battered credenza. I lit Camels for everybody and settled in.

I went to Southampton High School with Ross, but couldn't remember ever talking to him there. We were both loners, each in a separate universe, though he managed to make a name for himself by appearing on a TV quiz show. He won a partial scholarship, which he used to study English literature, which everyone knows leads invariably to a life in crime and punishment. I do remember him as the only socially inept kid the whole school was afraid of. Even teenagers can sense a vibe, and Ross Semple's said, "Don't underestimate."

"You know, Jackie," he said, "any time there's a fatal auto accident, we're obligated to look back on the prior twenty-four hours of everyone involved. Dead or alive."

So I told him what I told Jackie, which wasn't entirely everything that happened in the last twenty-four hours, but I didn't know how to explain finding Honest Boy Ackerman inside Amanda's pickup truck or how I came into possession of Elaine Brooks's coffee mug.

"I'm mostly interested in the connection between that poor girl's death and those two bozos who ran into the back of your car."

"Me, too," I said, "and I'm certain there is one. They didn't just ram into me, they tried to shoot me."

"I don't know if that's so strange, Sam," said Ross. "I can think of a lot of people who'd like to shoot you. Sometimes I want to shoot you myself."

"Ever heard of *El Cerberus*?" I asked. "That's who sent the killers, according to the killer who lived long enough to tell me."

"Cerberus? The ugly dog guarding the gates of hell?" he asked. "Christ, has that damn thing got loose again?"

Jackie rolled her eyes up at the ceiling.

"Honestly, Ross."

"What else did he tell you?"

"That pretty soon America will have out-sourced our entire civilization. But we knew that already."

"The Chinese can have my job any time they want it," said Ross. "They can figure out how to deal with Venezuelan hit men."

"So you know they were Venezuelan," I said.

"Geez, Sam, let's try something different this time. Why don't you tell me everything you know and I'll tell you everything I know, so we both end up knowing the same things?"

I tried again to remember everything I felt okay telling him, which was most of it. He returned the favor by telling me he was the Chief of Police investigating a homicide and didn't tell God what he knew until the case was cleared and the perp had died in prison or gone to the electric chair. Which sounds like a one-sided standoff, but I was good at reading between Ross Semple's tortured lines. He liked having me out there poking around this one, especially since he was reasonably sure I hadn't done it myself, which wasn't often the case. And maybe he'd get lucky and catch the next guy who came after me, which could uncork the whole mess. Better bait than a red herring any day.

So after tossing out a few more softballs, he let us leave without even strong-arming Jackie into running an ad in the Police Ball program guide.

"Don't get too comfy," said Jackie, as we scooped up Amanda and walked out to the parking lot. "You're not done with this yet."

"Not until I fix my car," I said.

"Oh, heavens. Why would you do that?" said Jackie.

"It's my car."

"It's not a car, dear. It's a battleship," said Amanda.

"So far on the winning side of the battle. When do you think the cops'll give it back?" I asked Jackie. "I'm a little worried about the frame. Be a bitch to find a straightener big enough."

I let Jackie give me the usual warnings, remonstrances and pleas for sanity before she left in her pickup and we jumped into ours, the official vehicle of the East End's local populace.

Amanda took the driver's seat and started the engine.

"Where to, boss?" she said.

"Oak Point."

"I know the place," she said.

"Proceed briskly, but keep an eye on the rearview."

"As unfunny as that is, at least you're beginning to take this seriously."

"Although prepared for martyrdom, I prefer that it be postponed."

"St. Francis?" she asked.

"Winston Churchill. A hedonist more to my taste."

"Indomitable?"

"Unrepentant."

———

Eddie had everything under control when we got back. He greeted me first, but fussed more over Amanda. I attributed that to her lavish distribution of Big Dog biscuits and crostini slathered with Fromage d'Affinois.

I tried to use the rest of the day to build lawn ornamentation for Frank Entwhistle, but my mind stubbornly refused to concentrate on the task. Instead, I sat at my drawing table and allowed discontinuous images of Iku Kinjo, George Donovan and dead Venezuelans to crowd into the under-equipped, overlit little workspace.

This was apparently a time-consuming enterprise, because I was surprised to get a call from Amanda telling me it was already well past cocktail hour and we were still without food or drink.

I took a shower, and then in accordance with our usual division of labor, I stirred gin and Tom Collins mix into an icy tumbler and Amanda filled a bowl with yellow grapes. We lugged it all out to the edge of the breakwater, along with sweatshirts and flannel blankets, embracing the cooling season on its own terms.

"So what are you thinking now?" asked Amanda. "You must be thinking something."

"I need to spend more time on the computer."

"You don't have a computer," she said.

"Not working on it. Finding it."

"Iku's."

"Sullivan's scouring Vedders Pond. Worth doing, but it could be in a landfill somewhere, gone forever."

"Unless the killer kept it," she said.

"That's what Bobby Dobson said."

She asked what I thought the computer would tell me. I said I didn't know, but probably a lot. It was a vast repository of data, ready to give up its secrets if you knew where, and how, to look. I talked about patterns and rhythms, but also how anomalies stand out against a background of consistencies, speed bumps on the smooth road surface. I told her you can read stress in even the most innocuous exchange, if you look for it. That you have to read the voice, not just interpret the words.

"Sounds like voodoo."

"More like jazz," I said.

"Okay."

"Human language isn't just the notes, it's how they're put together and played. Listen to a little early Coltrane before you boot up."

"You learned this at MIT?"

"First semester, freshman year."

From there we transitioned onto more productive topics, like the price of lumber and the relative merits of Tom Collins mix over standard tonic water and lime. Thus agreeably occupied, we burned up the early evening, which was relatively warm, and slipped into solid night, which wasn't.

"I'm cold," said Amanda.

"Cold, of course. Explains the shaking."

We each suffered an overflowing armload of grape stems, glassware and dog biscuits, and made our unbalanced way across the broad lawn. Eddie, always overjoyed to head for the next thing, whatever it was, bounded toward my cottage, thinking that was our destination.

Partway there he broke into a full run, barking furiously.

We both stopped and looked into the blacked-out space between us and the cottage, made more so by the dim glow of the light above the front door.

Eddie's bark went up another register.

I dropped the stuff I was holding and grabbed Amanda's arm, causing her to drop her own load. I bent over and ran, pulling her along, at least for a few seconds before she started to run in earnest. I held on to her hand, and she dragged me across the last few yards of lawn to the small porch on the side of the cottage. We slid between a pair of bushy yews and dropped to the ground.

"What do you think?" she asked.

"No idea."

"Maybe it's nothing. We're just being jumpy," she said.

"He never barks like that."

"He doesn't."

"Stay here," I said, and immediately felt her start to rise.

"I mean it," I said. "Just let me do this. I can't be worrying about you." She fell back down on the ground, letting my forearm slip through her fingers as she went.

"Write home."

I moved along the periphery of the house, inside the overgrown shrubbery, and worked my way around to the front, peering as hard as I could into the dark, which revealed nothing outside the ordinary. A white-painted wooden porch lit by a yellow bulb in a glass shade above the door, a galvanized milk box from my childhood I was too stupid to throw out and the three-quarter-sized baseball bat I used to hit tennis balls for Eddie and occasionally whack people over the head.

I reached through the bushes and wrapped my hand around the bat, pulling it silently toward me. The feel of the handle flowed up through my wrist and all the way to the middle of my body. Courage transferred through the hardwood fibers.

Thus emboldened, I walked through the bushes and past the porch and out to the front lawn. I could hear the nervous whine Eddie used when trying to flush a bird out of a stand of sea grass, or a tennis ball from under the living room couch.

He was out to the lawn, prancing side to side, and staring at the narrow alley that led though the mounds of antique yew bushes to the front door. I shot the flashlight through the hole and saw it right away. I yelled to Amanda to come and take hold of Eddie's collar. The thing was high up on the door, but well within his vertical lift.

"What? What?" she asked as she came around the corner.

"Just hold him," I said.

Even in the colorless glow of the flashlight I could make out the component parts. A slick mass of grey cauliflower partially covered by a photograph of Amanda in her work shirt and headband, sweaty, pointing at something above her head. The image was seriously compressed, the telltale of a big telephoto lens. At least 400 mm.

Both were pinned to the door with a long Japanese knife.

A dark bead dripped off the cauliflower and landed on the floor. I followed it with my flashlight. It looked black, but when I bent down for a closer look, it was dark red. Confirming what I already thought.

A brain. A big bloody brain.

SEVENTEEN

Hospital waiting rooms are designed to guarantee that the experience of waiting is so dreary, monotonous and dehumanizing that you'll think twice before ever going to the hospital again. Wait long enough and you'll begin to question relationships with people close to you who might sometimes need to go to the hospital, like your parents or children.

The person at the hospital who sat at the reception desk behind a small set of sliding glass doors seemed busy and engaged in what she was doing, so much so that it was impossible to make eye contact with her. A television, hung from a bracket off the ceiling, was set on a show where nice-looking people made sober accounts of the day's events while a confusion of ticker-tape messages scrolled along the bottom of the screen. Though Amanda had occasionally tried to explain modern television to me, I still found it impossibly strange. Luckily, the volume was below audible, reducing the thing to a simple distraction, like a spoiled child running around a train car, or a drunk in a nice restaurant.

"You're sure we shouldn't just take this directly to the police?" Amanda asked, pointing to the bundle I held in my arms.

"Nah. We've already wrecked the crime scene. And I can't wait for all the official pronouncements. We'll call Sullivan as soon as I get Markham's opinion."

The woman behind the glass doors finally noticed we were standing there. She slid one of them open.

"Yes?" she said.

"I need to see Dr. Fairchild," I said.

"What's the nature of the emergency?"

"I don't know. That's why I need to see him."

She slid a clipboard over the opening.

"Fill this out," she said.

After a few moments, she realized I hadn't taken the clipboard out of her hand. She looked up at me.

"I don't need to fill that out. I need to see the doctor. He knows me. Just give him a call."

"I'll call someone," she said, the words burdened with the weary residue of constant repetition. "But I need you to fill this out first."

Amanda leaned into me and stuck her head through the opening.

"Dr. Fairchild will be very disappointed when he learns we were here to see him and he wasn't informed," she said.

"You think so?" the woman said, slightly more sincere than sarcastic.

"I do," said Amanda.

She frowned, but picked up the phone. Amanda did her best not to look too pleased with herself.

It was another half hour before Markham showed up, time we spent playing a variation on "blissful ignorance" you might call "flagrant denial," dissecting the performances of the baseball players on the TV and utterly ignoring the fact that I had a brain in the gym bag on my lap.

I always felt Markham approach before I saw him. Probably because his density and mass affected the local air pressure.

I stood up to shake his hand. He looked me over.

"So I don't need a gurney," he said.

"Just a quiet place out of the public eye," I said, holding up the bag. "Something with stainless steel tables and running water."

He looked over at Amanda and smiled.

"Dis fella never fail to keep t'ings entertaining," he said.

"Indeed."

He took us up a level to where they did on-site lab work. The usual cast of anonymous people in white coats, blue scrubs and face masks wrapped around their necks buzzed around with a look of distracted intensity. They all smiled at Markham, but gave him wide berth, advisedly.

The room fit my specs. I set the gym bag on the table and handed out rubber gloves from a dispenser mounted on the wall. Markham shook his head at my offering and pulled a pair of his own out of his pocket.

"Triple XL," he said.

I used two hands to pull out the gallon-sized Ziploc bag and set it on the examination table, then backed away. Markham hummed with curiosity as he dug his hand into the bag and picked up the rubbery mass within. He held it up and turned it in his hand, squinting with concentration.

"*Ris de veau*. Who brought the chives?" he said, after a few minutes.

"Ick," said Amanda.

"Technically, *ris de taureau*. A big one," he said.

"Bull brains," I said.

"Not a definitive conclusion, but most likely. Unless you slaughter a bison, or maybe African water buffalo. Herbivore for sure, bigger den a deer, smaller den elephant. Much smaller. For that you need a bigger bag."

"Locally available?" I asked.

He nodded.

"For sure. Out on Montauk dey got a regular cattle ranch. I sometimes get to patch up holes these beauties leave inna cowboy's thigh."

"Can you trace the exact source? Through DNA?"

He enjoyed that thought.

"Not me, Mr. Acquillo. But maybe somebody can. They don't cover that at Georgetown Medical School."

I held the Ziploc bag open for him so he could drop it back in. I asked him if we could leave it in one of his refrigerators so the cops could pick it up in the morning. I had to endure some more jovial sarcasm, but he said okay. I thanked him for his time, and he did me the honor of letting it go at that.

When we made it out to the sidewalk I called Joe Sullivan, waking him up.

"I think I discovered the brains of the operation," I said.

I waited while he apologized to his wife and found a quiet place to talk.

"This had better be good," he said.

I didn't disappoint him. Except that I'd waited until then to call him. I didn't offer any sort of defense, and he was too tired to rail at me for more than a few minutes, so I got off the phone in relatively short order.

"So what now?" Amanda asked.

I looked around the hospital parking lot, searching for guidance.

"I know a place a few blocks from here that serves drinks by the glass," I said, as if assaulted by a revelation.

"How novel," she said.

"I think it's gonna catch on. With the right public support."

The hostess at the big restaurant on Main Street found two stools to pull up to the crowded bar, a courtesy I credited to Amanda's effective social graces. Between the pumped-up stereo and competing conversational blather, it was almost too noisy to talk. The ubiquitous flat-screen TVs blinked and flashed at the corner of my eye, but the vodka was cold and the light a warm amber glow, making the women look as great as they hoped for and Amanda impossibly beautiful.

"So," said Amanda, "as you'd say to me, theories?"

"You need to go stay with Burton. Have the biggest guys off your crew pick you up and drop you off. Maybe get a dog. Eddie'll write up the specs."

"You're concerned."

"I am. I'm not used to this kind of heat. A few meatballs here and there, no problem. But these people, out of my league. I don't want something to happen to you or Eddie because I didn't take it seriously."

"What people?"

"I don't know. That's why I need to concentrate, which'll be hard if I'm constantly worried about you."

Faced with that kind of indisputable logic, there wasn't much she could say.

"No way I'm being driven out of my own house. I've faced worse than this. Just give me one of those guns you took off Con Globe security. My mother taught me how to shoot," and more of the same.

I waited it out.

"I'll call Isabella," I said. "She'll get the east wing ready."

On the stagger back to the car she put both arms around me and squeezed.

"You don't want me to be horribly murdered," she said. "But you don't think I care if the same thing happens to you."

"It won't."

"You don't know that. I can't bear another gigantic loss."

Loss was something Amanda knew a lot about. When I first met her, she'd lost her only child and only parent. Her grief was most of what was left. And I was a fine one to turn to, addled by loss and regret of another sort. Now here we were, in a truce with grave misfortune, which I was threatening for no other reason than the death of my old boss's girlfriend.

"I'm in it, now," I said. "The only way out is through."

A faint breeze, cool and hollow, blew between us, but she squeezed harder and left it at that.

———

We drove back to Oak Point. While Amanda packed up her things and connected with Isabella, Burton's major domo, I put a few weeks' worth of Eddie's food, Big Dog biscuits, tennis balls, dog bed and the only chew toy he hadn't chewed to oblivion into a big garbage bag and brought it out to Amanda's Audi.

"He'll have to forage locally for rotten logs and bird carcasses."

"I didn't tell Isabella about a dog."

"Better a surprise."

On the way over Burton called my cell phone. I told him about what I knew, and what I feared. He backed the plan.

"I'll have Fernando and Jarek join her crew. Both handy with pneumatic nailers and throwing knives."

The atmosphere inside the Audi was tense and quiet. Eddie sat up in the back seat and panted. Amanda fiddled with her seat belt and sighed.

"You'll visit," she said.

"I'll visit, I'll call, I'll write long letters."

The big white gate that guarded the entrance to Burton's long driveway opened as we approached. We made the four-hundred-mile drive through the bordering privet hedges in decent time, and were met at the front porch of the main house by Isabella, along with a tall, tattooed ghoul with kinky pink hair and another hard case that looked like Charles Bronson's anemic, mentally ill younger brother. Part of Burton's domestic staff, most of whom had stayed on after his defense practice saved them from long jail terms, or worse.

Introductions were made all around, after which we got Amanda and Eddie settled in, and spent a few hours talking things over with Burton. By then it was pretty late, so it was easy for me to slip away and drive back to Oak Point, where I sat up for another few hours and smoked a month's ration of cigarettes, nursed a single tumbler of Absolut, listened to Etta James and pretended I wasn't spooked by every little sound in the night.

I was back where I'd started. On Oak Point, alone in the dark.

EIGHTEEN

LATE THE NEXT DAY I heard a sound I'd never heard before. I was in Amanda's pickup, which I almost ran off the road searching around the dashboard for the source, realizing eventually it was coming from my pocket.

It was my cell phone. A flashing alert told me I had a voice message waiting. I'd retrieved plenty of these before without all the frantic notification. I studied the little screen and saw that the message had been marked urgent. It was from Joe Sullivan.

"The doc was right about the brain," he said. "Riverhead says it could have come from any slaughterhouse. They're also working on the photograph of Amanda, but don't expect much."

I told him that I'd sent Amanda over to Burton's, which made him happy. He said Will Ervin would stay close to her during the day. I thanked him.

"You were also right about unknown prints A, B and C," he said. "Elaine Brooks, Zelda Fitzgerald and John Churchman, owner of the property, in that order. We interviewed Churchman already, doesn't know nothing about nothing, and why would he? He's living on his boat, a few slips down from Hodges at Hawk Pond, if you want to waste your own time."

I was only a few blocks from Hawk Pond, so I turned off North Sea Road and followed the creek that fed the pond that eventually flowed out into the Little Peconic Bay. First I knocked on the weatherboards on Hodges's old Gulf Star, but he wasn't home. In the process I stirred up his two shih tzus, whose crazed yapping attracted the annoyed attention of the next-door neighbor, a woman with round, apple-red cheeks and a cloud of white hair.

"Cute dogs, but noisier than sin," she said, her head poking up out of the companionway of her boat, her hand shielding her eyes against the pure sun of early fall.

"Do you know which of these boats is John Churchman's?" I asked her.

"Not that one. That's Paul Hodges."

"I know. He's a friend of mine. I'm actually looking for John Churchman."

She jerked her thumb to the left.

"Three slips down. Sportin' Life."

"That's his boat?"

She shook her head.

"The boat's name is *April 16*. The day after tax day. The guy's an accountant. My husband calls him Sportin' Life."

"Your husband given to sarcasm?"

"No," she said, lowering her voice and looking pointedly at something behind me, "jealousy."

I turned and saw a dark woman walking down the dock. She had a towel wrapped around her head and a terry cloth bathrobe that would have fit her if she'd been half as tall.

"Excuse me," I said to her. "Do you know John Churchman?"

She stopped abruptly, and unlike Elaine Brooks, collected the neck of her robe and gained greater purchase on a clear bag filled with bathing paraphernalia. She didn't know whether to look suspicious or smug.

"Funny you should ask." She looked toward her neighbor, who'd already ducked out of sight. "I'm staying with him. Who would be inquiring?"

"I'm a friend of Bobby Dobson, the one renting John's house off Vedders Pond."

"Johnny's still in the shower. Exfoliating. He'll be by in a sec."

She moved on down the dock with the kind of sliding gait that made you think of high heels and tight skirts. I followed her.

She stepped nervously across a short gangplank and into the cockpit of a modern sailboat, all clean rounded fiberglass and chrome, not a splinter of teak anywhere. She was halfway down the companionway before she saw me walking on the dock. She waved as she descended down into the boat.

"I'd invite you in, but I lack the authority. He'll be along soon."

I said something inanely apologetic and sat down on a plastic storage bin chained to the fence that ran along the dock. As predicted, Churchman showed up soon after, wearing a towel and the self-possession of a crown prince.

He had a lot of hair on his chest, but you could still see it was sculpted and fat free, and well represented by his posture, which was somewhere on the extreme end of ramrod. When I stood up from the bin and stepped in front of him a smile erupted on his face that would have been all perfectly straight, brilliant white teeth if it weren't for the cheerful lines sketched on his cheeks and around his eyes.

"John Churchman?" I asked.

"Absolutely," he said, thrusting out his hand.

His grip was a shade tighter than it needed to be, so I squeezed back before letting go. I expected him to be startled by that, but instead he looked impressed.

"I'm Sam Acquillo. I found the dead girl in your house."

"How shitty was that?" he said, his face shifting smoothly into sympathy mode.

"Very. Can I bother you for a few minutes?"

"I already gave my statement."

"I'm not a cop. The thing's just got me bugged and I thought you might be able to help."

He nodded, smile back in place.

"Absolutely," he said for the second time. "Let me get decent and we'll chitchat." He looked at his boat. "Wait'll you meet Brigitte. A one-woman babe-a-thon."

"We met."

"Lucky you. Come on."

It took a while for him to get decent. I suppose that involved moisturizing, achieving a razor-sharp part in his straight brown hair and picking out the right outfit—a soft rayon shirt tucked with precision into a pair of pleated trousers. Brigitte came up the companionway directly behind him and put her arm around his waist. Her dress looked like it was made from the same material as his shirt, in a contrasting but nicely coordinated color. They stood there for a moment so I could take it all in.

"We're about to have our evening drinkies," said Brigitte. "Care to join?"

"If you got vodka and ice, sure," I said.

Churchman patted her on the rump when she turned to go back down the companionway.

"Ever windsurf?" he asked me, after sitting down on the cushioned cockpit seat across from me.

I said no. "I like a boat around me."

He looked disappointed.

"Too bad. I was going to suggest you move up to para-surfing. Learned it down in Cancun. Much bigger rush. I'm going out tomorrow if the wind kicks up like it's supposed to."

"So you live here during the season?"

He shook his head with another expansive smile, giving me a chance to see what teeth can look like under the proper management.

"Year-round when I'm in the country. Just do a short haul in the spring to paint the bottom. Usually while I'm staying at my apartment in Montmartre."

"Quelle chance."

"You a local?" he asked.

"My grandparents were from the *onzième*, but I've never been there."

"I meant Southampton."

"Yeah. Up in North Sea. So Bobby Dobson rents Vedders Pond full time?"

Brigitte called to him to help her with a tray piled with wine, cheese and bread, and my vodka on the rocks. He swept it out of her hand and slid it onto the cockpit table without a pause or clink of glass.

"Great tenant. Marvelous. Doesn't know which end of a screwdriver drives the screw, but that's what landlords are for."

"So you don't mind the subletting."

"I choose to call them guests, and who cares as long as the rent is paid and there're no problems?"

"Like a woman getting murdered?"

He wasn't sure if I meant it as a joke, but he kept the grin when he pointed his finger at me.

"You make an excellent observation. Murder was not part of the lease."

Brigitte used two fingers to tap his thigh, in a parody of an actual swat.

"Heavens, John. How awful."

"You're right," he said, putting his arm around her as she sat down next to him. "It's not funny."

"John likes to laugh in the face of death," said Brigitte. "Jumping out of planes, skiing down mountains—occasionally at the same time."

"It's a bad habit."

"So no opinions on what happened?" I asked him. "No ideas?"

He looked at Brigitte as if to help him remember.

"Not really. I stay pretty clear of the place during the high season and never met the Japanese girl. One of the cops said he went to the house on a complaint and found her drunk with the music blasting and bawling like a fountain. Don't the Japanese like to commit hari-kari when they're bumming over something?"

Brigitte looked like she wanted to say "How awful" again, but instead she took a big sip of her white wine.

"It wasn't suicide. The body was moved from the rear patio to a bedroom in the basement. Don't worry. No blood. The killer was unusually tidy."

"Then I could use him to clean up when the cops let me back into the house. They left a mighty mess."

"How well do you know Robert Dobson?" I asked.

"I do his taxes. And the old man's. I'll always know if they can afford the rent."

"Dad pays?"

"Oh, yeah. Bobby's a bit of a disappointment financially, but he's their kid, you know?"

Brigitte nodded briskly at this, as if she'd asserted the same position herself just that morning.

"It must be quite a responsibility knowing everybody's dirty secrets," I said, finishing what little vodka Brigitte fit into the thick-walled glass. A clear example of false advertising.

"Why does everyone assume there're dirty secrets?" Churchman asked. "What's wrong with slightly soiled?"

"What're Bobby's?"

"Tish-tish. I wouldn't even tell that to the cops. Not without a court order."

I toasted him with my glass full of ice.

"Do you believe in coincidence?" I asked him.

"Accountants don't like statistical improbabilities."

"Neither do engineers."

Brigitte finally arrived with more ice, and oh joy oh bliss, a bottle of Grey Goose. French vodka. Of course.

The conversation took a sudden diversion when Brigitte told Churchman she'd screwed up on scheduling the next day's tennis game, which might cut into his parasailing time. Though battered by disappointment, he took it well enough. She suggested a longer stint at the gym, but he thought they should get the mountain bikes back out of storage and check out the new trails being cut through the Northwest Woods above East Hampton.

I strived to look interested until Churchman remembered I was there and tried to get me into the conversation.

"What do you do for exercise, Sam? You look pretty fit."

You could hear "for an old guy" hanging there in parenthetical midair.

"I hit things. Bars, nails and bags full of sand."

"Sounds very therapeutic," said Brigitte.

"If you want to try it out, I'll set you up."

A little shift in mood passed behind Churchman's eyes. I took the hint and guzzled the rest of my second drink before he could say what he said right after that:

"Personally, I'm getting ready to hit Bobby Van's."

He patted his washboard stomach with a broad open hand as if to share the resonance of his hunger.

"Then you should go," I said, standing up. The sun was mostly buried under the horizon by now and the resulting chill had caught up with Brigitte, who was trying to rub heat into her shoulders. Churchman pulled her to her feet and wrapped his long arms around her.

"Sorry, baby. Let's get you a pashmina."

I stood up and stuck out my hand for Churchman to shake.

"Thanks for the drink and chitchat, folks. Enjoy your dinner."

I grabbed one of the split backstays and was about to swing myself up over the transom and across the gangplank when Churchman remembered something.

"Hey, Sam. I just remembered. I've got a client who used to work for Con Globe. It was a referral from Bobby Dobson, actually."

I swung myself back into the boat.

"Really."

"Yeah. Retired, like you. Your age. You gotta know him. What the hell's his name?" he asked Brigitte, who looked panicked that she didn't have the answer. "Funny name. I'm thinking black-and-white TV. Sixties?"

"Lucy?" Brigitte asked, exhausting her knowledge of the subject.

"Ricky's dad. Went to work every day as a bandleader in a suit and tie. Made no sense."

"Ozzie?" I asked.

"Christ, yeah. Oswald Endicott. Can you believe that?"

"Ozzie worked for me," I said.

Churchman suddenly looked almost bereaved.

"Jesus, really? Well I'm the asshole."

I hate self-flagellation. Especially when expressed by someone so unpracticed at it, like John Churchman.

"How come?"

"Well, you say North Sea, and I'm not thinking those big places up on the ridge."

I sat back down on the cockpit cushions.

"Sorry, man. Not following," I said.

"Ozzie worked for you? Weird bastard, but what the hey. Money'll do that to you. What are you doing with yours? I do a little financial planning for my bigger clients. Just mentioning."

"How much money? How much money makes you weird? Round numbers."

He struggled with the answer.

"Eight figures? That usually gets you over the threshold. Ozzie's comfortably inside the building."

"We're talking about Ozzie Endicott?"

He nodded, almost apologetically.

"Hey, you want another drink? Brigitte, get some more ice."

I grabbed the backstay and hauled myself back on my feet.

"I've already taken enough of your time," I said.

Churchman looked resigned to the inevitable, but still cheerful.

"Sure. Fine. Nice to see you. Stop by any time. Right, Brigitte?"

She nodded like it was her idea.

I found Amanda's pickup in the dim light that filled in between the setting of the sun and the lighting of the big post lamps dotting the marina. I'd been planning to go into the Village to buy a newspaper, sit on a park bench on Main Street, and maybe get a burger later at one of the joints that still marginally catered to the locals. But after the visit with Churchman, the mood was lost.

This used to happen to me when I was a process optimizer. When I was on the cusp of a solution I'd suddenly start to feel nauseated. I didn't actually have the solution itself, but I knew that I would momentarily. This would cause a physiological reaction, a feeling of nervous revulsion. I used to wonder if it was the by-product of the frenzied calculations going on in the back of my mind, my overworked subconscious.

But the trouble didn't come from the process. It was when the conclusions being generated seemed untenable. Preposterous. Yet, like Churchman, I was ultimately a quantitative guy. In any contest between empirical data and logic and reason, the data almost always won.

I drove back along North Sea Road and stopped at the place where I'd first read Bobby Dobson's real estate file. The same bartender was working the bar. He didn't remember me, thankfully. When I ordered Grey Goose he looked at me like I was speaking French, so I acquiesced to whatever he had in the well.

As some of the truth about Con Globe, Ozzie Endicott, George Donovan and Iku Kinjo started to leak into my jostled mind, I said "Oh, fuck, can't be," to the bartender, since he was the only one within earshot.

"Always is, partner," he said, swabbing down the space in front of me and then moving on to the prospect of a better conversation farther down the bar.

NINETEEN

HALFWAY THROUGH THE NEXT DAY I was outside working at a folding bench, hoping to put a few hours into the teak planters I'd promised Frank Entwhistle. And maybe take advantage of the fair weather and the recuperative qualities of manual labor to regain my senses.

So even though I was getting ready to make the call myself, I was disappointed when the little screen on the cell phone told me George Donovan was on the line. I looked out toward the bay, wondering if I still had the arm to go the distance. Then I answered the phone.

"I thought you would have contacted me by now," he said.

Not if I'd been doing my best to avoid you, I said to myself.

"I was about to."

"We need to talk," he said.

"We do."

"It's happened."

"What?"

"I've been approached."

"Where are you?" I asked.

"In Montauk. You can't come here. Arlis is out with the dogs. We need a place to meet."

I thought about it.

"You know the park at the bitter end, the one with the lighthouse? Find a comfortable place. I'll find you."

"You're still honoring the deal?" he said. "I need your assurance."

"I already honored it. I found Iku. We're now in the 'find-the-one-who-killed-Iku' phase."

"That wasn't part of the deal."

I thought he might say that.

"I know it wasn't, George, but now it has to be."

More painful silence.

"I'm afraid not. I will see you in an hour."

Then he hung up.

———

Montauk always felt like what it was, an outpost at the end of the known universe. There used to be a little downtown, like the ones lining the highway to the west, but the hurricane of 1938 wiped it out. The subsequent reconstruction came mostly after the war, so a lot of the commercial buildings had that spare, expedient, post-war look. But the people living there retained the pride of frontier survival, and managed to express in their endurance an obvious love of place.

The day did its part by being brightly lit and well ventilated. I know there are a lot of beautiful places in the world, but this was the only one I knew that felt as good as it looked. As if to dramatize the thought I hit a band of cool, hazy air blowing in off the ocean over a field where you could pick your own strawberries. Some of the Latinos who had been bent over the ground hugging green mounds stood and looked toward the sea. The others held their focus, plucking and tossing the fruit to rows of children held reluctantly in tow.

The park I'd suggested to Donovan encompassed the easternmost tip of the South Fork, hence the lighthouse that in the old days kept ships from losing themselves on the treacherous shoals, with limited success.

Donovan was there waiting for me on a park bench at the base of the sandy path that led to the lighthouse.

I pulled the pickup into a raised parking lot where I could look down on where Donovan was sitting. He wore white slacks, a blue blazer, soft leather slip-ons without socks and a pink and white pinstriped shirt. He still didn't look very good, even at that distance.

The park was nearly empty, with only a small herd of tourists halfway up the path to the lighthouse and a couple sitting on a blanket on the lawn leading down to the sea. No Venezuelan assassins, at least within view.

I waited another five minutes before shutting off the engine, then walked down to the park bench. He didn't see me until I was almost on top of him.

"Hi, George."

"Sam."

"I almost brought a friend along, but I didn't think you wanted the extra company."

I sat next to him on the park bench. Up close, he looked even worse. Thin and drawn, as if he'd partially evaporated, and a death-grey pallor that added ten years to the way he looked when we last met in Greenwich. Circumstances had finally caught up to him, cancelling his exemption from the penalties of old age.

"This friend of yours, what have you told him," Donovan asked, "about my situation?"

"Everything I could think of."

"Which he'll undoubtedly only discuss with you."

"As long as I'm alive," I said.

"Then I wish you a long life."

"I'm depending on that."

He leaned back in the bench and crossed his legs, putting his arm up on the backrest. He looked out across the park, as if assessing the quality of the groundskeeping.

"Did you know there's an inverse corollary between an exceptional IQ and the likelihood of professional success?" Donovan asked.

"I've heard that. More mediocritist propaganda."

"Not if you look at the two of us. I'd say we're proof positive."

"My carpentry career's clicking right along. So you must be right."

"You know the difference between the brilliant and the merely accomplished?" he asked.

"Net worth?"

"Perspective. Smart people see too much, know too much. They're too easily distracted by insight and revelation. The thoughts pile up until there's too much to filter. Perceptive people are ultimately crushed under the weight of their own comprehension. They know the merciless realities of life."

"Can't accuse me of that. All I have are happy thoughts," I said.

"This is what I seem to have lost. Perspective. And predictably enough, my financial prospects are suffering the consequences. Yet I'm no wiser. If anything, I feel as if my intelligence is leaking out of my ears. Doesn't seem fair."

"Your brain's not the only organ you've been thinking with lately."

Donovan uncrossed his legs and sat up straight on the bench. His hand was only a few inches from mine. Like his face, it was the color of rotting dough, covered in tan age spots and etched with veins more black than blue.

"I suppose I deserve that, but I don't care what you think about me. A typical aging narcissist falling prey to a beautiful young woman. It might have been that, but felt like more. Up until the moment she stopped calling me, I was sure she felt the same way. And I still do. If I'm a fool, so be it. Now that she's gone, my mind's a cloud, a blur of outlandish emotion, and all I want to do is run, as fast and as far away as I can."

"So do it, George. You got the money. Go sit on the porch in Montauk and watch your grandchildren dominate each other out on the front lawn. You've got nothing to prove to anyone."

"If it were that easy."

"Oh, right. You've lost perspective. I'd help you get it back but I'm too busy underachieving."

Donovan grunted and tried to get more comfortable on the wooden bench.

"Not quite," he said. "From what I hear you've been both busy and productive."

I tried to look modest.

"I've done a few things," I said.

He looked at the sky, then directly into my eyes.

"It all needs to stop."

"Who got to you, George? What did they say?"

"You know what they said. The worst possible thing. An offer is on the table. I have the opportunity to choose among an array of potential catastrophes."

"Let me help you, George."

He shook his head.

"The only way you can do that is go back to your cottage and forget any of this happened. I'm holding up my end of the arrangement. Our outside counsel is preparing to contact your attorney. A stroke of the pen and you're a wealthy man."

"They know about Iku?"

He made a low, humorless sort of laugh.

"Know? They know everything. In intricate detail. Every correspondence, every assignation. I've seen the evidence. Damning is too tame a word."

"Who killed her, George?"

He leaned forward in the bench and put his face in his hands. When he spoke his words were muffled, but I heard what he said.

"One proviso attached to every option I've been given is that I force you to cease and desist your efforts in that area."

"What do they want from you?"

He took his face out of his hands.

"One would think a man who gave up on a nearly perfect life would be a little less persistent," he said.

"I'm a late bloomer."

"They want my company. Nothing more than that."

"I didn't think that was up to you. The Mandate of '53 and all that." He put his head back in his hands. It looked like a comfortable position, and I considered trying it myself. Instead, I lit a cigarette. Without looking up, Donovan moved slightly away from me. Health nut to the end.

"The Mandate of '53 became moot the day you turned our board meeting into a brawl."

"Hardly a brawl. One punch. Well deserved."

"I'd say misplaced," said Donovan. "You should have saved it for your financial director. Far more deserving."

"Ozzie Endicott? You asked me about him at your house. You wanted to know if I still talked to him."

Donovan flicked errant bits of wind-borne tree fluff from his bright white pants.

"Back before you left the company, Marve Judson came to me with an interesting bit of information about Mr. Endicott. He'd been held by the Stamford police for questioning in regard to a drug transaction. Subsequently released, but Marve had an acquaintance on the police force who alerted him. At Marve's suggestion, we mounted a discreet internal investigation."

"Discreet for sure. I never heard a thing."

"Endicott was, in fact, a rather committed drug user. Amphetamines, which are apparently highly addictive. And expensive, especially if your goal is to keep your habit under wraps."

I finally had a firm picture of Ozzie in my mind. A little wild-eyed, a little frantic, but usually good humored. I'd known the type for years. Driven by the job to go way beyond the job's requirements. That's all I thought it was. I never made the effort to know any more than that about Ozzie, or any other employee.

"He embezzled money," I said.

"Oh yes. Quite a bit. Very clever scheme. The man was remarkably capable. You can achieve a lot if you never go to sleep."

"Like destroying your job. How come he didn't?"

Donovan smiled something like a genuine smile.

"I always said you were the smartest guy in the company. Don't disappoint me now."

I stood up and shook out my joints, trying to get a little extra blood to flow up into my brain. I tried to picture Marve Judson talking to Donovan, then sitting down with Ozzie. Relishing the moment of omnipotence. Wielding the delicious power of dangerous information.

Ozzie's beloved career in the palm of his hand. What pleasure. What delightful leverage.

I snapped a look at Donovan, who was waiting calmly on the park bench for me to catch up.

"You had him by the balls. He'd do anything you wanted. What did you bastards do to him? Ah, Jesus," I said, as the jolt of realization thrilled across my mind. "I know what you did. Holy crap."

I sat down on the grass, unable to move any closer to Donovan at that moment. Afraid of what I might do.

"You had him cook the books so you could sell off my division without seeming to violate the Mandate of '53," I said. "All he had to do was hide enough revenue to keep TSS under a certain size. Fontaine got the bargain of the century. You and the other insiders got a tidy jump in stock value and the worst that happened was Mason Thigpen got a sock in the nose."

Donovan looked a little like a proud parent.

"See? I knew you could do it," he said. "Unfortunately, that wasn't the worst that could happen."

I lay back on the grass and looked at the sky. It had been blue, but was beginning to haze over. I could hear seagulls, but they weren't in view. I pictured them circling above the north shore, plucking up bivalves to smash on the rocky beach below.

"Somebody found you out," I said, propping back up on my elbows so I could see his reaction. "How did that happen? Iku?"

His face stayed in neutral.

"How no longer matters," he said. "The fact is, there are people who know that the sale of your division was not only based on intentional fraud, but that it has exposed the entire company to hostile takeover. You can imagine how my wife and her family will take the news."

I stood up and brushed off my blue jeans. Not as neatly pressed as Donovan's white slacks, but more resistant to messy tree life or the salt mist coming in off the sound, which had begun to condense on the park bench. The sun was over my shoulder, so Donovan had to squint to look up at me.

"So what are you planning to do?" he asked.

"Find out who killed Iku Kinjo."

"If you continue down that path it will cost you a tremendous amount of money. If you're lucky, that's all it will cost."

He said that last part to my back, since I was already heading down that path, walking back under the greying sky and through the freshening breeze, with one eye on a nearby stand of trees and the other on Amanda's pickup. My hope was to make it all the way back to Oak Point, home of the little bay and the dog, the fading light and a brighter life than I deserved.

The conversation had still left a lot of things unresolved, but at least one burden had been lifted from my already over-burdened heart.

I was done with George Donovan. This time for good.

TWENTY

"BUT WHY, SAM?" said Jackie. "Why when I'm so overbooked and tired and in need of personal hygiene, starting with a soapy shower and dental floss?"

"It's way too early to be in bed," I said. "You still have that old computer at home, right?"

I was on the landline back at the cottage. Before she could fill the phone with complaint I caught her up on the past few days. It was enough to revive her attention, if not her spirits. I told her I really needed her to find some things on the Web. She asked me for the millionth time why I didn't get a PC of my own and look it up myself. I told her I could do that, but then she'd miss out on all the fun.

"What a doll."

I waited for her to go to the back porch and boot up the good old HP. Through her portable phone I could hear the sound of keys tapping, ice in a glass and a match being struck.

"No dope until you do the search," I called into the phone.

"I'm not even going to dignify that," she said, coming back on. "What am I looking for?"

"Not what. Who. Oswald Endicott. Located somewhere in Connecticut."

"Westbrook, according to Tucker."

"Okay, Westbrook," I said.

I waited through another minute of key taps.

"Whoa," said Jackie, in a barely audible voice.

"What?"

"We're too late," she said.

"We are?"

"He's dead."

"He is?"

"Give me a second to read."

I gave her a few minutes, which I used to light the first of the next day's Camel ration.

"This from the online edition of *Shoreline News*," said Jackie. "Oswald Endicott, sixty-one, was found at four a.m. in a car parked at West Beach in Westbrook with a fatal bullet wound to the head. Police are investigating what they say is an apparent suicide, but have not released additional details. Endicott, a native of Flint, Michigan, has lived in Westbrook since the late nineties. He retired there following a nearly thirty-year career as a financial manager for Consolidated Global Energies in White Plains, New York. Divorced in 2000, Endicott has no living relatives. A memorial service will be held at St. John's Episcopal Church in Stamford."

She read the time and date.

"That's tomorrow."

Jackie was quiet on the other end of the line, but I could hear the keys rattling like machine-gun fire.

I took the phone with me out to the screened-in front porch and sat at the pine table so I could look at the bay.

The sun was barely angling above the line of mist on the eastern horizon, just below the tree tops, so I didn't see it, but saw the effect on the surface of the water. The air was clear enough to see the North Fork lit up along the horizon. I liked looking at it better than the images forming in my head of the table in some airless, joyless conference room where Ozzie and I would go through the monthly financials, him patiently explaining the numbers and teaching me for the hundredth time the accrual method of accounting and the difference between labor and material inventories.

"This from the archives of *The Wall Street Journal*," said Jackie, coming back to life. "Con Globe announced on Monday the early retirement of another key executive within its Technical Services and Support business unit, which was spun off last month in a sale to the European oil giant Société Commerciale Fontaine. Oswald Endicott had been Director of Finance at the division for more than a decade. His follows a series of similar departures, beginning with TSS Divisional Vice President Sam Acquillo, whose resignation immediately followed announcement of the TSS sale to Fontaine. According to Con Globe spokespeople, Acquillo's decision to resign was for personal reasons unrelated to the sale . . . Wasn't the reason you personally socking Mason Thigpen in the jaw?"

"In the nose. Important distinction."

So Ozzie had bailed out with the rest of the old TSS hands. Not surprising, since we all knew what Fontaine would do with our operation—essentially chop it up and scatter it across their organization, which was even more global than Con Globe, and probably three times the size. There might have been some nice opportunities in playing on a bigger stage, so it might not have been the smartest thing to do, but it didn't surprise me. We'd built TSS from next to nothing, operating with relative autonomy outside the attention, and thus meddling, of corporate management. The better of our people would never stomach working for people they hadn't chosen. They were too independent and obstinate.

Of course, Ozzie probably had a few other incentives. Probably a whole bucketful of carrots and sticks.

I asked Jackie what he did post–Con Globe.

"As far as I can tell, nothing," she said.

"No jobs, no hobbies, no charities?"

"No nothing. If I didn't have his address in Westbrook, and the news clip, I wouldn't know he even lived there."

I ask her to look up his ex-wife, admitting, to my regret, that I didn't know her name. I probably never knew her name.

"I can find it by checking genealogical records. Or it might be on the title to his house, since they were still married when he bought it."

"Great. I'll wait."

"Gee thanks."

While I waited I tried to remember the names of the secretaries we shared. There were a lot of them, so I should have recalled at least one. But I didn't really see the need for a secretary, so I didn't give them much to do. There was a typing pool in the sales department that took care of my letters and I didn't want anyone answering my phone. I was perfectly capable of saying hello all on my own.

Ozzie gave them too much to do, so it should have balanced out, but it was really too much. He was always respectful and polite, but with the exception of an ex-cop who was going to night school for accounting all of them quickly succumbed to the tidal wave of work flowing from his office.

"How does Priscilla sound?" asked Jackie.

"Like it goes with Oswald."

"Until 2000."

"Who got the house?" I asked.

"He did, apparently, since it's still his address. You didn't tell me he had money."

"He does."

"Well, the place cost him over five million dollars in the mid-nineties," said Jackie. "You can triple that now."

I switched on the light beside the pine table and pulled a yellow pad out of the magazine rack. I sat down and started to draw boxes and arrows. I couldn't help it. Next to looking at the Little Peconic Bay, nothing worked as well to organize my brain.

"What do we do now?" Jackie asked.

"We take a trip."

"No we don't."

"Just a short trip."

"To where?"

"I'll bet Priscilla lives in Stamford," I said.

The line went quiet for another few minutes.

"She does. Unless it's a different Priscilla Endicott."

"Then that's where we're going. In time for the memorial."

"You're not going to share this theory with me, are you. What happened to full and free disclosure?"

"I'll fully disclose on the way to Connecticut. I'll pick you up at nine. We'll take the ferry. Suck in a little sea air. You'll love it."

"You're going to hang up on me, aren't you? After all I've done."

"You'll love it, I promise," I said, then hung up on her and called Joe Sullivan.

———

The water in the Little Peconic Bay would usually stay warm well into October, but warmth is a relative thing. That night it was plenty cold, though not enough to discourage me from stripping off all my clothes and jumping in and swimming out as far as I dared.

As more of a thrasher than a swimmer, keeping close to shore was advisable, even when I feel energetic enough to swim to the North Fork and have a beer at a bar I know off Corey Creek.

Looking at the Little Peconic was great for clearing the mind. Jumping into it even better.

Especially since it gave me the opposite vantage point, looking in at the cottage, with its screened-in porch, now lit by a single standing lamp next to the pine table on which sat a yellow pad filled with a fresh set of schematics and calculations.

I didn't like seeing Amanda's house mostly in the dark, only brushed by the glow of the post lamp next to her driveway. I'd seen it like that before, during the bad times when I'd lost her to the lunacies of the moment. For George Donovan, that loss was unrecoverable. How did it feel for Ozzie Endicott when Priscilla packed her bags and walked away from the big new house? Who was grief-stricken and who relieved?

Burton once told me that behind every murder was either love or greed.

Or both.

—

I spent most of the next morning in bed. I'd woken up later than usual, lulled by the absence of the near bark Eddie used to roust me to make breakfast.

I lay there for another hour running the numbers—the probabilities, however half-baked and ill-conceived. I missed Amanda's warm body, though it was probably better not to have the loss of concentration, of focus. I called her to tell her that.

"I'm concentrating on fresh melon, prosciutto and a mocha latte with cinnamon sprinkled on top," she said.

"So Burton's feeding you all right."

"Food, shelter and a small security detail. Fernando and Jarek are actually quite the carpenters. Eddie stays here with Isabella. She's teaching him Spanish. He already knows 'come eat' and 'no pissing on the furniture.' But believe it or not, we'd still rather be back at Oak Point."

I briefed her as well as I could, sticking to what I knew, and letting the theories stay theoretical. She acted as if that was good enough for her, which was good enough for me.

After hanging up I went into the kitchen and brewed a large pot of Gevalia chocolate raspberry coffee, which I drank as accompaniment to my first Camel ration. I brought the pot into the outdoor shower where I spent the next half hour pondering the plan. And as usual I failed to advance the plan, even fractionally. But I did get through the whole pot of coffee.

—

Jackie was in full mourning regalia: black leather jacket over a black cashmere sweater, black pleated miniskirt over black woolen tights, black motorcycle boots out of which poured thick-knit black socks.

"Do you think this is formal enough?" she asked.

"Not for the Hells Angels. They'll probably be there."

"I don't have a lot of black."

My daughter could've helped her there. That's all she had. Claimed it saved on laundry bills, but I knew it meant fewer decisions to make in the morning.

The day was fresh and clean. The sunlight hard and clear. We were in Amanda's red pickup with the windows down so we could smoke without smelling up the upholstery. The soft air, blessedly dry, swirled around and created a pleasant side benefit: the resulting noise gave me an excuse to avoid anything so complicated as an explanation.

"But you're going to tell me when we get on the ferry," she said.

"Definitely."

As it turned out a swarm of motorcycles was unloading from the ferry when we got there. I told Jackie to slide down in her seat.

"You can't have her," I said, as they roared by. "She's mine."

The sun reflecting off Long Island Sound as we crossed was nearly blinding, but we stayed topside, leeward of the hard breeze and secure in a pair of white plastic chairs.

"So," said Jackie.

"So it's quite a day."

"Come on."

"When I was a troubleshooter in the oil refineries I liked it when things didn't make sense."

"Typically perverse."

"That meant I didn't need to waste my time with the obvious. That I could focus everything on the unlikely, the unanticipated."

"So what doesn't make sense about Iku Kinjo's murder?"

"It's obvious."

She swatted my shoulder.

"Come on."

"Sometimes Occam's razor needs to stay in the drawer."

The look she gave me complimented her outfit.

"You're not going to tell me, are you?" she said. "I knew you wouldn't tell me."

"There's nothing to tell you that you don't already know. Only a few figments of my imagination."

"Criminy," she said, and let it drop.

I celebrated by getting us both coffee and spending the rest of the trip describing the potent currents of Long Island Sound, how they flowed like a bastard to the east for a while, then switched and flowed like a bastard to the west, making sailing a complex triangulation between wind, tide and expectations. And fishing an adventure in riding the chop above the shoals. She acted like she didn't care, but I knew she was paying attention. Among Jackie's more reliable afflictions was an uncontrollable interest in arcana. A sucker for a good fish story.

I hadn't seen Bridgeport in almost ten years, and it looked a lot better than I remembered, especially around the harbor where the ferry pulled in. At the time, I was fresh out of Con Globe and fully invested in Jack Daniels, so the details were a little fuzzy, though I remember the lifestyle offered a marked contrast to the one immediately prior. I wondered how my associates in the inner city had fared after that thing with the dead guy and the shotgun.

To get to Stamford from Bridgeport you had to go down the coast and up a few socioeconomic strata. It was a short trip, with one stop to let Jackie pee and me refill my mug.

"Does the heart attack tell you when you've had enough coffee?" she asked me.

St. John's Episcopal Church sat on a small hill, exaggerating the impression of a towering fortress. It was built out of Connecticut brownstone and establishment presumptions. You had to park in a lot to the side and walk up the hill to the front doors. There were only three vehicles in the lot, including a panel truck pulling a lawn tractor on a trailer.

One of the cars was a nondescript General Motors station wagon, the other a familiar Volvo.

I let Jackie hold on to my arm as we slogged our way up to salvation.

The priest came out the door before we were halfway there and walked down to meet us. He was startlingly young, with round frameless glasses and a smile that looked beatific, though that was probably influenced by the setting.

He held Jackie's elbow when he shook her hand, as if to maximize the strength of the greeting, then did the same with me.

"Here for Ozzie, I hope," he said.

"We are, Father," said Jackie.

He nodded, obviously pleased. Then he took us each gently by the arm and guided us up the hill.

"I didn't know him myself, but Priscilla is a regular here at St. John's. She said she was doing this for herself and didn't care if anyone came, but one always cares, right? Are you family?"

"Ex-coworker," I said.

"His lawyer," said Jackie, jerking her thumb toward me. "Here for moral support."

"Lovely to have you," said the priest. "Moral support is one of our specialties. By the way, I'm Hank Ortega," he added, turning to walk backwards so he could get our names.

He looked at his watch.

"We're actually about to start," he said. "I was just checking for stragglers. Come meet your fellow mourners."

The inside of the church was predictably dark, with vaulted oaken arches absorbing the meager light from the tall stained glass windows and incandescent lanterns. We walked down the center aisle past the empty pews to the last row before the altar and sat down. At the far end was a beefy, grey-haired white guy in a flannel shirt. Next to him was a woman Ozzie's age, squat, with a fleshy face and thin blonde hair.

Sitting next to her was Bobby Dobson.

TWENTY-ONE

I WAS GETTING USED TO his look of alarm, so I just reached across Priscilla and patted his knee. This was a little alarming to Priscilla, though her attention was quickly regained by Father Ortega.

He told us he was going to read a few prayers. We were welcome to follow along in the prayer book and could either kneel or sit, depending on our preferences. I sat, Jackie knelt, with her back straight and hands clasped in front of her like a school kid.

The prayers were nice picks. Father Ortega had them memorized and spoke the words like he really loved what they said. They made me think of Ozzie a little differently for the first time, more positively, which I guess was the idea.

Then Father Ortega sang a hymn, joined only by Jackie, who turned out to have a beautiful singing voice. It was deep in the alto range, with a hint of rasp and spot-on intonation. I was even more impressed that she read the music out of the hymnal.

After the hymn the priest closed his book and walked out from behind the little portable pulpit he'd been working from. He stood with his hands clasped in front and resting comfortably among the folds of his vestments.

"I didn't know Ozzie," he said, "but I heard a lot about him from Priscilla. For many years she and Ozzie enjoyed a very happy marriage, bolstered by the affection of friends and a close and loving family. And then Ozzie entered a period of grave difficulty. Like many natural achievers, success only drove Ozzie to work harder and harder. And then harder again, driving himself unmercifully, until he became untethered from those priceless human connections that give us perspective, that help us understand the true priorities in life: love of God and family, the companionship of friends and the blessings of a composed and peaceful heart. This left Ozzie vulnerable to a different type of association, the dark and unforgiving fraternity of illegal drugs—amphetamines to fuel his unrelenting drive and ambition, and cocaine to soothe the agony of his troubled soul.

"Yet we're not here to condemn Ozzie, but rather to honor him, for in the moment of his deepest despair, he found within him the true beauty of his character and sought help for this cruel affliction. And he found it, and after many years of trial, also found sobriety, and, if not peace of mind, at least personal satisfaction for having conquered what many believe unconquerable.

"We're also here to honor Priscilla, who stood by Ozzie even as their marriage fell asunder. And Robert Dobson, who spoke to Ozzie every day from the moment they were joined together in rehabilitation, whose loyalty and steadfast faith in his friend was likely the most powerful influence on Ozzie's daily recovery.

"We also thank those who have come to say goodbye to Ozzie—Richard, Sam, Jackie—and ask that you now join us in prayer. Our Father, who art in heaven . . ."

I stopped listening after that. First off, I knew the prayer. Secondly, I didn't think God would mind if I mentally drew in the lines between a few of the boxes on the yellow pad back at the cottage.

"Holy Toledo," I heard Jackie say under her breath, more than once, so at least one of us was still in a religious mood.

We all stood up when Father Ortega signaled the end of the service by walking down from the altar and leaning over to hug Priscilla. Jackie was already out of the pew and moving around to the other end, where Richard had Bobby conveniently boxed in.

I was ready for him to leap into the pew behind us and make a run for it, but he stayed put until Richard cleared out and Jackie could get a grip on his arm. I abandoned my position and went around to help her. Father Ortega and Priscilla were talking and hugging, oblivious to the situation.

I took Bobby's other arm.

"Let's chat," I said, in as low a voice as I could.

If you can look terrified and smug at the same time, that's how Bobby looked. Then he looked over at Priscilla.

"I don't have to say goodbye," he said. "She hates my guts."

He turned and started walking down the side aisle. I dropped behind, but Jackie kept a grip on his arm, though looser, more like an escort than a prison guard. He didn't seem to care either way.

—

Outside the sun half-blinded us after the murky atmosphere of the old church. Bobby put his hand over his eyes
and moaned.

"Just right for a headache," he said. "I gotta sit down."

I pointed to a gigantic copper beech growing partway
down the hill.

"How about over there, in the shade?"

"I guess," said Bobby. "It doesn't matter."

"There's the spirit," I said.

I waited until we were sitting under the tree to ask the
obvious. The black miniskirt presented Jackie with some
logistical challenges, but she worked them out.

"Why did Ozzie shoot himself?" I asked Bobby.

"He was a miserable, paranoid, antisocial, depressive
junkie. Other than that, who knows?"

"You met in rehab."

"Roomies. I guess they thought an older guy would mentor a younger guy, and the younger guy would lend some
energy and optimism. They were right."

"So you guys shared everything," I said.

He looked at me carefully.

"Why don't you just tell me what you think you know,"
he said.

"Yeah, Sam, why don't you," said Jackie, helpfully.

Like the father said in there, Ozzie loved to work. Loved it
more than anything. Probably too much. Now I knew how
he could work past midnight, then be back at his desk at
seven in the morning looking like he'd just come back from a
week in the Caribbean. Why he never exercised but kept
losing weight. I was oblivious to stuff like that.

"Some people think confession is part of recovery," I
said. "I don't know about that. I've never recovered. But I can

see how Ozzie would need to unload a little. Rehab's an intimate environment. They encourage you to open up. And he did, didn't he? To you, his young craphead roommate."

"Cokehead. More or less the same thing," said Jackie.

"Then you turned around and told Iku, didn't you? An old throb from the glory days of Princeton. There she is, sitting in the house on Vedders Pond. Letting off steam that had built up over months in a high-pressure project. Letting down her guard. Entertaining the group with stories of trysts with corporate bigwigs and takeover conspiracies with scary hedge fund operators. She talks about the inner workings of Eisler, Johnson and Phillip Craig, which was interesting enough, but then she gets to Con Globe and you're thinking, 'Holy shit, I know those guys. I know what's going on here. I'm not supposed to, but I do. And she has no idea that I know.' You got off coke, but you still drank. Enough to let down your own inhibitions. Enough to betray bosom rehab buddy Ozzie Endicott, selling out his secrets in return for Iku's attention. Finally impressing her. It was just too irresistible."

Bobby's face registered a tinge of triumph to accent his sullenness and fear.

"Brilliant analysis, smart man. Try proving it."

He stood up, slapping the dust off the seat of his pants. Jackie stood up as well and pointed back to the ground.

"Not yet, hero. We're still talking," she said.

He shrugged and plopped back down.

I was glad for the interruption, because it gave me a chance to think. It was time well spent, however brief.

"I am a dope sometimes," I said to Bobby, looking over at Jackie for validation, which she gladly provided. "I keep confusing duplicity with ordinary shallowness. They're not the same, though you seem to manage both quite handily. Jerome Gelb must really love you."

Sullenness and fear seemed to deepen, squeezing out the triumph.

"What was the deal, Bobby?" I asked. "A better job, a piece of the action, a ride in the corporate jet? It had to be pretty good to sell Ozzie down the river. Was it worth it? Was it worth the poor guy's miserable life?"

"I'm not admitting anything," he said.

"You don't have to," I said. "You didn't just tell Iku. Bringing in Gelb was an even better career builder. He was Iku's boss. Her mentor. She was the perfect link to both Con Globe and Angel Valero, but Gelb added the management horsepower. You loved pulling this together, getting on a more equal footing with Iku Superstar. Have her notice the lowly nebbish from the help desk. The nerdy underachiever chafing at the end of his parents' leash."

"Fuck you," Bobby said, almost convincingly. He finally looked ready to clam up. I knew the expression. I'd seen it on my daughter plenty of times, beginning when she was two years old.

"Did Angel ever stop by your house?"

He shook his head.

"Iku made us promise not to tell anybody where she was," he said. "And I didn't. I don't care if you believe me or not. That's what happened."

Before I could press him further he stood up and starting walking back down the lawn to the parking lot. Jackie looked ready to tackle him, but I shook my head. Instead, we just followed a few steps behind. Before he reached his car, I gave it one more try.

"What the hell happened, Bobby?" I asked. "What went wrong?"

"You tell me," he said, turning around so he could look at

me. "Everything was fine until you showed up. Looking for Iku, freaking everybody out."

Then he got in his Volvo and peeled out of the parking lot, not unlike he did the first time I met him, when I watched him flee into the dark and deceitful night.

TWENTY-TWO

THE FIRST THING I DID the next morning was wake up
Angel Valero. I was barely awake myself, having had only
two cups of coffee in preparation for my morning shower.
I'd plugged my cell phone into the same outlet that fed the
coffee pot, and when I went to unplug it, Angel's number
popped up on the screen at the top of my contact list. The
phone was always performing these spontaneous demon-
strations, undoubtedly caused by the inexperience of
the operator, but I took it as a hint from above and hit the
send button.

"I told you to wake me at six. It's only four in the fucking
morning," he growled on the other end of the line.

"Not here it isn't. Where the heck are you?" I asked.

"Who's this?"

"Sam Acquillo. I think we might have a friend in common.
You know a guy named Ozzie Endicott? Actually, the late
Ozzie Endicott."

The line was quiet for a while. I thought he'd hung up, but the little time counter on the screen was still going.

"Angel, you there?" I asked.

"You're not going to go away, are you," he said.

"Not if I can help it."

"We can settle this," he said.

"We can?"

"Not over the phone. We need a sit-down. You probably have a figure in mind. It's gonna be more than I'm willing to pay. So save yourself the disappointment and start discounting now."

"Ah. That kind of settlement."

"What other kind is there?"

"Okay," I said. "When and where?"

"You'll be contacted tomorrow when I get back from L.A. Don't call me again," he said, then hung up.

I poured the rest of the coffee out of the pot and into an insulated mug with the Yankees logo on the side. I brought it along to the outdoor shower, where I invested a week's pay in hot water. I don't know why showers, administered externally, have such a powerful effect on a person's internal vitality, but they do. Mentally and physically.

I dressed for the day in work boots and a pair of shorts with big pockets on the legs, a sleeveless T-shirt and a black Yankees cap, to further express my abject loyalties.

Then I drove down from Oak Point, through Southampton Village, to the sea. It had rained the night before—thundershowers—so there were large puddles creating an obstacle course along Dune Drive. Amanda's pickup handled the challenge with distinction.

When I reached one of the few public access points through the dunes, I parked the truck and proceeded on foot. The sun was up on the horizon, but the air was still cool from all the rain and the gradual shift from summer into fall.

It took almost a half hour to reach Angel's big white box. It's not always easy to identify houses usually approached from the road by their beachside facades, but Angel's architect had made it easy. The other clue was a bit of luck on par with my lucky call first thing in the morning: the sight of a brunette in a yellow bikini sitting at the edge of the surf on a chaise lounge, plowing through the final chapters of *The Agony and the Ecstasy*.

"Which is it for you?" I asked her, pointing at the cover.

Jesse shaded her eyes when she looked up at me. Then she looked at where I was pointing.

"A little of both."

I sat down cross-legged, grateful to be finished with the uncomfortable slog across the sand.

"Mind if I join you?" I asked.

"You already have."

She dog-eared a page and closed the book, resting it on her naked belly. I noticed a bracelet tattoo on her ankle.

"My father had a tattoo of an anchor on his chest," I said. "Hip before his time."

She held up her leg.

"It's a string of pearls," she said.

"Which came first, the pearls or the swine?"

She smiled.

"I did enjoy the way you handled Angel. Though not so much his mood afterwards."

"Sorry. Not my fault."

"But this is. Visiting me on the beach. How do you know he's not on his way to join me?"

"Can't get here that fast from L.A."

Jesse took the thick book in two hands and tilted it up on end, showing off a little more tanned belly.

"So you made a special trip, just for me," she said.

"I did."

"Do you think staying in a rich person's house, along with several other girls, in return for the occasional sexual favor, constitutes a form of prostitution?" she asked.

"To some people, I guess. Not to me."

"Interesting. You handle loaded questions even better than bullies."

"Just a lucky answer. It's been going that way for me all morning."

She seemed satisfied with that.

"So, what are you trying to get lucky with now?" she asked. "Me or Angel's business?"

"Are those my only two choices?"

"They're the two I'm most familiar with."

"Okay. Let's start with business."

She gave the air a gentle punch.

"Excellent. What damaging things can I tell you?"

"It's heartwarming to see such loyalty," I said.

"Swine is a good choice of words. Though it might be understated."

"Did you ever meet a young consultant named Iku Kinjo?"

"Iku? Sure. She was here all the time. She worked for Angel, indirectly. Part of a consulting business. Can't remember the name."

"Eisler, Johnson."

"That's it. Business freaks. Always in black suits and ties. Carrying big black cases full of chart packs and projectors."

"So Iku wasn't the only one he worked with."

She shook her head.

"There were others. They all look the same to me, same clothes and haircuts, so they kind of blur together. All but the big scarecrow. Much better dresser."

"Jerome Gelb."

"That's it. Angel called him Jerry, which you could tell he hated, which is why Angel did it."

"Was he here a lot?"

"He usually came with Iku. That girl was intense, but I liked her. I'm not surprised she killed herself. Wound that tight. But I feel really bad for her. She always said hi, noticed I was there."

"When Iku and Gelb were here, did they work off their laptops?"

"They all do these days. That and the little handheld things. Next they'll have something jacked right into their skulls. That's why it's sort of funny," she added, her voice trailing off.

"What is."

"That Iku would leave it here. Her laptop. You'd think her family would want it back."

"Oh, but they do," I said, immediately pissed at myself for blurting it out. "They've been searching for it all over."

"Really."

I stared at her as the plea floated unspoken between us.

"You're joking," she said.

"I'm not. He doesn't need it. You'll be making some nice people very happy."

I reached involuntarily for my cell phone, fingering the stubby antenna on top, but keeping it in its holster. I didn't know how much time I had before Angel got back from the Coast, but it was probably less than needed for Sullivan to get the story in front of Ross, and then in front of a judge willing to invade the privacy of a semi-public figure, all without Angel catching wind of it and getting one of his household thugs to take a quick trip to the middle of the Shinnecock Bay.

Jesse shrugged.

"Sure. Why not," she said brightly.

I felt myself let out a long held breath. I hoped it didn't show.

"Excellent. How about now?"

She opened her book to the dog-eared page, refolded the corner and shut it again.

"Hold your horses there, Lone Ranger," she said. "I got to figure a way to sneak it out of the house."

I tried to look apologetic.

"Of course. You're right. How much time do you need?"

She looked at her watch.

"Angel's not back till after six, but I'm not taking any chances. Let's meet at noon. Name the place."

I told her how to get to the Pequot, figuring it was the one place on the East End where she was least likely to be recognized. I said if I wasn't there, to leave it with one of the owners, Dorothy or Paul Hodges. I'd give them the heads-up.

"You trust them?" she asked.

"With my life."

"Then I guess I can trust them with mine."

—

On the return slog I had enough time to weigh all the possibilities, and worry about timing, and Jesse's safety, which I might be seriously endangering without her knowledge, and the safety of others who might get caught in the crossfire.

But by the time I reached the pickup, my mood from the earlier part of the morning was back in place. The worries were still there, but I had a technique for keeping them at bay. All I had to do was remember Iku Kinjo sitting on the edge of a chair in my office at the company, impatiently scribbling down notes on a small pad of graph paper, checking her watch, the consummate neurotic, eager, alive and just starting to find her way.

———

My relief was almost overwhelming when I saw Jesse come through the doors of the Pequot, with a large wicker bag and a look I'd last seen on Honest Boy Ackerman confronting the distinctive ambience for the first time. Luckily Dotty was nearby to greet her and put her at ease, as well as a woman with chartreuse-and-black-striped hair can do.

"This place was a lot farther away than I thought," she said, reluctantly accepting my offer to sit at the table.

"You got away clean, I hope," I said, looking hopefully at the wicker bag.

"It's in there. I'm not sure how clean I am. Probably clean out of my mind for even contemplating this, much less doing it. You're a very persuasive person."

"Thank you," I said, reaching into the basket and pulling out the dark grey plastic slab and tangle of power cords before she succumbed further to second thoughts. I tucked it under my arm and fought the desire to make an immediate run for the truck.

"So maybe I can persuade you of one more thing," I said.

She looked attentive, but suspicious.

"And that would be?"

"You've already met Dotty. You want to talk about a girl with a brain. You'd love spending a little time with her. Like, tonight. Her roommates all pick their teeth with filleting knives. Safest place in town."

Suspicion grew into annoyance.

"I'm not safe?"

"It might be a good idea to exercise a certain caution. Just for tonight."

"So, I'm not safe," she said.

"I don't know. Angel might discover the laptop is gone. He'll be very upset."

"And what about the grieving Kinjos?"

"They'll still be very happy. Wherever they are."

I did the best I could to sell her on the idea, though she hadn't entirely capitulated by the time I left. I thought she would. Paul and Dotty were giving her the full blast of their distinctive charm, something few souls could resist.

I brought the laptop back to the cottage and out to the lscreened-in porch. I set it on the table next to Randall's PC primer and the tumbler filled to capacity with a whole day's ration of vodka on the rocks. No better way to sharpen the concentration.

———

I thought peering into the private cyberlife of a recently murdered woman would be a little unnerving, and I wasn't disappointed. True to the torqued-down professional I remembered her to be, Iku's folders were clearly labeled and alphabetically arranged. With the exception of headings like "Reports" and "Analysis," I didn't know what any of it meant, even after opening the documents. It was all boxes and arrows, tables and rows of data, a familiar language, but in a distinctly foreign dialect. I once had a penchant for deciphering meaning from all forms of data, however alien, but I was out of practice and the sheer, numbing volume of the information was daunting.

I clicked out of the heavy stuff and went looking for easier prey, like "Correspondence."

After divining a way to open the file "Saved Emails" I ran smack into another form of impenetrability. The language here was unexpurgated corporate-speak—or worse, consultant-speak. In this Iku was so masterfully fluent I almost began to admire the opacity of the prose, her deft handling of euphemism to evade precision, and the use of passive voice to express near-poetic ambiguity. It was clear from the exchanges that, by comparison, her clients and fellow consultants were rhetorical pikers.

Angel Valero, on the other hand, didn't even compete. His style was refreshingly loutish and blunt, poetic only in the absence of capital letters, as if using the shift key was too big a time commitment. The subject matter of their correspondence was ordinary to the point of banality—though, as with the technical files, I sensed there was meaning in the interpretation. The syntax varied, but the import was the same.

Bobby Dobson was vague and filled with complaint. Jerome Gelb was imperious and brusque, without Valero's rough charm. Elaine Brooks was flirtatious. Zelda, poetic and erudite, trying to live up to her name. But with an edge, as delicate and keen as a razor. Anger masquerading as clever wit, highbrow repartee.

George Donovan, on the other hand, was tender and kind, and playful. Affectionate in the earnest, self-deprecating way people are when they really mean it. It was an adult affection, restrained only by fear of exposure. But it was clear—Donovan had fallen off the cliff. For him it wasn't conquest, it was redemption.

I resisted being ensnared by the correspondence and pulled into a deep dive. There was too much surface to peruse, too many layers to peel away, holding areas to uncover and decant.

As I clicked along, my nervous system began to light up. There was a chase afoot and I was getting used to moving the little arrow around and remembering which key did what, speeding the process: validation of Sullivan's theory that computers addict the unwary. Maybe, I thought, lighting a Camel and sipping the top off my drink, but only if you have an addictive personality.

Whatever success I managed to have on the job was probably based on a knack for pattern recognition, starting with recognizing what were patterns and what weren't. This is what made me an official problem-solver for most of my professional life. Yet I was always a little superstitious about examining the process, afraid that understanding how I worked through a problem would ruin my ability to do it.

As I cruised around Iku Kinjo's cyberlife, I could feel the process starting. A scan of the data in search of a gestalt, an image of meaning camouflaged by its context, yet visible to the objective first-time observer.

What I saw, in addition to Iku's gift for obfuscation, was the burning need to obfuscate. It went beyond conforming to corporate jargon. She had things to hide. Lots of things. But also a need to communicate over a medium that was as insecure as it was indispensable.

The solution was to operate in plain view, by writing messages that conveyed twin meanings—one routine, the other, anything but.

This is what I recognized almost immediately. A thing you know is there, even if you don't know what it's telling you. A cipher wrapped in a puzzle inside a code. My favorite thing.

———

It took the rest of the day, and the balance of the night, but by the time the Little Peconic Bay began to glow with the nascent dawn, and the birds were in full chatter and chirp, I had it cracked.

I had it all.

TWENTY-THREE

"You must be kidding me," said Zelda Fitzgerald, through a crack in the window next to her front door. "I'm just sitting down to breakfast."

"Sorry about the timing. I only need a few minutes."

She huffed and slammed the window shut. The door lock clicked and the door opened.

"Acquillo, right?" she asked.

"Sam is good enough."

"For you," she said, walking away before I had a chance to follow her through the sepulchral dinge inside the house. I made it all the way to the kitchen without getting lost.

"Sashimi and wheat toast," she said, pointing to a tidy place setting on the kitchen table. "I'd offer you some but I only buy for one."

"Ever tried North Sea fin tail? It's all I eat."

"You want tea?"

I said no thanks and watched her pour herself a cup and settle down in front of her meal.

I picked a small framed photograph of her with Bobby and Elaine off a shelf filled with jars of flour and colorful dried pasta. I looked at it, then looked at her.

"You lied to me," I said.

Zelda had a hunk of pink salmon gripped between a set of chopsticks, about to shove it in her mouth. She paused.

"Pardon me."

"You said Bobby brought Iku home to Vedders Pond, but it wasn't Bobby. It was Elaine."

She ate the salmon and shrugged.

"It was one of them. I wasn't too with it myself that night."

"It wasn't the first time Elaine dragged somebody home in a drunken stupor. But this was different. Iku Kinjo wasn't just another girl. She was a force. A brilliant, beautiful force. Attractive doesn't even begin to describe her. You've known that since living with her at Princeton, where she made you feel invisible. You were half in love with her yourself."

She tightened up and slammed her chopsticks down on the table.

"That's enough," she said.

"It's like a nightmare. Your rival, long since gone from the scene, suddenly back again. Bobby and Elaine fawning all over her. Inviting her to stay at the house. I can see you watching Elaine as she watched Iku's every move, licking her chops."

"That's disgusting."

"What part?"

She took a bite of her breakfast, then pointed her chopsticks at me, as if taking aim.

"I loved Iku," she said. "But not in that way. I admired her. Look what she did with her life, coming from next to nothing.

And look at me. Coming from everything and achieving nothing. I was worried when she started staying at the pond, I admit it. Even if I don't have to. But it wasn't long before I only felt pity. I've never known a person so stressed out and exhausted. And heartsick."

"Heartsick? What do you mean, heartsick?"

"Oh, please."

"Tell me," I said.

"In love? Ever heard of that? The poor girl was gone, all the way. Weeping like crazy over George, whoever the hell George is."

"You didn't ask?"

"Don't know, don't care. All I know is she thought she'd betrayed him somehow, ruined his life. You want to talk about guilt. Half of it was pure babble, but I got the gist. He started out as the devil and ended up St. George. She'd gotten mixed up in an illegal business deal, and in the process betrayed him. She said she was afraid to ever face him again. When I tried to talk her out of it, she said she was too ashamed. She wanted to go to the cops, to make things right, but was worried about George. After watching her down endless bottles of Campari and spill her guts all over the place, I could see the problem. Those creeps she worked for sent her in to entrap George, and instead she gets trapped herself. Ms. Genius falls in love with the old bastard. Like crazy in love."

I sat across from her at the kitchen table and plucked a piece of salmon off her plate.

"So how did it feel to finally have the upper hand?" I asked. "Which came first, the pity or the triumph?"

"What a strange thing to say."

I suddenly didn't like being that close to her, so I stood up from the table to get a little distance.

"Ah, come on. Quit with all the phoney sanctimony. Having Iku around wasn't the best thing that could have happened to you. It was the worst. The best was having her dead."

She finally put the chopsticks gently on the table, capitulating to the inevitable: this was not going to be just another lively tit for tat.

"I want you to leave," she said.

"When I'm ready. If you don't like it, call the cops. They'd love to get in on the conversation."

Her shoulders dropped, and she cast her eyes down to where her hands were clenched in her lap.

"If I'm not mistaken, you're about to accuse me of something," she said.

"Why's would I? Because you invested hours consoling and extracting dangerous information from the very woman who was ripping up your carefully crafted world? A woman you might have admired, likely envied, but most certainly feared and loathed, who is conveniently found murdered in the bedroom next to yours."

"You don't honestly think . . ."

"Who else?" I asked, in a voice that was likely louder than I meant, because it made her jump in her seat.

"You can't," she said.

"Who else knew?"

"Knew what?"

"About Iku's change of heart? Who else knew?"

Zelda grabbed the abandoned chopsticks and snapped them in half. "What difference does it make?" she said. "It wasn't exactly a secret around the house. Everybody knew. Elaine. Bobby was just sick about it. Just sick. And her boss, what's his name. He was concerned, too."

"Jerome Gelb."

"That's right, he called too. On Iku's cheap little cell phone. She was passed out, and I thought, what's the harm? He was a very interesting man. Very articulate."

"What the hell did you tell him?"

"I don't remember. We just talked."

"You told him how she felt about George."

"I guess. Probably. What was the guy's name again?"

"Jerome Gelb," I said.

"That's right. Jerome. He said he wanted to come see her, so I gave him directions to the house. Didn't do him much good. Couple days later she was dead."

"So you told Gelb where Iku lived, even though she made you all promise to keep it a secret."

Zelda dismissed the thought with a sneer.

"Ridiculous. There are no secrets in this world."

She used the back of her hand to sweep her half-eaten meal and the broken chopsticks off the table. There was more I could have said to her, but we both knew it was pointless. So I let myself out into the glimmering East End light, where I stuck my face in the freshening breeze and fled the evil banality that clung like mist to her grim fairy-tale home.

———

Hoping to hide from caller ID, I drove all the way back to North Sea so I could use the landline in my kitchen to roust Angel for the second day in a row—with any luck, jet-lagged and groggy from his trip in from the Coast.

"Who's this?" he said.

"Sam Acquillo. How're the nuts? Still working?"

It was quiet a moment.

"I told you not to call me."

"I've never been good at following directions."

"What do you want?"

"Your ass. Now that I've met the rest of you, it's irresistible."

"I told you I'd meet with you."

"You did. I'm ready now."

I tapped a Camel far enough out of the pack to pull it out with my teeth. I lit it with one hand, bending the match in half and striking it with my thumb, a move I learned in high school. The hell with rations, I thought. Not today.

"My patience has just about run out with you, Acquillo."

"You remember where they found Iku?"

"Vedders Pond."

"Meet me there at exactly twelve noon. That's almost two hours from now."

I hung up and finished my cigarette and made a pot of coffee, which I took out to the Adirondacks to drink while watching the morning sun burn off the haze and heat up the day.

On the way to Vedders Pond I listened to public radio, which was promoting a Mozart festival at Southampton College. That was a nice surprise. Mozart always had a calming effect on me.

I knew Angel would want to arrive a little early, so I got there a little earlier than that. The sun was reaching its high point of the day, so there was still plenty of light falling through the trees and glancing off the surface of the pond.

I lit a cigarette and sat down Buddha-style in front of the statuette of the Virgin Mary, who accepted the irony without remark.

Angel's black Mercedes AMG showed up a few minutes later.

He had a sideman with him who looked a little like Frankenstein, tall as a tree with a squared-off jaw and crew cut. Everything but the little bolts in his neck.

"Hey, who's your handsome friend? You guys going together?" I said, trying to set the right tone.

"Don't mind if we stand," said Angel, looking around the rocky, weed-infested lawn.

"I'd rather you sit. More friendly."

He didn't like it but he dropped his lumbering bulk to the ground and ordered his pet ghoul to follow suit.

"So, what're you peddling?" he asked me, after getting semi-comfortable.

"That's all the foreplay I get?"

"Enough of that shit," said Valero. "What's the deal?"

"Okay. Silence. That's the offer on the table. You pay me whatever I think it's worth to stay quiet about your conspiracy with Jerome Gelb and Iku Kinjo to," I used my fingers to tick off the list, "threaten exposure of Con Globe's fraudulent sale of the TSS division, in return for George Donovan agreeing to break up the company, and to sell the most valuable assets to you. How am I doing so far?"

"Depends on what you have to back that up," he said.

"What about you?" I asked his silent partner. "What's your opinion?"

He just stared at me.

"His opinion is he's looking forward to ripping off your arms and legs," said Valero. "But don't let that distract you."

"Okay," I said. "You want back-up."

I reached in the laundry bag and pulled out Iku's computer. Angel frowned.

"It's hers. You can see the little Eisler, Johnson sticker on the bottom." I showed him. "It's got her name and some kind of code. I've already had a night to go through the files. It's all there. Even some of Ozzie's ginned-up spreadsheets. Is that what you showed him before he killed himself?"

"Okay," said Angel.

"Okay what?"

"Okay. What'll it cost me to get that computer back?"

"You told me to start discounting. So I did, and got all the way to zero."

"You don't want anything?" he said.

"I'm not saying that. I don't want any money. Just a single piece of information."

"What?"

"Why did you kill Iku Kinjo?"

The tall guy started to stand, looking at Angel for the go-ahead. Angel leaned back against a tree stump and waved him forward.

"Get me that computer," he said.

The guy was so long and awkward, it took him forever to get all the way to his feet, plenty of time for me to knock over the Madonna and retrieve Marve Judson's gun. I pointed it at Angel's head.

"Up to you," I said. He opted to have Frankenstein retake his seat.

"Answer," I said, now aiming the barrel of the gun at Angel's chest.

"Gelb told me she was losing it, on the verge of blowing the whistle. He was freaking out, but I said it was just a case of pre-deal jitters. Happens to people. I'd already put the thing on hold when she stopped returning our calls. I figured she'd snap out of it. I'm a patient man. I could give it a month. After that, who needs her? We had the goods from Endicott. The only one who'd want to fight us was Donovan, and he was dead man walking, thanks to Iku. It's all documented in there," he said, pointing to the computer. "Which you probably know."

I held up the laptop with the hand not holding the automatic.

"And you killed her for it," I said.

He shook his shaggy head like the enraged bull he was.

"Gelb, that pinheaded geek, showed up at my house with her computer. He said people were nosing around his office, so it was safer here with me. He didn't say where he got it, but when I heard the news about Iku the next day, I figured it out. I should've never got involved with that piece of crap, but that's business."

I could see it all starting with a phone conversation, or a harried meeting. Bobby Dobson telling Jerome Gelb some guy's looking for Iku. The description fits Floyd Patterson. Alarms start to go off. Dobson says this couldn't happen at a worse time. Iku's having some kind of emotional breakdown. He tells Gleb that she's fallen hard for George Donovan, and that her remorse over what she'd set out to do was about to drive her into the arms of the state's Attorney General. Gelb is now really starting to panic. He tells Bobby that he has to see Iku, to talk some sense into her. In a rare display of character, the weak-willed Dobson holds out, though he gives up Iku's disposable cell number. Gelb then hits the jackpot with Zelda. She gives up everything, including the location of Iku's bedroom, right inside the patio door, which is completely hidden from the street and the other houses. He knocks, and in her semi-stupor she opens the door.

As the head of Eisler, Johnson's Tokyo office for ten years, Gelb knew something about Japanese ritual suicide, but hadn't counted on her putting up such a fight. After trying without success to slash her throat, as the practice dictates, he was forced to jam the knife straight up into her brain. A faked-up suicide was still a worthwhile misdirection, so he cleaned up as well as he could and staged Iku in the middle of her bed. Then he unplugged the computer, dropped the Cat 5 cable down behind the dresser, and strolled back out the way he came.

I shared this thinking with Angel Valero.

"All I gave a shit about was leveraging Donovan's wandering dick into a takeover of Con Globe assets and a quick liquidation," he said. "I liked that girl. I didn't kill her."

I put down the computer and took the digital recorder out of my inside jacket pocket. I shut it off and set it on the ground.

"Maybe not directly, but you played your part. So did everybody else. Even the ones who loved her," I said.

We heard sirens in the near distance. Angel's face had reddened considerably during our conversation, but the tone now shifted toward purple. I hoped he wouldn't pop an artery before the various authorities were done with him.

"I might forgive you for nailing a brain to my door and sending two of your countrymen to kill me, *El Cerebro*, but their families probably won't," I said, watching the blue lights from Sullivan's undercover and a pair of patrol cars light up the surrounding trees, mixing uncomfortably with the golden red glow off the pond as it reflected the sun at the apogee of its daily arc.

TWENTY-FOUR

HODGES'S BOAT ISN'T MUCH of a speedster but it's easy to handle in heavy air, which is what we had that day out on the Little Peconic Bay. Burton was at the helm, his preferred location. Hodges was below cooking lunch and the rest of us were sprawled around the cockpit trying not to spill our cocktails as we dug fresh fruit out of the plastic bowl Amanda was passing around.

Eddie was forward, warning creatures of the deep to stay clear, and occasionally monitoring the sky for incoming birds of prey.

The Nat King Cole Trio was on the stereo and the only discordant note was coming from Jackie Swaitkowski, who was trying to engage Burton in a legal debate.

Jackie thought I still had a good case for pursuing my share of the intellectual property settlement from the shattered remains of Con Globe, most of which had now been absorbed into the Société Commerciale Fontaine.

Burton differed, citing the clarity and underlying validity of my original severance agreement, though he pointed out that the indictment and subsequent resignation of George Donovan, and the fraud he help perpetuate, might render the entire agreement moot.

With Angel Valero, Mason Thigpen and Marve Judson selling Donovan and each other out as fast as their lawyers could write up their statements, it looked like Honest Boy would get his wish. Everything and everybody relating to Con Globe was blown to smithereens and scattered on the wind.

Including Jerome Gelb, though the FBI had yet to discover where the wind had scattered him to. They felt the circumstantial case was strong enough to charge first-degree murder, but my better hope was that one of Angel Valero's remaining Venezuelan associates would get there first and render that argument permanently moot.

"Well, I'm not ready to give up on Sam's financial prospects," said Jackie. "It's the only way I'm going to see any money out of that client."

I didn't have the heart to argue with her, but the fact is, I was happy with things they way they were.

I worked my way from amidships to the pulpit, where I sat down to watch the water race under the bow, put my arm around my dog, and ponder the ineluctable modality of pure dumb luck.

ACKNOWLEDGMENTS

Thanks to Mary Farrell for indispensible help and understanding. Thanks to Marty and Judy Shepard, wonderful editors, publishers and human beings. Likewise, Marion Garner of Random House Canada, and her associate Anne Collins, who put a lie to the notion that there are no great editors left in the world.

Beloved readers Randy Costello and Sean Cronin were again critical to getting the book off the ground, with special thanks to Sean for instruction in lethal weapons of personal destruction. Thanks to Bob Willemin for a tour of the financial lunatic fringe, and to Rich Orr, Cindy Courtney and Norman Block for legal guidance (all fiction-related, mind you).

Abiding thanks to Anne-Marie Regish for astounding logistical accomplishments, and my Mintz & Hoke partners Bill Field and Ron Perine for the airspace and generous support.

Heidi Lamar and Laurence Willis helped me understand what you can and cannot do with secure data streams and laptop computers. Susan Ahlquist continues to fiercely attend to production detail. My brother Whit, with tweaks from Randy Costello, cleaned up my Spanish. Paige Goettel was responsible for the profane French, so if you're offended, blame her.

CHRIS KNOPF is a principal of Mintz & Hoke, a marketing communications agency. Occasional copywriter and cabinet maker, Knopf lives with his wife, Mary Farrell, and their wheaten terrier, Samuel Beckett, in Connecticut and Southampton, Long Island. He is the author of three other Sam Acquillo novels.